House of Love

by Jason M. Dry

House of Love
by Jason M. Dry

This book is a work of fiction. Names, characters, places and incidents are either the product of the author's imagination or are used fictitiously, and any resemblance to actual persons, living or dead, events, or locales is entirely coincidental.

Published by Germane Media

http://www.jasondry.com

Author: Jason M. Dry
ISBN: 978-0-9845309-0-8

"And God shall wipe away every tear from their eyes. There shall be no more death nor sorrow, nor crying; and there shall be no more pain, for the former things have passed away."

Revelations 21:4

"Well, there he is."

"He ain't much, is he? But he's a cute little booger."

"It don't seem right to me that such a little boy oughta be livin' like that with old folks."

"Well, he could do a lot worse. They say his mama ain't in the best condition to take care of him, anyway. An' he don't have nowhere else to go. I guess his mama feels real bad about it."

"You think his ol' granny'll make him go to church with her?"

"I doubt it. She don't go nowhere nowadays. Wouldn't be so bad if she would take him to church. Might give 'em both somethin' to do besides sittin' around all day an' feelin' sorry about what happened. But I expect he'll have plenty to do around here."

Lavelle closed the curtain as her daughter Cindy left the kitchen to put on her makeup. Lavelle continued to wash the dishes and smoke a cigarette.

Outside, Mama Ray and Daddy C unloaded the bags of their young grandson, Paul. They were all dressed in funeral clothes. Little Paul was also dressed in black, even though he hadn't been allowed to attend the funeral. He hung tightly to a baby doll that his mother had given him a long time before, one that could talk and eat. He was a little worried about his baby doll, because she was so silent now and hadn't been hungry for the last few days. So many things had happened that even *she* seemed to have trouble processing it all.

Paul surveyed his grandparents' house on Bellview Street in Sulphur Springs, Texas. He knew it from before. He had been born in that town and had spent his first Christmases in that house after he, his mother, and brother had moved in with his new step-daddy. He wasn't sure how to think of it, really. They had said he would have to be there for some time, that his mother had to rest a while. Somehow he would have to think of this as home. For a while. What was "a while?" "Just a while" was the answer, which gave no clarity to his question.

"Let's go in with the first load, kiddo. We gotta get all this stuff in the house, then I'll get some supper ready," said Mama Ray, trying hard to sound cheerful. She certainly did not *look* cheerful, all dressed in black funeral clothes. She had been crying since she had arrived in Kingsland, Texas, for the funeral, and most of the day on the car ride back from Paul's parents' house. He knew it was his fault that she was crying. And he knew that she knew it — that *everybody* knew it — too. He did not want to live with her and his grandpa, because they knew what he had done. He was so ashamed of it, even though it had been an accident, even though he had not meant to kill his little sister.

"Come on, Doll," said Daddy C, whose enthusiasm seemed to be more comforting. He had not cried in Paul's presence, and this made Paul feel safer, like he did not hate him. At least it made it easier for him to believe this. Daddy C patted Paul on the back and grabbed suitcases. Mama Ray and Daddy C carried the bags, and Paul followed them with Baby Doll in tow.

His grandparents' house had that cold familiar feeling that he remembered well from those Christmases. It was a mixture of old people and mothballs, perhaps. And a faint smell of stew or bacon grease, or maybe a combination of the two. The house was not as big as his house in Kingsland, and it was much older. The furniture was also older. Not antique and fancy, just old.

They walked through the living room, which was rarely used. The sofas were covered with cushions, and there was a dilapidated gramophone against one wall. Paul saw a plastic electric organ in a corner of the room. The walls were covered with photographs of family members. Paul noticed some photos of his mother when she was younger. He saw his baby picture, and one of his older brother, Frank. Next to his own picture was one of his little sister, Jennifer. Paul stopped to look at her.

"Come on, Doll," Daddy C said, ushering him through the living room.

Mama Ray and Daddy C took Paul's bags, all his toys, and games into what would be his new room. He had slept there before. There were twin beds which had been used before by him and his brother when they had visited. Now he would sleep there alone. It was hard to imagine having to sleep in that bed without his brother in the one beside him, that bed standing cold and empty in the dark.

"Well, this is your room, Doll, but you know it already," Daddy C said. "This time it's all yours. You don't have to share it with nobody, except that little dolly if you want to." Daddy C always called Paul "Doll." It used to bother him because it seemed like a name for girls, but now it didn't seem to be so bad. He even had started to like it in the last couple of days. Perhaps he needed to feel like someone's doll now, soft and protected in somebody's arms. And loved. "We'll get your things unpacked after supper." Mama Ray was already in the kitchen, and the house had begun to smell like food again. "Do you wanna take a nap before supper?"

Paul hated taking naps, and when he had had to take them at school he had always tried to pretend it was a game. He had tried to hold still as long as he could and keep his eyes shut. He had tried to day dream, but for him it was so uncomfortable to be still and silent for so long that he thought of it as a punishment. In fact, his mother had often used it as a punishment. "Don't come out till I tell you to," she would say, and sometimes he would stay in bed for hours, waiting for her to give him permission to leave his bedroom.

"Do I have to take a nap?" Paul asked, hoping that his grandpa would say no.

"No, Doll, you don't have to. I just thought you'd be tired after everything. It's been a long trip, hasn't it?"

"Yeah, but I'm not tired, though. I'll just stay in here." Paul wanted to stay out of his grandparents' way, so that they wouldn't change their minds about letting him stay there with them. He didn't want to have to go back to the neighbors' house where he had stayed before the funeral. It had also occurred to him that he might have to go to an orphanage if he messed up his chance with his grandparents. He wondered what they would do to a boy who had killed his sister at an orphanage.

"Okay, if you want to you can come an' watch TV with me. Ain't nothin good on, but that's where I'm gonna be. There in the den. Just come in if you want to." Daddy C started for the door.

"Okay."

"Have fun, an' don't let that doll eat too much." Daddy C winked at Paul.

"She ain't hungry," Paul answered.

"Well, maybe she oughtta try Mama Ray's good cookin'." Daddy C chuckled. "Maybe she's too big for that bottle."

"She don't like real food," Paul said.

"Who said Mama Ray's food was real food?" Daddy C smiled and leaned closer, in a conspiring whisper: "It may not be real but it'll fatten you up. An' your little dolly too."

"We don't wanna get fat!" Paul protested.

"Ain't nothin' wrong with gettin' a little loose around the belly," Daddy C said. "It'll give you an' your little dolly both more to love an' more to hold onto."

Paul shook his head and made a sour face at the idea.

"Well, you know where I am if you wanna come an' watch TV." Daddy C laughed and left the room, closing the door behind him.

Paul picked up Baby Doll and held her. She looked up at him with her big blue eyes as he spoke. She was smiling, but he knew that she was sad and scared. She had a lot of questions for him, and Paul was afraid that he wouldn't be able to answer all of them.

"Yeah, Honey, this is our new place," Paul told her. "But it's just for a while."

"I don't know how long a while is, Honey, but it's not a long time."

"They need time to rest, that's all, Honey."

"Yes, you can sleep with me. And we can ask Mama Ray if we can keep the light on. It'll be okay."

"I promise it'll be okay."

"You don't hate me, Honey?"

"I'm glad, Baby Doll."

"I love you, too."

Mama Ray had put on her loose purple housecoat and house shoes, and was in the kitchen at the stove. Cooking was one of the smooth regularities of life, something that could be counted on and always needed to be done. It was nice to slip so easily back into the routine of cooking after what had happened. The sizzling, the smells, and the hot and sticky steam of oil frying brought back to her a feeling of normality.

She thought of little Paul in his room as she peeled away at a potato. He seemed too old to be playing with dolls, especially for a boy. Mama Ray supposed that if his mother had thought it was okay, then she could hardly say otherwise. Maybe he would grow out of it soon.

Paul was surely hurt by what had happened, but Mama Ray couldn't be sure how hurt, and she didn't know how to talk to a seven-year-old anymore. She didn't really know how to talk to anybody, for that matter. Not even her husband, it seemed. They had lived together for almost 40 years, and instead of getting closer and knowing each other better, it was more as if they had drifted slowly and irrevocably apart.

Mama Ray had two daughters, Lorene and Connie. Lorene was her daughter by her first marriage. Mama Ray had left her parents to marry when she was very young. She had been just sixteen when Lorene was born. Lorene's father was killed in the Second World War. Mama Ray was pregnant when her husband had been shipped off to Holland, but she had not known it at the time. She told her husband in a letter, but she never got an answer back. She did not know whether he had been killed before he had received the news, or whether he had gotten the news before he had died, and hadn't had the opportunity to answer her. It broke her heart to think it was possible that he had died without knowing that he had created a child in her, but she told him every chance she got, both at his grave and in her prayers.

Mama Ray sat down with the bowl of peeled potatoes and began to slice them. It had been a long time since youngsters had been in her house. It didn't seem right to her. She didn't feel that she would be good for her grandson. Not as a mother anyway. She felt like a good grandmother, and she liked doing grandmotherly things like baking cookies and sending birthday cards, but whatever maternal energy and instincts she once had possessed had left her heart and womb many years before. She wasn't sure that she had ever had them. It wasn't difficult to feel that she had failed somehow as a mother the first time around, the way her children had turned out.

Her daughters hadn't been failures in the long run. Both Lorene and Connie were married and had beautiful children, but the road to that point had been long and scandalous, and Mama Ray was afraid that those threads that held the surface of her daughters' lives together would break again and leave their lives, and her own sense of accomplishment as a mother, in shambles. This had also been a frequent subject of her prayers.

Now she prayed that God would somehow give her the strength and energy she would need to take care of little Paul. He was very fragile, and he held so much guilt inside him. Her own guilt was festering, because she had not been able to take him in her arms, look him in the eyes and tell him that it was not his fault. She had been too confused and upset. That beautiful baby Jennifer, that sweet little girl had never hurt anybody, and they had left her all alone for that to happen. She knew it wasn't Paul's fault. He had been left alone too, and he was too young to be expected to look after her. But Connie, their mother, had left them both alone to take a nap. Maybe Connie had been really tired that day, and had needed to lie down for a few moments. But those few moments were enough for that sweet little girl to fall into the lake and die.

Mama Ray had not trusted those children living on that lake. It was too dangerous, she had told their parents, but they never listened to her. She had prayed that Connie's husband would move them to another place away from the water, but it didn't happen. God didn't stop it, either. She tried to make sense of it all as she emptied the sliced potatoes into the frying pan.

She would have to find a way to talk to Paul. She had to tell him that it wasn't his fault; but she couldn't say that it was his mother's fault, either. What would happen if he asked whose fault it was? Do little children understand that things just happen? Perhaps it would even be easier for him to understand it that way. Maybe it was only adults who always looked for someone to blame things on. Then she remembered the questions that her daughters had asked when they were little. What is the sun? Why does it shine? Why do people die?

After seeing an episode of *Dragnet* in which a character had died, Mama Ray's oldest daughter, Lorene, had once asked, "Mommie, when a person on TV dies, do they find someone who wants to die an' then kill him?" It had all been so real to Lorene. Mama Ray couldn't even remember how she had answered the question. How could she explain to Paul, that sweet little boy, that he hadn't hurt his little sister Jennifer? How could she explain why it had happened, when she didn't understand it herself? Could she say that God had taken Jennifer away? But, then, what would God think of that answer? He was probably already angry enough with her as it was for choosing the husband that she had.

Mama Ray didn't believe that God had killed Jennifer, but it had crossed her mind that He had stood back and let her die. She had even felt angry with Him and had thought a few times that all her prayers had been wasted on nothing. She still had the rest of her family, at least; and now God had put that sweet little boy in her house, and he was suffering, she knew. She would have to find that strength again, and that voice that parents use to talk to children when they are hurting. She would have to take his pain away, and that guilt, when she could not take her own pain away. She couldn't help but feel that somehow she had been the seed that caused it all, that she had been a bad mother when her daughters had needed her to be something different from what she was and had been brought up to be.

Daddy C sat opposite Paul at dinner. Mama Ray sat at the end of the table where she could easily reach the pots of food that were on the stove. Paul watched his grandparents eat. Daddy C, dressed only in his T-shirt and underwear, shovelled chunks of salad into his mouth and crunched hungrily, as if he hadn't eaten in days. The way he ate reminded Paul of a starving dog, or a pig. He expected his grandfather to snort at any moment. The thought of this made him want to smile, but he was still on edge and feeling formal. Besides, he loved Daddy C and didn't want to hurt his feelings. And he needed all the allies he could get.

Mama Ray ate much more daintily than Daddy C. She cut her food into small bites and chewed slowly, occasionally wiping the corners of her mouth with a paper napkin. Paul noticed, however, that her elbows were propped on the table as she ate, and she used both hands. That was something his mother never had allowed. "Only trashy people put their elbows on the table," he remembered his mother saying. Paul couldn't help but wonder if his grandmother was trashy.

Mama Ray swallowed a bite and chased it down with iced tea. She turned to Paul. "Honey, there's somethin' I want you to know." She paused a moment. It seemed to Paul that she was a little nervous, or that maybe she hadn't swallowed her food right. "Honey, you didn't have nothin' to do with what happened to your little sister. It wasn't your fault. And that's what I want you to know." Mama Ray put the napkin down beside her plate and rested her hands on the table. "Some things just happen and there ain't no explanation for 'em."

Paul was surprised. Even Daddy C looked a little surprised at first. As Mama Ray began to speak, Daddy C stopped eating for a moment to look at his wife, and then at Paul. He must have assumed that it was better to stay out of it, because he promptly grabbed a forkful of potatoes and started to eat again.

"But it *is* my fault," Paul said. "I didn't watch her like I was supposed to. And Mama told me it was my fault when we found her. But I didn't mean to do it. I didn't want her to die."

Mama Ray picked up her napkin again and clenched it in her hand. She opened her mouth, about to speak, and then stopped. Finally, she banged her fist against the table. "I ain't gonna say nothin' against your mama right now, but it wasn't your fault that she gone off and left you alone with your sister. You ain't old enough to be a baby sitter. She shouldn't a done that. Look at me, Honey. Honey, look at me."

Paul looked at her.

Mama Ray spoke very carefully and tried to remain calm. "You didn't do nothin' wrong. What happened was an accident. What happened is between God an' your mama, and it didn't have nothin' to do with you. Maybe you can ask God to forgive your mother, but you don't have to ask Him to forgive you for nothin' at all. Do you understand me?"

Paul didn't understand her, really. Mama Ray was the first one to have talked to him about the incident in the five days that had passed since his sister's death, except for his mother's anguished words at the side of the lake after she had dragged Jennifer's body to the shore. "How could you let this happen? How could you!" his mother had screamed as she held Jennifer's body, limp as a dishrag, in her arms. Paul had been sent to stay at their neighbors' house after that, and they had avoided the topic altogether. In fact, the neighbors had not said much at all to Paul. They had simply given him food and a place to sleep until his grandparents had arrived to get him.

"But I killed her," Paul insisted.

"You didn't kill nobody. It ain't your fault." Mama Ray seemed to be getting more distressed. She didn't know how to make her grandson understand.

"If it ain't my fault, then whose fault is it?" Paul asked.

Daddy C chimed in. "That ain't for us to decide, Doll. But just remember that you didn't have nothin' to do with it." He looked sternly at Mama Ray, as if warning her not to go further.

Mama Ray looked at Daddy C and returned his glare with equal sternness. "I ain't decidin' nothin'," she said. She turned to Paul again. "There's a lot of things nobody understands, Honey. No matter how old an' how many wrinkles you get. But you couldn't have done nothin' to help your sister. I want you to understand that. I want you to tell me that you understand. Even if you don't fully understand it right now, I want you to tell me. And you'll understand it soon enough. Tell me you understand me."

Paul looked at Mama Ray. He wanted to tell her that he understood, partly because she had obliged him to, but mostly because he wanted to believe her. It would be a great relief to the burden he had been carrying around. Still, for five days he had been convinced that he had been responsible, and it seemed impossible to change this feeling just because of his grandmother's words, no matter how well-intended they were. He gave in to his need for release of the guilt and conceded. "I understand," he said.

"Now tell me that you know you didn't have nothin' to do with what happened," Mama Ray insisted.

"I didn't have nothin to do with it."

"Good, now we can finish eatin'," Mama Ray said.

"Amen," added Daddy C, and he put another bite into his mouth. Paul began to pick at the food on his plate, not much convinced that he could continue eating. Daddy C looked over at him and made Paul an offer. "If you clean your plate, I'll take you around town with me tomorrow in the truck. I gotta go down to the produce stand and see what ol' Runny Joe an' Cowboy is up to. Gotta see if they been robbin' me blind."

Paul liked to ride with Daddy C in his pickup, and so he ate everything on his plate, even the blackeyed peas.

That night Mama Ray tucked Paul and Baby Doll into bed together. She brought in a night light, so that both of them would feel safe. As she started to leave the room, she turned to look at her grandson. She had heard a noise. She could see Paul curled up with his doll in the soft glow of the night light. "Did you say somethin', Honey?" she asked.

Paul turned and looked up from his bed at Mama Ray. "No," he said. "I didn't say anything."

12   Jason M. Dry

"I could've sworn I heard somethin'," she said. It had sounded to her like a distant whimper, or like perhaps someone had been trying to speak.

"It wasn't me," Paul said. He rested his head again on his pillow. Mama Ray waited a moment longer and looked around the room, but she could no longer hear the noise. Perhaps it had just been her imagination. Finally, she shrugged her shoulders and left Paul's bedroom.

The next morning Paul and Daddy C were on the road. They were accompanied by Buster, Tinker, and Dawn. Paul had left Baby Doll in the house, because she didn't like the dogs at all, and he was afraid that they would chew on her. Paul got along with Buster okay, but Tinker and Dawn were erratic. They always had been. Sometimes they would wag their tails and seem happy to see him, but Paul had learned early on from his Christmas visits that this was just a ploy to lure his hand toward their mouths so that they could bite the hell out of him.

Tinker was a brown chihuahua, whose small size was yet another deception. One would not suspect that she could be so ferocious, but Paul knew better from experience. His fingers had been ensnarled by her vicious chops too many times. Tinker was also deceptively fast, and it seemed that she always had perfect aim when it came to fingers and hands. Now she was squatted on her haunches in the floorboard, staring up at Paul and growling. Daddy C seemed oblivious to this showdown. He was driving merrily along, just happy to be on the road again with his dogs and his little grandson.

Dawn was Tinker's daughter. Although no one could be absolutely sure that Buster was Dawn's father, it had always just been assumed to be true. Indeed, one had to admit that the resemblance was strong. Dawn looked just like what one would expect to be the product of illicit intercourse between a chihuaha and a gray mut like Buster. Dawn was small and bushy, with bug eyes and an excessive underbite. Her lower jaw protruded about half an inch farther than the upper. She would have been an avid biter like her mother, and just as ferocious, but her dental problems impeded this.

Dawn was in the floorboard beside her mother. She was not on guard like Tinker was, but curled up and enjoying a morning nap. Buster was in Daddy C's lap, his snout out the window, and his tongue flapping joyfully in the summer wind.

"You hungry?" Daddy C asked.

"Who? Me?" asked Paul. He was not sure whether his grandfather was talking to him or to the dogs.

"Yeah. We ain't eat no breakfast yet, and if you want I'll take you over to Mrs. Celecia's for some huevos rancheros."

Paul didn't know what a huevo ranchero was, but he liked to eat breakfast with his grandfather. They had eaten many breakfasts on the road together. His older brother Frank had always been there with him, and they had been high times. His brother was about six years older than Paul, but their resemblance was nonetheless striking. One time the three of them had been in a truck stop together, and the waitress seemed dumbfounded by them. "You two are brothers," she had said as she wiped the counter. "On the outside, y'all are the spittin' image of each other, but inside y'all are as different as night and day." Paul did not know which one of them had been night and which one day, but he missed his older brother. Frank had always helped him to put up a good fight against Dawn and Tinker when they were on the road. Tinker and Dawn had always seemed to like Frank, anyway, and so they had normally been at their charming best. Paul had even thought once or twice that Tinker and her daughter might have been competing for Frank's affection.

"I remember Mrs. Celecia," Paul said. She made the best Mexican food he had ever tasted. He liked Mrs. Celecia, and she seemed to like him, too. She had always given him extra beans and Spanish rice with his enchiladas, and would often sit down with them to shoot the breeze.

"We'll go there after we run by the fruitstand. I gotta check on Runny Joe an' Cowboy before they rob me blind. We'll pick up some vegetables for Mrs. Celecia an' take 'em to her when we go." Daddy C always took vegetables to Mrs. Celecia's restaurant. She had started out as a customer of his, buying vegetables to cook in her restaurant. But over the years they had become friends, and Daddy C would take her avocados and tomatoes which were overripe. She used them in her guacamole, which was the best around. Daddy C had a lot of friends in town. He didn't always sell all of his produce, but that didn't seem to be the point of his business. It was more of a way to stay active and moving, and to keep in contact with people.

There were many a people in and around Sulphur Springs to whom he simply gave his wares, knowing that they could hardly afford a good meal otherwise. He often traded his vegetables for other things when people couldn't pay. What he got in exchange was often useless junk, but he didn't mind. It was a way to allow his customers to feel that they had given something in exchange for the fruits or vegetables that they took. He would take home these items that he had traded for, presenting them as if they were small treasures, often to Mama Ray's horror. The garage had become full over the years of useless junk. Sometimes, however, he would get in exchange something that pleased Mama Ray — like a good kitchen pot, or a blender — and Mama Ray would smile gleefully. There wasn't anyone around who didn't know Daddy C, and Paul couldn't imagine anyone who didn't like him, either — except, maybe, for Mama Ray.

"Okay," Paul said. He smiled and couldn't help but feel happy, despite the fact that Tinker was staring him down relentlessly from the floorboard. Paul looked out the window to avoid her and enjoy the view. The Texas sun shone brightly now, high above the houses of the town.

"Whaddaya know, Runny Joe?" Daddy C said out the window as Runny Joe walked up to the pickup.

"Not much, Señor," Runny Joe replied. He wobbled a little as he walked. He was a tall and thin black man in his mid-fifties. He and Cowboy lived in the little fruit stand that Daddy C owned. It was not much of a place to live in, but they had a little heater for the winter and a fan for the hot summer days. The fan didn't help much, and so Runny Joe and Cowboy spent most of their time outside, drinking Wild Turkey from a paper bag and watching the cars drive by. There was no shower at the fruit stand, and so Runny and Cowboy mostly went without bathing, except from time to time when they dipped a rag in the sink to wash themselves.

Runny Joe's real name was Ronny Joe, with an "o," but Daddy C's twang made it sound like "Runny," and Paul didn't know the difference. To Paul he was simply Runny Joe, and he had never been able to figure out why on earth a mother would name her son "Runny."

One time Paul had asked his grandfather, "Why do they call him 'Runny Joe?' Is he runny? Does he have the runs?" "That's just his name," Daddy C had answered. "Just like your name is Paul an' your brother's name is Frank. His name is Runny Joe." After a while Paul gave up trying to understand that one, and soon enough he had accepted it as another fact of life.

"I got my grandson here with me," Daddy C said. "You remember Paul, don't you? Paul, you remember Runny Joe."

Runny Joe leaned his head into the window from Daddy C's side. He looked in at Paul and smiled widely. His face beamed. "Why sho I 'member that lil' booger. Why, last time I seen you, you was just a little thang. No bigger'n the corn on my toe. Now you's a big boy. 'Course yo' Mama Ray's cookin'll put some meat on yo' bones. She a good cook, yo' Mama Ray." Runny Joe smiled at Daddy C, then he went around to Paul's side of the pickup. "It sho' is good to see you again, Seño'." He reached in to shake Paul's hand, and as he did, Tinker bolted alert and went in for the kill. She jumped up and bit Runny Joe squarely on the hand. She landed on Paul's lap and then jumped down into the floorboard. Paul screamed, and Runny Joe screamed louder. "Ouch!" screamed Runny Joe as he retracted his hand. Paul noticed that the skin was torn.

"Tinker, haah now!" Daddy C said. He scooped her up from the floorboard and put her on top of his lap. Her paw landed on top of Buster's back, and Buster, in turn, snapped at her ear. Tinker growled and bit back. Dawn, on the floor board, woke up, at first dumbfounded by the commotion and, realizing that there was action, she began to howl wildly, so as not to be left out. Daddy C pulled Buster off of Tinker, and Tinker, still indignant about being reproached, bit Buster on the tail. Buster then turned back to get a bite in on Tinker's little rump. Tinker whined.

Dawn continued howling. Paul couldn't stand the noise. He was also afraid of becoming the next target, and so he opened the door and bolted out of the pickup, inadvertently hitting Runny Joe in the shoulder as he escaped. Runny Joe doubled over and hollered again. Dawn, not wanting any prisoners to escape, jumped up from the floorboard and out the open window. She scraped Runny Joe's forehead with her claw in her flight. Runny Joe cried out again.

Daddy C spanked Tinker and put her on the floorboard. "Haah now! Stop that!" Then Buster jumped from Daddy C's lap onto the floorboard and went at Tinker, snarling. "Dad gummit! Cut that out now!" Daddy C grabbed Buster, opened the pickup door, and put him out.

Meanwhile, Dawn had landed and found her footing again. She started after Paul's heals, snapping madly. Paul was so scared that he kicked her. She fell over and let out a bellow. She quickly recovered, and then made a jump up at him. She didn't make it back to the ground. Runny Joe caught her in mid-air. Paul thought that if Runny Joe hadn't caught her, she would have surely gotten his throat. Dawn must have been caught by surprise, because when Runny Joe caught her, she stopped barking immediately and began to whimper. Runny Joe noticed a warm, wet sensation moving down his arm.

"Oh my gooness! This thang peed on me!" Runny Joe exclaimed, horrified. Paul looked at the yellow liquid still dripping out of Dawn onto Runny Joe's arm. Paul thought later, maybe that was why they called him runny. Runny Joe dropped Dawn in disgust. She fell on her side, but quickly rolled over onto her feet and ran under the pickup.

Paul began to laugh in spite of himself, but his laughter seemed too loud and artificial. It was the first time he had laughed since what had happened to his sister. It seemed strange to him, almost foreign, as if the laughter was coming from someone else.

"It ain't funny. I don' know why yo' laughin'," Runny Joe said. "I saved you from the damned thang."

"I'm sorry," Paul said. He really did feel bad, and he was grateful to Runny Joe for having intervened. He just had not been able to help himself. He decided to make up a lie to save himself and to make Runny Joe feel better. "I wasn't laughing at you. I was laughing at the dog. You sure did show her."

Runny Joe looked thoughtful for a moment and began to smile. "I guess I did," he said; his smile grew wider and wider, showing his big white teeth, and he began to chuckle as he shook the urine from his arm.

Paul, already ashamed and startled by his initial expression of joy, stifled his own laughter.

Daddy C opened the pickup door and got out. He walked around to where Paul and Runny Joe were. Buster and Tinker followed behind him, wagging their tails. Dawn came out from under the pickup and joined in, wagging her tale in unison with the others. They seemed to have forgotten about the whole struggle that had ensued just moments before.

"You all wet, Runny Joe," Daddy C said. "I'm sorry about that. They ain't normally so high strung. I guess they're just a little bit excited with our grandson here."

"I shoulda knowed it was yo' fault," Runny Joe said, looking at Paul. Paul got a little nervous, but then Runny Joe began to smile. "Aw, I's just teasin you. It ain't yo fault. Those dogs is just mean an' crazy. They been 'round Mama Ray too long." He chuckled again, but, looking at Daddy C and seeing that he was not amused by the comment, he stifled his glee. "I gotta wash this dog pee off of me," he said. He took off his shirt. Paul could see a curved scar on Runny Joe's chest as he used his shirt to wipe Dawn's urine from his arm.

"Here, Runny Joe, give that shirt to me. Mama Ray'll wash it for ya." Runny Joe gave his shirt to Daddy C, who then tossed it into the back of the pickup. "Where's Cowboy?" Daddy C asked.

"Aw, he still sleepin', I guess," Runny Joe said. "'Less he done gone out the back while I whuddn't lookin'."

"Well, what's been goin' on while I was gone? We done sold all them cantaloupes?"

"Yeah, we done sold most of 'em. People kept comin' back fo' mo'. They was real sweet, like honey. A few done gone sour, but we done sold right near all of 'em. People was askin' 'bout you. They sho' was real sorry to hear 'bout what happened." After he said this he looked at Paul and immediately regretted having mentioned it. "I'mmo go in an' git me anotha shirt. Come on y'all two, an' see if we can wake Cowboy up. It's almost eight o'clock. An' he'd sho' be upset if he missed seein' you, little Paul."

They all followed Runny Joe into the fruit stand. It had once been a washateria, and by now it was pretty run down. There were still several old washers and dryers which had been pushed to the back of the old building. Scattered among the machines were also many of the items of junk for which Daddy C had traded at the fruit stand and at flea markets throughout the years. The concrete floors of the fruit stand were covered in dirt, onion peels, corn husks, and peanut shells.

In the very back of the building was a sofa, an old black-and-white television set, and an ancient white refrigerator which miraculously still functioned. Cowboy was asleep belly-up on the sofa. He had his hat over his face, and his arm and leg draped off the side. Runny Joe walked to the back and reached into a cardboard box where he kept his clothes. He grabbed a wrinkled shirt, shook it bruskly, and put it on without buttoning it. "Cowboy still sleepin'," he said, not at all trying to whisper for Cowboy's benefit. "He sleep 'bout half his life away."

Daddy C was looking at the fruits and vegetables, checking which ones had sold, which ones hadn't, and which ones were beginning to rot. "Damn, Runny Joe, these tomatoes here's done rotten." He was already picking the rotten ones out and putting them in a paper sack to throw out. "Ain't no customers gonna buy no rotten tomatoes. You gotta pick 'em out, or all of 'ems gonna go bad."

"I know it, Señor. We been real busy," Runny Joe replied. At this he gave Paul a conspiratorial smile. "Just look at Cowboy there. He done tired out fom all the work we been doin'."

"Hell, I know all about the work you been doin'," Daddy C said, a bit annoyed. He continued picking through the produce. "Workin' on two bottles apiece the whole night. You know about as much about China as you know about workin'. Why don't you tell me about Jack Daniels, if you wanna sound like you know what you're talkin' about. Here, Paul, these apples is good. You want an apple?"

Paul looked at the apple in Daddy C's hand. It looked brown and sticky. Daddy C noticed that Paul was looking at his hand. "Not this one, Doll. This one's done hog slop. Take one of these." He put the rotten apple in the sack and picked up a fresh golden delicious. "These ones is real sweet an' juicy."

Paul took the apple. "Can I wash it before I eat it?" he asked. He looked around and didn't see a sink.

"You can wipe it on yo' shirt. It won't hurt none," Runny Joe suggested. "Least it ain't got dog pee on it."

"Naw, we're gonna wash it for him," Daddy C said. "Eatin' dirty fruit's just like stickin' dirty money in your mouth. Your mama taught you real good, Doll. My grandson's brought up right, Runny Joe." Daddy C looked proud. He took the apple and went back to the small restroom to wash it in the sink for his grandson. As he passed the sofa to get to the toilet, he reached down and pulled on cowboy's foot. Cowboy snorted.

Daddy C came back to the front and gave the apple to Paul. Paul bit into it heartily.

"We done open?" The sound came suddenly and startled Paul. Daddy C, Runny Joe, and Paul looked around to see where the voice came from. It was Cowboy, now roused from his slumber.

"Hell, yeah, we done open," Runny Joe answered. "Been done open fo' hours. I done sold yo' boots an' 'bout five pounds of taters."

"My boots?" Cowboy looked around, still dazed, for his boots. Finally he found them still on his feet. "You didn't sell my boots. I still got 'em."

"Yeah, I sold yo' boots, Cowboy," Runny Joe said. "A man came 'round 'bout six o'clock this mo-nin'. Paid me for them boots an' said he'd come 'round this afternoon to pick 'em up. We tried to get 'em off you, but we couldn' do it 'cause yo' feet so big. He wanted yo' hat, too, till he saw how filthy it is. I tried to give him a cheaper price, but he wouldn't take it nohow."

"My feet ain't big. *You* got big feet, and they ugly too. An' they stink. An' you didn't sell my boots, 'cause you know I'd kick yer cotton-pickin' ass if you did."

Daddy C intervened. "Haah now. Be nice, Cowboy. My grandson's here. Ain't you got no better manners than to talk like that? And Runny Joe didn't sell your boots. He was just jokin' with you."

Cowboy pulled himself up into a seated position on the sofa and squinted his eyes to look for Daddy C's grandson. "Why, hello there, Frank! I didn't see you before. It sure is good to see you again."

"I ain't Frank," Paul said. "I'm Paul, his younger brother." Paul didn't mind that Cowboy had mistaken him for his brother. It happened often. Even though he was several years younger than Frank, many old people had trouble telling them apart.

"Well, my lands, son," Cowboy said, bewildered. "I sho' did think that you was Frank. You look just like him. You sound like him, too. But I guess it's 'cause the last time I seen him he was as big as you are now. I guess he'd be a lot bigger by now. How's life been treatin' you, little Paul? I sho' am glad to see you."

"I'm fine," Paul said, still eating the apple. It was juicy and sweet, just like Daddy C had promised.

"I guess he's gonna be with us for a while, huh, Boss?" Cowboy asked Daddy C.

"Yeah, an' we sure are proud to have him," Daddy C answered.

"Maybe it'll liven things up a little havin' a young 'en around the house," Cowboy said. "But of course you'll have to fatten him up a little. He ain't big enough to shake a stick at." Cowboy was big himself. He was about 26 years old, around six feet tall, and had a gut that protruded far past the waistband of his Wrangler jeans. He wore a large belt buckle that he had bought at a rodeo, but its prominence was hidden beneath his belly. Cowboy always wore western shirts, and his dirty old Stetson hat, and so it was no mystery as to where he got his name.

"Well, we gonna take care of that, ain't we Paul?" Daddy C replied. "We gonna go right now down to Mrs. Celecia's an' load him up on her huevos rancheros. He likes those. Don't you, Paul?"

"Yeah," said Paul, although he still wasn't sure what huevos rancheros were. He figured he would find out soon enough, and, if Mrs. Celecia made them, then they must be good.

"Paul!" cried Mrs. Celecia as she saw him come into her restaurant with Daddy C. "I ain't seen you in forever!" She ran up to Paul and bent down. She hugged him tightly, giving Paul a start. Then she looked him over and put her hand through his hair. "Calvin, you brought your little grandson back with you. He gonna stay with us a while?" Mrs. Celecia always called Daddy C by his first name, which was "Calvin."

"Yes, he is. He might start school here, too. We think he'll like it," Daddy C said.

"Oh, that's wonderful! I bet you're happy to have him," Mrs. Celecia said.

"We sure are!" Daddy C smiled.

"Come, sit down, both of you." Mrs. Celecia signaled them to sit at a table near the counter. "What can I get for y'all?"

"Huevos rancheros," said Paul carefully, struggling to get the words out in exactly the way that Daddy C had said them.

"Oye, ¡Qué bien!" Mrs. Celecia said. "You said that real good." "You speak Spanish, too?" she asked, teasing Paul a little.

"Is that Spanish?" Paul asked. He didn't know that he had just spoken Spanish.

"Yeah, that's Spanish," Daddy C said. "See there how smart my little grandson is, Marie?"

"Yes, I see. He's real smart, and handsome, too. Just like his grandfather." Paul noticed that Mrs. Celecia winked at Daddy C when she said this.

"Y ¿Qué quieres de beber, mijo? What do you want to drink, sweety ?"

"Iced tea," said Daddy C.

"Not, you, silly. I was talking to Paul." Mrs. Celecia laughed, and wrote down the drink order.

"I want iced tea, too," Paul said.

"Okay, two iced teas and two huevos rancheros. Coming up!" Mrs. Celecia disappeared into the kitchen, but her voice was still audible.

"Órale, que Mr. Sewell está aquí con su nieto. ¿Te acuerdas? Ay, ¡Qué guapo es el niño! ¡Está cada vez más guapo! ¡Se parece a su abuelo! Ándale, pues, ponles dos huevos rancheros." Mrs. Celecia came out with two large plastic cups of iced tea. Paul noticed that the tables were covered with a thick plastic wrap, and underneath were postcards from Mexico. On the walls of the restaurant were old posters advertising bullfights, and prints of beautiful Mexican señoritas. There was a print of a sad-looking donkey over the cash register.

"You want sugar, Calvin? Your grandson, he sweet enough without none, he he." Mrs. Celecia pinched Paul on the cheek.

"No, Marie, I don't take sugar no more. I'm tryin' ta cut down, you know. When you're too sweet, the ladies don't want you. You know how it is." Daddy C grinned and took a healthy swig of his iced tea. The sun outside was getting hot, and the cold drink felt good going down. "Sit down and stay a while, Señorita. Take a load off."

"No, you know, I been so busy as you can see. I gotta wait around and see if anybody else comes in." Mrs. Celecia looked around at the empty room and smiled to make her sarcasm obvious to them. Paul looked around, too, and wondered why Marie had said that she was busy. He thought that maybe she had a lot of work to do in the kitchen. Mrs. Celecia sat down with the two.

"Times is hard all over, Marie. What with this new Republican President and all. He wasn't even good as an actor, much less as a President." Daddy C was a die-hard Democrat. He still had portraits of Franklin Roosevelt and John F. Kennedy hanging on the walls. One of his proudest moments had been when he was invited to the inauguration of Lyndon B. Johnson as President. He didn't attend the ceremony, but he still had the invitation mounted proudly on his wall, between the portraits of Kennedy and Roosevelt. "Who knows what'll happen next."

"I don't think it got nothin' to do with who's President, Calvin. I think the people aroun' here just don' like to eat frijoles. They don't want good home cookin'. They wanna eat grease burgers and french fries. I wouldn' feed that stuff to my dogs, much less to my children. What they need is some good enchiladas an' a bowl of menudo for breakfast. My mama fed us menudo every day for breakfast, and we didn' grow up to be fat little ungrateful slobs like most gringo kids. Of course, your children didn' turn out that way, Calvin. There must be some Chicano in your blood." Marie laughed, but Daddy C didn't seem amused by the thought of having Chicano in his ancestry.

"Yeah, people just don't know good ol' down-home cookin' anymore," Daddy C said. "But I like to have a burger now and then myself, if it ain't all-too-often."

"I like hamburgers," Paul added to the conversation.

Mrs. Aguilar shook her head in disapproval. "Well, honey, that's because you haven' tried my enchiladas in a while," she said, deciding to give Paul another chance. "You tell your grandpa to bring you aroun' in the evening, and I make you some good enchiladas, and you'll never want a hamburger again. You need to eat more enchiladas anyway, Mijo."

"Okay," Paul said, looking at his grandfather for a sign that it was okay. Daddy C nodded back at him.

"I almost forgot, Marie," Daddy C said. "I brought you some tomatoes. They ain't many, but, you know we been gone a few days. The other ones was done rotted, but these is real good. You can put 'em in your salad, or your menudo or whatever." Daddy C handed the paper sack to Marie. Marie made a mock frown as she took the tomatoes from him.

"Calvin, you din' hafta do that. You know I got plenty tomatoes. But I sure appreciate it, 'cause they ain't none of 'em as good as yours." She opened the sack and smiled widely. She looked at Paul. "You see what a nice man your grandpa is?" Paul was in the middle of swallowing some tea, and so he nodded. "He does lots of good things. You gonna learn a lot from him, and from your grandma, too." Mrs. Celecia leaned over to Paul and whispered in his ear. "There a lot of people in this town, they don't like your grandma. But I know her for a long time, and she's a good woman, so you don't listen to what the other people say 'bout her." She leaned back again and nodded sternly at Paul. Then she put her finger over her lips, indicating that he should keep quiet about what she had just said.

"You tellin' secrets, Marie?" Daddy C asked, looking over his big cup of tea, which he had raised to his mouth.

"I'm always telling secrets, Calvin. You know that. That ain't nothin' new that happened since you been away. I just told your grandson that you drive the ladies wild. But he woulda figured that out on his own."

"Well, yeah, that ain't no mystery, Marie. But they drive me wilder." Daddy C grinned.

Marie laughed, and got up from the table. "I go get your huevos. I don' want them to get cold. Cold huevos is worse than those darned fat burgers. You gotta eat 'em hot or they make you constipated. That's how I got revenge on my husband, served him cold huevos an' he wouldn't be able to go to the bathroom for days." Marie disappeared into the kitchen.

Paul and Daddy C ate their huevos rancheros quickly because they were delicious, but also because they didn't want to get constipated. Paul was not sure what constipation was, but the word itself was enough to make him want to avoid the condition.

As Daddy C and Paul were leaving, Mrs. Celecia said, "You bring your little grandson back to see me, Calvin. I want him to meet my little granddaughter, Daniela. She real sweet just like him, and I think they would be good buddies. And bring Wanda Ray with you. She don't get out enough."

"Will do, Marie. We'll all be cravin' your enchiladas 'fore too long anyway," Daddy C replied. Paul waved at Marie, who blew them both a kiss as they walked out the door.

Mama Ray was in the kitchen with her mother, Martha, who, after Connie and Lorene were born, became "Big Mama." Big Mama lived in the house just next door to Mama Ray and Daddy C. Thus, they saw each other often, for better or worse. Big Mama had a full life of her own, and, therefore, did not intrude much on the lives of her daughter and son-in-law. In fact, she was very helpful to them most of the time. She had taken care of Buster, Tinker, and Dawn while Mama Ray and Daddy C were away at the funeral. Mama Ray was very thankful to have her mother living near them, but Big Mama possessed some eccentricities that often tried her daughter's patience. Big Mama had stopped going to Sunday school and church many years before, claiming that it was a waste of her time. She also claimed to talk to spirits. Mama Ray did not believe that her mother actually talked to spirits, although there had been many times when Big Mama had known things before they had happened. Mama Ray did know, however, that just the simple notion of conjuring spirits was the work of the devil, and she wanted none of that in her house. Her preacher seconded this opinion, and he had convinced Mama Ray to have a second Baptism in order to ensure that she was freed of any wicked influence that her mother might have had on her. In spite of all Big Mama's eccentricities, Mama Ray loved her, and finally they both had reached an agreement to avoid the topic of spirits and preachers altogether.

Big Mama and Mama Ray were sitting at the table, having tall glasses of iced tea. "You think you still got it in you to go out an' kill one of them chickens?" Mama Ray asked her mother.

Big Mama was puzzled by her daughter's question. "What chickens?" she asked.

"Them that's out in the back yard," Mama Ray answered. "I know I shouldn't do it, but I just can't have 'em out there shittin' all over the place an' eatin' up the grass."

Big Mama knew that house backwards and forwards, including the back yard, and she hadn't seen any chickens there in years. "Honey, there ain't no chickens out there in the back yard," she said.

"The hell there ain't," Mama Ray replied. "Go out there an' look for yourself. They're eatin' up the grass an' shittin' all over the place."

Big Mama put down her iced tea and scooted her chair back. She waddled over to the window that was above the kitchen sink. She peered out and squinted her eyes through her horn-rimmed glasses. She could see the swing set, and to its left the tool shed that Daddy C had put out there to store some of the junk he was always bringing in from trading at the produce stand and the flea markets. Farther back, near the fence, she was finally able to see a group of white hens pecking away at the dirt.

"Where did them things come from?" Big Mama asked, still watching the chickens.

"What do you mean, 'Where did they come from?'" Mama Ray said. "They've always been out there, ever since Calvin brought the darned things home when they was babies."

"Honey, them chickens wasn't out there before," Big Mama insisted. She turned around to look at her daughter. "I remember you used to have chickens, but that was a long time ago."

"You must be goin' crazy, Mama," Mama Ray said. "They've been out there this whole time."

Big Mama knew that she was not going crazy, but she wasn't so sure about her daughter. "You put them chickens out there, didn't you?" Big Mama asked.

Mama Ray was bewildered. Why would her mother accuse her of putting those chickens out there, when they had been there for years. She had warned Daddy C before that her mother was going mad, but he had always insisted that she was wrong. Now it seemed that she was most definitely losing her mind. "Now, why in the world would I put them chickens out there?" she asked. "You know I can't stand 'em. They done eat up all my grass."

Big Mama simply shook her head. She went back over to the table and sat down. She was not as worried about the chickens as she was about the fact that her daughter insisted that she had not put them there. If Mama Ray had forgotten that she herself had put the chickens out there, then there was no telling what else was happening in her mind. "What do you remember about the funeral, Honey?" she asked.

"Why are you askin' about that now?" Mama Ray said. "I'd just assume forget about it."

"I'm just curious, is all," Big Mama said.

"Well, what do you think I should remember about it?" Mama Ray asked. Big Mama could have asked her what she had thought of the funeral, or if the preacher had been a good one. To ask her what she remembered about the funeral, however, was absurd. Her mother seemed to be questioning her ability to remember the funeral altogether, when Big Mama was the one who filled in the gaps in her faulty memory with delusions. *She* was the one who had been claiming for years to communicate with the dead, after all.

"I just thought I'd ask what the funeral was like," Big Mama said, trying to soften the previous question. She sensed that her daughter was getting defensive.

Mama Ray put her iced tea on the table with a thud. "Oh, it was a lot of fun," she said. "I got a thrill out of puttin' on a black dress an' watchin' my little grandbaby bein' put down in a hole."

"What did Paul think about it?" Big Mama asked. She was being very cautious now not to be too direct. She knew that her daughter was getting upset with her questions, but she could not yet understand the reason for her anger.

"Paul didn't go," Mama Ray said. "He had to stay with the neighbors. It was better that way."

"Why did he stay with the neighbors?" Big Mama asked.

Mama Ray seemed to be calming down a little. At least she was calm enough to pick up her glass and take another swig of iced tea. "He was real upset," Mama Ray said. She stopped herself. It had been difficult enough to think about what had happened. To put it into words, to *talk* about it, made it feel even worse. Mama Ray's voice trembled as she continued. "He thinks he caused his sister to drown. It would've been too much for him to be there."

Big Mama shook her head. "Why does he think he killed his sister?" she asked. "I never heard of such nonsense."

"I know," Mama Ray agreed, "but he was there when she died, an' for some reason he thinks it's his fault. I done told him it wasn't, but I still don't think he believes it."

"He was there when *who* died?" Big Mama asked. She was having difficulty following what her daughter was talking about.

Mama Ray sighed loudly in frustration. "His sister! Jennifer!" she said. "Mama, have you gone completely out of your gourd? Why do you think we went an' picked him up in the first place?" Mama Ray was beginning to really worry about her mother. She knew that she should not be so hard on her, but it was frustrating to have to explain the situation again. The words alone seemed to bring the events back to life, and it was too much for her. Big Mama was very old, she had to remind herself, and it was normal for old people to lose their minds. But one would think that she would be able to remember the death of her own great-granddaughter. Mama Ray feared that she would have to take her mother to a doctor soon.

Big Mama tried to think of a way to bring her daughter back to her senses. She had apparently forgotten everything that had happened. What had happened to her? First she was imagining chickens, and now she had forgotten all about why she had gone to Kingsland. She started to try to explain. "But, Honey, Jennifer's—"

"Mama, could we please just drop the subject?" Mama Ray interrupted. "I don't wanna talk about it no more. It was real hard on all of us, an' I don't think you should talk about it to Paul, either."

Big Mama looked her daughter squarely in the eyes, trying to see what was going on inside her head. Mama Ray seemed completely convinced of what she was saying. Now, Big Mama realized that she would not only have to deal with little Paul, but with Mama Ray, as well. She decided that it was best to just abandon the topic, for the moment. In the meantime, she would just let her daughter think that she was crazy. Crazy people always thought that everybody else was insane, anyway.

Big Mama decided to change the subject. Over the years, she had developed a real talent for getting her daughter's back up, and, luckily, she was equally skilled at calming her down quickly. "When are we gonna go an' catch us a chicken?" Big Mama asked with an grin. If her daughter had put those chickens in the back yard, then they might as well fry one up for lunch, she decided.

It had been a long time since Big Mama had wrung a chicken's neck, and now she had begun to look forward to it. She had owned a small farm many years before, and at that time wringing a chicken's neck had been like second nature to her. Big Mama's fried chicken was widely known as the best around. She had satiated the appetites of many a kin folk with her juicy chicken, and she was excited to fry up a batch for her great-grandson. There was nothing like a freshly-killed hen for her prized fried chicken. She preferred killing them herself to buying the plastic processed meat that was sold in stores, but since she had sold her beloved farm, she had gotten used to a life of consuming body parts sold in plastic bags. It seemed to her that people were not even aware anymore of the fact that they were eating an animal, that something had died to be put upon their plates at dinnertime.

"Well, I guess we might oughtta go ahead an' kill one of 'em," Mama Ray said, a bit distracted. She was still thinking about her poor mother, and what she was going to do about her. She hoped that the problem would not continue, because the last thing she wanted was for the whole town to know that Big Mama had gone mad. Everybody knew that insanity runs in the family, and, if she had to put her mother in the loony bin, people around town would probably start suspecting her of being crazy as well.

Mama Ray had devised a plan to serve little Paul up a batch of Big Mama's down-home fried chicken. She knew that there would be unpleasant consequences, however. Daddy C had brought home ten baby chickens which he had been given at the flea market. Two of them had died within a week of their arrival. Later, upon reaching adolescence, one of the hens was apparently killed by a neighbor's cat, which had left blood and feathers all over the yard. Soon after, another hen had just disappeared. Daddy C had said that the teenage chicken had run away out of sadness after the loss of her sister. They had been left with six hens that had grown up to become a flock of white pecking beasts that even Tinker was afraid of. They lived in the back yard, and when the dogs would have to go outside to do their business, the hens would hiss and chase them around, sometimes pecking them on the rear. Not even little Tinker's ferocious bark would scare those chickens away. Daddy C did not notice their frequent acts of terrorism against the dogs. Instead, he had grown to love them and think of them as his pets.

The hens had pecked away all the grass, which left the yard with nothing but dirt and looking like a waste land covered in chicken and dog droppings. Mama Ray had thus vowed to cook their gooses as soon as possible, and Paul's arrival made the perfect excuse to celebrate with a fresh fried chicken. Unable to bring herself to do the dastardly deed, she had retrieved Big Mama as soon as Paul and Daddy C had left to the fruit stand that morning.

"I guess we'll just tell Calvin that it run away," Mama Ray said. "I guess they could fly over the fence if they wanted to. I wish they'd all do it."

"Oh, don't you worry none about Calvin," Big Mama said. "He'll get over it. He knows you can't have chickens as pets." Big Mama knew that Calvin would not care one way or another, since the chickens were only products of her daughter's overactive imagination. In any case, she was looking forward to getting ahold of one of them. She wanted to prove to herself that she still had it in her to wring a chicken's neck.

"Let's go get one," Mama Ray said. She was determined to get it over with before she began to have second thoughts again. Overcome with sudden conviction, she put her glass of tea down on the table and got up quickly from her chair. She wanted to get it over with before she lost her nerve.

"Wait a minute. Hold your horses, now," Big Mama warned. "You can't just go out there runnin' around an' expect the darned thangs to come a runnin' up to you an' lovin' on you. They wouldn't do that. They don't like you, remember?" Big Mama laughed.

Mama Ray didn't take the comment personally, because the chickens did not like anybody except for Daddy C. They *tolerated* Mama Ray, or, better put, they ignored her. Perhaps this was what annoyed her most of all. She had even tried to be friendly toward them at times in the beginning, giving them scraps and corn. But they never would go up to her like they would to Daddy C. They would sit in his lap and let him scratch their heads. But they just ignored Mama Ray and only ate her scraps when she had gone back into the house and was out of their way.

Mama Ray stopped and stood with her hand on the back of her chair. "Well, how do you expect to get one, then?" she asked.

"We need to have a plan. Chickens is smarter than you think," Big Mama said. The wheels of her brain were already turning, concocting a plan.

Mama Ray looked at her mother, whose eyes were glowing, indicating that she was thinking up a scheme. She shook her head and sat down again, hoping that this plan would not take long to devise. However, she had known her mother long enough to know that, to Big Mama, half the fun of the act itself was in the creation of a plan. To her it was like living out the fantasy in her mind, as if it was actually happening in her head even before the act was committed. Mama Ray put her hand through her hair, streaked with brown and gray, and propped her elbows on the table. She tried to be patient, although a feeling of unease began to creep upon her.

"If you go a runnin' up on one of 'em, it'll run off and start a squawkin'," Big Mama continued. "Then they'll all start a squawkin' and a screamin' bloody murder. Then they'll be a flappin' all over the place, and you won't never get to one of 'em."

"Well, what do you plan to do, then? Hypnotize 'em?" Mama Ray asked.

"Somethin' like that, but not exactly," Big Mama answered, with widening eyes. "You done seen me wring a plenty a chicken's necks. Don't you remember that?"

"Mama, that was a long time ago," Mama Ray answered, trying to hide her impatience, which was mounting. "I don't remember that." She was just fifteen when she had left the farm to get married.

"Well, then, this'll be like a new experience for you," Big Mama gleamed. "You're gonna go up behind 'em an' walk real slow toward me. I'm gonna be in front of 'em, and you're gonna herd 'em up in my direction. I need you to do that 'cause of my leg. I don't think I can run as fast as I used to." There was a reason why they called her Big Mama. Since the end of her farm days and after several divorces, she had begun to sit at home much of the time, and much of that time she spent at home was dedicated to cherished activities like eating her prized fried chicken and other down-home delicacies to which she liked to treat herself and her many guests who passed by to pay a visit.

As her reputation as the best cook and most hospitable hostess around began to grow, so did her physical size. She was a very lively woman with a naturally stout build, and so the additional pounds seemed to add to her legendary status. She was still very active, except that the excess weight had impaired her circulation. She was still able to walk wherever she wanted to with a cane, and did so often. However, her poor circulation prevented her from sitting for long periods, and had prevented her from accompanying Daddy C and Mama Ray to the funeral. Big Mama was happy to have stayed home and kept the dogs for them, however. She didn't believe in funerals.

"Well, come on, an' let's get it over with," Mama Ray said, eager to put the deed behind her.

"Yeah, boy!" Big Mama shouted, unable to conceal her zeal. She put both hands on the sides of the chair and pushed herself up. She grabbed her cane, which was hanging on the back of the chair next to her.

Mama Ray noticed that her mother had grabbed her cane. She normally only used it for walking long distances, and so it surprised her. "Do you need your cane?" she asked.

"Well, I might," Big Mama said. "If I have to go a runnin' after one of 'em. You never know what they might do when they realize what we're up to. They ain't stupid, you know."

Mama Ray followed Big Mama through the kitchen and den, and out through the sliding glass door to the grassless back yard. The hens were all together, still pecking happily at the dirt. Big Mama spotted them and walked slowly off the porch. She lifted her big flowered dress up above her knees, showing the tops of her stockings, and began to crouch down. She turned to Mama Ray and put her finger to her lips, indicating that she should be quiet. "Now go over there behind 'em. But be slow," she whispered.

Mama Ray followed her mother's order, walking slowly along the chain-linked fence at a safe distance from the chickens. She wondered what Big Mama had in mind to do next. From the other side of the yard she saw her mother begin to sway awkwardly, her dress still lifted above her knees and feet out. It reminded Mama Ray of a hippopotamus.

Big Mama slowly maneuvered herself until she was a few feet in front of the chickens, which still didn't seem to have paid any attention to her. She stopped and began to stare at them. Her eyes bulged out and she began to move her head back and forth. Her cane in hand, she began to slowly flap her arms, with elbows out and hands pressed against her shoulders.

"What are you doin'?" Mama Ray asked, bewildered. Her mother really was going mad, she thought.

Big Mama stopped flapping her arms. "Shhhh, be quiet! You're gonna scare them chickens," she said, annoyed that her daughter had interrupted her fun. She figured that if Mama Ray already suspected that she was crazy, then she might as well give her a good show to add fuel to her suspicions. She began to flap her arms again.

"*You're* gonna scare 'em if you keep doin' that," Mama Ray said.

"I ain't gonna scare 'em. They *like* me. They think I'm a chicken, too. Now be quiet," Big Mama said.

"Yeah, a three-hunnerd-pound chicken with a walkin' cane an' half a brain in its head," Mama Ray said softly to herself.

"I heard that," Big Mama said.

Big Mama couldn't possibly have heard what Mama Ray had said. She had said it much too softly for her mother to have heard it from the other side of the yard. Maybe she had expected her daughter to make a sarcastic remark, and had just reacted out of expectation.

Big Mama began to sway her hips and move up closer, stretching her neck out and kicking at the dirt. The chickens still did not look up from their pecking and scratching. Still flapping her arms, Big Mama let out a bellow. "Bawk, bawk, bawk, bawwwwk," she said, giving her best chicken impersonation.

Mama Ray was looking at her, still in disbelief. As she witnessed Big Mama's earnest expression, her eyes bulging out beneath the black horn-rimmed glasses on her chubby face, her arms flapping, and the mad bellows that she let out, Mama Ray could no longer control herself. The sight of her mother seemed so absurd to her, so funny, that she let out a bellow of her own, a loud, uncontrolled, roaring laugh. "Aaaaah ha ha!" she cried, and slapped her knees, unable to control her laughter. "Aaaaah ha ha ha!"

At this the chickens started. They flapped their wings and ran toward Big Mama. Big Mama screeched and swung around. As she turned around, one of the chickens tried to fly away. Disoriented, it flew up in her direction, its wings flapping in a frenzy. Big Mama swung at it with her cane, hitting it in the head. The chicken fell back to the ground and made another leap to get away. Big Mama dropped her cane, and she grabbed at the chicken. In the confusion she thought that she had missed it, but she looked down at her hands and saw that she had its neck squarely in her clutches. Almost instinctively, she held the chicken in the air and began to jerk it quickly back and forth, feeling the strength come back to her with every movement. "I got me one!" Big Mama cried triumphantly. "He he! I got me one!"

The chicken squawked hysterically as it jerked in Big Mama's grip. In a frenzy, the other five chickens scurried away, also squawking madly, flapping, half flying, half running, in Mama Ray's direction. When Mama Ray saw them coming, she began to run, feeling their wings brush against her. "Shoo! Shoo!" she screamed. "Get away from me!" She swung her arms at them, and one of the chickens scraped the back of her hand with its feathers. "Shoo!" Mama Ray screamed. "Shoo!"

A neighbor opened the shutters to see what the commotion was about. He leaned his head out the window. "Where are those damned chickens?" the neighbor cried.

By this time the chickens had made their way past Mama Ray and were scuttering to safety in a far corner of the yard.

Mama Ray turned to the neighbor as Big Mama continued strangling her prize. She did not recognize the neighbor. He must have moved in freshly, since their old neighbor, Old Lady Prewitt, had passed away. Old Lady Prewitt had been a kind elderly woman who had lived in that house across the fence for many years until, one day, she passed on gently in her sleep.

"I'm sorry about the noise," Mama Ray said back to the neighbor. "We was just gettin' up a chicken to fry."

The neighbor peered out past both of them to some distant point. Mama Ray thought that he was ignoring them. "Damned squawkin' chickens!" he said, and then closed the window, paying no attention to the two women.

"There now!" said Big Mama. Mama Ray turned to her. Her mother had lowered her arm, and the chicken was dangling limp and lifeless in her large fist. "There now! It's all over. Poor little chicken. He he!" She looked up from the hen and at her daughter. "That wasn't too bad. 'Course I'd a done it a lot faster in my younger days. I hate to make the poor thangs suffer too much. But it's dead now, so I guess we can go ahead and pluck it."

"Let's go on in the house with it, Mama," Mama Ray said. She was feeling uneasy. She did not want to draw too much attention from the neighbors, lest they bear witness to the deed.

"We oughta pluck it outside," Big Mama said. "You'll have them feathers an' blood all over the house if we ain't careful."

"Just bring it in the house, Mama," Mama Ray insisted. She started toward the porch without waiting for a response.

Big Mama shrugged her shoulders and followed her daughter into the house. "I never heard of pluckin' a chicken indoors before," she protested as she carried the hen by its feet through the den.

"I don't wanna be out there where that new neighbor can see our business. He seemed kinda weird to me," Mama Ray said. She also didn't want to leave a trail of blood and feathers on the ground outside for Daddy C to find. Any stains would be easier to clean up from the linoleum floor.

They went into the kitchen. Mama Ray got out a long baking pan and put it on the table. Big Mama put the chicken on top of the pan as her daughter scooted the trash over to the sink to put the feathers in.

"Oh, that neighbor ain't gonna bother us," Big Mama said. She knew that he most likely hadn't even noticed that they had been out there. "Who is he, anyway? I didn't know that nobody lived there since Ms. Prewitt left."

"I didn't either. He must be new. He sure didn't seem very friendly. Gave me the creeps." Mama Ray took the pan with the chicken on it and put it on the counter beside the sink.

"Best to just stay out of his way, and he'll stay out of yours," Big Mama said, "the way the world is goin' nowadays. Every man to hisself."

"I ain't gonna go 'round him. That's for sure."

"I sure never heard of pluckin' a chicken in the house before," Big Mama repeated, in case she hadn't gotten her point across the first time. "But I guess these is modern times," she added.

The two women stood around the chicken. The both grabbed some feathers and began to pluck. As soon as they began to pull the feathers out, the hen began to scratch furiously and flap its wings. Mama Ray and Big Mama gasped in disbelief, as the chicken raised its head and started to squawk. Mama Ray screamed. Big Mama cried, "I thought it was dead! Hold it down!"

They tried to restrain it, but the chicken continued to squawk and struggle. Mama Ray tried hard to hold its head down so that it couldn't peck her. She looked down and saw terror in its eyes as the hen tried to get free.

"Hold it down!" Big Mama cried again as she shuffled in a drawer. She pulled out a big butcher knife and held it over the chicken. "Move your hands clear of its neck," she said. Mama Ray looked up and saw the butcher knife, and moved her hands away from the hen's neck. She looked down and saw the chicken, who by now had stopped squawking but continued to struggle to get loose. It was breathing rapidly.

"Stop!" cried Mama Ray, as her mother raised the butcher knife, ready to hack into the chicken. "Wait!"

"What?" said Big Mama, a little annoyed.

"Just let the poor thang go," Mama Ray said. "Put the knife down."

Big Mama put the knife down, feeling disappointed. "What do you mean, 'Let it go?'" By now the chicken had stopped struggling, but its body was rigid and it was still breathing heavily.

"Just let the darned thang go," Mama Ray repeated. "It's a sign from God. He don't want me to kill Calvin's pet chickens." She felt a little relieved that the chicken was still alive. She didn't want to have to face Daddy C when he came home and found his pet chicken served up with biscuits and mashed potatoes.

"How do you know it's a sign from God?" Big Mama asked, still holding the butcher knife, half hoping her daughter would change her mind. Mama Ray ignored the question. She took the frightened chicken in her arms firmly, careful not to let it claw her, and carried it out to the back yard. She put it down onto the porch. The hen seemed dazed. It almost fell over at first, but then somehow managed to find its feet. It waddled and zigzagged, not going in any particular direction. Suddenly it spread its wings and ran over to the other chickens, who were again pecking and scratching away at the dirt. The hen started to peck along with the others. Suddenly, it looked up and let out a long, loud squawk. As it fell over and died amongst the other chickens, Mama Ray felt a tinge of sadness course through her.

Big Mama heard the squawk and came trotting out to the porch. She came up beside her daughter, who was still standing on the porch, and she saw the dead hen lying amongst the others. "'A sign from God,' my ass!" Big Mama said. She went over to the dead hen and scooped it up. "I knew that I had killed the poor thang. You can go an' eat a hamburger if you want to, but today I'm gonna cook up some fresh fried chicken for my great-grandson." She walked past Mama Ray with the chicken in her hand and went back into the kitchen to start the plucking.

It had been a long time since Big Mama had plucked a chicken, but she felt the skill quickly coming back to her, and in a few minutes all the feathers had been efficiently removed. Mama Ray was still getting used to the idea that the deed had actually been done, that the chicken was dead and would soon be in the frying pan. Now she and Daddy C both would just have to accept it. It was done, and could not be undone.

"You get started on the apple pie," Big Mama said. "This won't take too long now." She had cut the chicken's head off and was letting the blood drain into the sink.

Daddy C and Paul came in around noon when the food was almost ready. Mama Ray and Big Mama were sitting in the den watching a soap opera. "You're missin' *Search For Tomorrow*," Mama Ray said, as they walked into the room. She knew that Daddy C had no interest in soap operas, but it was her way of saying hello to them. Daddy C looked at the television set and grunted.

"Well, hello, there, little Paul!" Big Mama said. "Come over here an' hug your Great Granny's neck." Paul looked at his great-grandmother. He had never seen her before, but he had been told many stories about her. He remembered hearing that she had lived on a farm. Big Mama was bigger than he had expected, and her horn-rimmed glasses looked strange to him. They seemed to sink into her broad cheeks as she smiled.

"Well, hello, there, Calvin," Big Mama smiled.

"Hello, there, Big Mama," Daddy C answered. He was very fond of Big Mama, and had often defended her before against Mama Ray's accusations that her mother was insane. He went into the bathroom to wash the grit of the morning off his hands.

As Daddy C left the room, Big Mama looked at Paul again. She noticed his apprehension as he looked back at her. "You don't remember me, do you?" she said.

Paul shook his head as he looked down at his shoes. "No, Ma'am," he said.

"Well, I'm your great-granny, Big Mama. I was there when you was born. Right there in the Hopkins County Hospital. I remember it like it was yesterday," she said. "You was just a little thing. An' I used to change your diapers sometimes when your mama an' granny was a workin'. But you was too little to remember that. You was just a baby. But I remember you, though." Big Mama opened her arms wide. Paul noticed that the flab of her arms sagged down from the short sleeves of her dress. "Now come over here and love my neck, son," she said.

"Go on an' hug your Big Mama, now," Mama Ray said to reassure Paul. "She won't bite you too hard." Mama Ray giggled.

Paul couldn't understand why he didn't remember ever meeting his great-grandmother. He knew that babies couldn't remember anything. He had tried before to remember his life when he was a baby, but never could. His first memory was from when he was three or four years old, going to pre-school. Paul hesitated, but walked over and bent down to where his great-grandmother was sitting on the couch. He put his arms around her belly, and he felt her bosom press against his face. Big Mama closed her arms and squeezed him. Paul was afraid for a moment that he would not be able to breathe. She rocked him back and forth in her tight embrace. Paul felt a little hot as Big Mama continued to rock him. The hug lasted only a few seconds, but it seemed longer, due to his fear of being smothered. Big Mama released her embrace and Paul pulled back. It had not been as bad as he had feared. He still felt hot, though.

"You sure are a little sprout. How old are you?" Big Mama asked.

"Seven," Paul answered as he stood in front of his great-grandmother. He wondered how old Big Mama was, too, but his mother had taught him that it was not polite to ask old ladies how old they were.

"When's your birthday?" she asked.

"On the twenty-third of July," Paul said.

"Well, that ain't far off," she replied.

"It sure ain't," Mama Ray said. "He's gettin' to be a big boy fast."

"We'll have to throw you a birthday party," Big Mama said.

"That's a good idea," Mama Ray agreed as she enthusiastically nodded her approval of the idea.

Big Mama began to wiggle and push against the cushions beneath her. "Now let your great-granny get up. I got a surprise for you." Paul backed away from the couch as his great-grandmother pushed herself up and went into the kitchen.

"You smell that?" Mama Ray asked.

Paul smelled the room. He noticed that someone had been cooking. It smelled good, too. He was hungry now after having gone around town all morning with his grandfather. It seemed like many hours since they had eaten at Mrs. Celecia's. "What is it?" he asked.

"Big Mama and me done made you somethin' special to eat," Mama Ray said. "We been cookin' all mornin'."

"It smells good," Paul said.

"It *is* good," replied Mama Ray. "Just you wait an' see."

Daddy C came back into the den and sat down in the Lay-Z-Boy recliner next to Mama Ray's. Between the two recliners was a stand with a box of Kleenex and some coasters to set their iced teas down. The Lay-Z-Boys were covered with flowery afghans that Mama Ray had crocheted and placed on them to keep the dog hair and food stains off. All the furniture in the house was covered up, either with such afghans that she had crocheted, or with white doilies that she had knitted. Paul could not understand why she would be afraid that someone might stain the furniture, since it already looked old and dirty anyway.

"We was down at Marie's this mornin'," Daddy C told Mama Ray. "She said to tell you howdy."

Mama Ray, like Daddy C, had known Mrs. Celecia for many years, since she had arrived in town. They didn't have a lot in common, but that wasn't very important in a small town like Sulpher Springs. They got along pretty well, and because of that they had been able to develop a sort of friendship over the years. Of course, they had grown distant over time, especially since Mama Ray had gone into the hospital and been forced to stop working because of her diabetes. She had started to stay home more and more, until finally she had lost contact with most of the people she had known. Mama Ray only went to town once a week to go to the bank and the grocery store. Since her exile, she had only bumped into Mrs. Celecia on occasion in the Piggly Wiggly grocery store when she had been there shopping. "Well, you tell her howdy for me, too, an' that I sure do think about her. How is she?"

"Oh, she's fine," Daddy C said. "Same ol' Marie, you know. Feisty as ever. She sure does like little Paul, too. Wants him to meet her granddaughter, Daniela."

"I didn't know she had a granddaughter," Mama Ray said.

"Yeah, she's around little Paul's age. Her daughter graduated with one of ours. I don't remember if she went to school with Lorene or Connie, but she graduated with one of 'em," Daddy C said.

"I think I remember somethin' like that, but I ain't real sure which one it was, either," Mama Ray said. She was not really sure whether she remembered that, or much of anything, anymore. Her memory seemed to be slipping by her, since her diabetes had gotten her really down and she started staying at home. Sometimes she found it awfully difficult to remember things. "Well, I bet Paul would like someone to play with," she added. "He needs to meet some friends."

"She said to come around some time in the evenin', to eat enchiladas. Maybe then we'll see her little granddaughter. Marie wants to see you, too, a course," Daddy C said.

"That'd be real nice," Mama Ray said. Suddenly she thought of the dogs. She hadn't seen them since early that morning, when they had left with Daddy C and Paul. "Where are the dogs, Calvin?"

"They're in the back yard," he said. "I'll let 'em in. They done had plenty of time to do their business." Daddy C got up from the Lay-Z-Boy and opened the sliding door.

Mama Ray felt a sudden lump in her throat. If Daddy C had been out in the back yard, then he must have seen the chickens. Apparently he had not noticed that one was missing, or he would have said something. This gave her a feeling of relief. She had decided that she would pretend that the chicken she and Big Mama had cooked was store-bought, and just act as if she didn't know what had happened to the hen when it turned up "missing." It would be the safest way. Then Daddy C would not blame her for murdering his "pet" that had destroyed her yard. She and Big Mama had put all the feathers and excess parts into the trash bag and put it out on the curb for the garbage men, and she had made her mother promise not to tell about the act.

"Haah, Buster! Haah Dawn! Haah Tinker! Haah!" The dogs came running into the house one by one, and Paul felt his stomach tighten. He was prepared to face the enemy again, but Dawn and Tinker just ignored his presence and jumped into Mama Ray's lap. They began to lick her arms and face. Daddy C seated himself again in the recliner, and Buster jumped in with him.

"Well, hello, my Sweeties!" Mama Ray said. "Yeah, give your Mama some sugar." The dogs wagged their tails excitedly and continued to lick Mama Ray's face, giving her their sweet sugar. Paul looked away from the displeasing sight and into the kitchen at Big Mama, who was moving around near the oven.

"It'll be ready in just a minute, little Paul," Big Mama said, without turning around to look at him. Paul wondered whether she knew that he had been looking at her. "Go get your hands washed," she added.

Paul looked at his hands and wondered why he had to wash them. They didn't look dirty. He was still new to the house, however, and didn't want to wear out his welcome. What would he do if they changed their minds about letting him stay with them? His mother didn't want him at home with her. He would have no place to go if his grandparents got tired of him and made him leave. He got up and went to wash his hands, careful not to attract the attention of Tinker and Dawn, who were lying calmly now on either side of Mama Ray's lap.

After washing his hands, Paul went into his room to check on Baby Doll. She was lying on the bed. "You okay, Baby Doll?" he asked. When she didn't answer, he realized that she was sleeping. She must have gotten tired of waiting for him to come back. He hoped that she wouldn't be angry with him when she woke up.

"Come an' get it!" cried Big Mama from the kitchen. "Come an' get it!"

They were all seated at the table. Big Mama was sitting next to Paul. "The drums sticks is for me an' little Paul, so don't y'all go tryin' to get 'em," she said. Her favorite part of the chicken were the legs. She put one drumstick on her plate, and the other on Paul's. She took Mama Ray's plate. "Wanda Ray, you like the breast, don't ya?" Big Mama called her daughter by her birth name, "Wanda Ray," but most everybody else in the family called her "Mama Ray."

Mama Ray nodded. Big Mama put a breast on her daughter's plate. "An', Calvin, you like the thighs, if I remember correctly."

"That's right, Big Mama," Daddy C answered. "Especially yours." Daddy C laughed. "Your fried chicken thighs, I mean."

Big Mama laughed. "Ha ha! I didn't even think about that one, till I realized you was makin' a joke. I always been drivin' the men crazy with my thighs."

Mama Ray rolled her eyes. Paul was not sure what Big Mama and Daddy C were talking about, but he was getting impatient. The food smelled good, and he was ready to eat.

"That's 'cause your thighs is always so good an' juicy," Daddy C continued.

Big Mama blushed a little, but she laughed again. "Hoo hoo! I think we better stop this now, here in mixed company," she said. "An' let's start eatin'. My thighs ain't too juicy when they's cold, anyhow. Y'all help yourselves to the vegetables an' biscuits. I'll help little Paul get started." She took Paul's plate again. She reached over the table with her other hand and put generous portions of mashed potatoes and green beans on the plate with the chicken leg. She looked at Paul and smiled, her cheeks pushing up her horn-rimmed glasses. "You want gravy, too, Honey?"

"Yes, please," Paul answered. Big Mama poured some gravy over Paul's potatoes as Mama Ray and Daddy C filled their plates.

It was the best fried chicken Paul had ever eaten. He had always liked to go to Colonel Sanders', but this was even better. He ate heartily, but not as heartily as Daddy C, who had already cleaned his plate by the time Paul had gotten half-way through his chicken leg. "That sure was good, Big Mama. Can I have some more?" Daddy C asked.

Big Mama, who was busy enjoying her own down-home cooking, looked up proudly from her plate. "Well, sure you can," she said. Her speech was garbled because her mouth was full. "Help yourself." She chewed a little more, her cheeks pushed out by the food. Paul noticed a speck of fried chicken on one of the lenses of her glasses. "But that chicken didn't have but two thighs. If you want more after that one, you'll have to take a wing or the back, unless Wanda Ray don't want that second breast."

Mama Ray looked up, her elbows propped upon the table with a paper napkin in one hand. Her mouth was also full. "No, you go ahead an' eat that other breast, Calvin, if you want it," she managed to say. She was still feeling guilty about having killed Daddy C's chicken, and so she didn't have much of an appetite anyway. She kept seeing the chicken in her mind as it had struggled to get free over the sink.

She really had believed that it was a sign from God that the chicken had not died the first time. But, then again, maybe it had been a second sign from God when the chicken died the second time. Maybe that had meant that the chicken was supposed to die, that she was not responsible for it. After all, she had tried to repent and let the chicken go when it was in the kitchen squawking after the first time they had thought that it was dead. How could she have known that it would keel over when it returned to the back yard? Somehow this thought made her feel better and enabled her to continue eating the chicken breast. She still hoped, however, that it would be a while yet before Daddy C would see that the chicken was missing. She hoped that at least the trash men would come and take away the evidence before Daddy C noticed its absence. There were five other chickens still out there, anyway, and it was not likely that he would go out and take roll call just to see if one was missing.

"This chicken sure is good, Big Mama," Paul said. He couldn't remember the last time he had eaten so well.

"Well, thank you, little Paul. I'm glad you like it," Big Mama answered, pleased. "I made it just for you. I'll teach you how to make it some day." She reached over and rubbed his back.

Paul noticed that Big Mama had a dirty napkin in her hand, which she had been using to wipe the chicken grease from her mouth and hands, as she rubbed his back. He didn't mind too much, though. He looked forward to learning how to make fried chicken with his great-grandmother.

After lunch, Mama Ray and her mother cleaned the kitchen. Big Mama then went home, and the others went to take a nap. Paul was not tired, but he didn't want to disturb Mama Ray and Daddy C, and he wanted to spend some time alone with Baby Doll. She was still lying on the bed where she had been when he had checked on her before lunch. Paul sat down on the bed next to her and looked down to see if see was awake. "Baby Doll?" he said. "Baby Doll? You still sleeping?" She didn't answer. Concerned, he lay down next to her and held her in his arms as she continued to sleep.

Mama Ray and Daddy C were in the next bedroom. They had twin beds which stood next to each other. Upon the night stand between them was a lamp, an orange radio, a tube of Ben-Gay, and Mama Ray's Bible and insulin kit. Buster, Tinker, and Dawn were sleeping in their little beds, which were between the beds of Mama Ray and Daddy C. "You think he's okay?" Mama Ray asked across to Daddy C, who was lying in his bed, his face toward the wall. He turned around to face Mama Ray.

"He's fine," Daddy C assured her. "He don't talk about it, though. I think it's best to just let it all come out on its own, when it's ready to come out."

"I don't know what to do about him," Mama Ray said. She moved the pillow under her head. "I don't know how he's adjustin' to all this."

"He'll do just fine," Daddy C assured her. "Little kids is easier than grown-ups. It won't take him long."

"I hope not," Mama Ray said. She lifted her head suddenly, with a fright. She gasped.

Daddy C noticed that his wife had been startled. "What's wrong?" he asked.

"Shhhhhhhhh!" Mama Ray said. She turned her head to hear better. "Do you hear that?" she asked.

Daddy C listened. "Hear what? I don't hear nothin'."

"That cryin'," Mama Ray said. "Sounds like someone's cryin'."

"I don't hear nothin'," Daddy C repeated.

"Well, it stopped now," Mama Ray said. "It sounded like a little girl a cryin'." Mama Ray continued to listen, but now she couldn't hear anything.

"Maybe it was little Paul," Daddy C said.

Mama Ray thought for a moment, then shook her head, doubtful. "Maybe," she said. "But it sounded like a little tiny girl."

Daddy C shrugged his shoulders. At that time, the door to Paul's room opened slowly, and Mama Ray and Daddy C heard soft footsteps coming up the hallway. "Paul, is that you?" Mama Ray called out. Suddenly Paul appeared in the doorway.

"Yeah, it's me. I'm sorry. I couldn't sleep. I didn't mean to wake you up," Paul said. He couldn't see the dogs. They were hidden by Mama Ray's twin bed, which was nearest the door. He could hear the unmistakable sound of Tinker growling at him, however.

"You didn't wake us, Doll," Daddy C said.

"Paul, was you cryin', Honey?" Mama Ray asked.

Paul was surprised by the question. He hadn't cried around his grandmother. He had cried a lot since what had happened, but he hadn't been crying in his room. He was embarrassed that his grandmother had asked him such a question, because he knew that boys were not supposed to cry. "No, I ain't been cryin'," he said, a bit defensive. "Why?"

Daddy C, satisfied with Paul's answer, rolled back over to face the wall. He had thought that Mama Ray's imagination had been working overtime, anyway. Since the funeral, she hadn't seemed herself, but he wasn't sure what was wrong with her. She had never talked much about what was going on in her own mind. She had always only speculated about the mental fragility of everybody else around her.

"No reason," Mama Ray said. She put her glasses on to look at Paul's eyes. They didn't look as if he had been crying. "I just thought I heard somethin', that's all. What are you gonna do if you ain't gonna take a nap?" she asked.

"I thought I'd go out an' play on the swings in the back yard," Paul said. As Paul answered, he could hear Daddy C, who was already snoring away. His grandfather snored loudly, and it reminded him of the sound of a bulldozer. Paul smiled to himself as his grandfather continued to snore.

"Well, you be careful around them chickens. They's mean. Take that broom with you beside the door, in case they come after you," Mama Ray said.

"Okay," Paul replied, not really sure whether his grandmother was serious.

Mama Ray took off her glasses and put them down again next to her insulin bag. "If one of 'em comes up to you, try to hit it in the head with that broom," she said, as Paul turned to leave.

"I will," Paul said. He left and could still hear Daddy C snoring as he walked down the hall.

He opened the sliding glass door in the den and went out to the porch. He saw the broom beside the glass door, but he decided to leave it there. He wanted to swing, not to fight with a bunch of hens.

As he walked out into the yard, he didn't see any chickens. Perhaps they were taking a nap like Mama Ray and Daddy C. It seemed that everything around there took a nap after lunch. He went to the swing set and sat in one of the swings.

Paul faced the house as he swung. He looked at the windows and tried to discern to which rooms they corresponded. He noticed that the white bricks were dirty, and that there was no grass in the yard. An empty bird bath stood in the center. Paul thought of using the water hose under the kitchen window to fill it up, but he didn't want to get in trouble. Suddenly he heard a voice.

"Hey, kid! Hey, you!" said the voice. Paul stopped swinging and looked around to find where the voice was coming from, but he couldn't see anyone. He felt scared. "Over here!" said the voice. He couldn't tell if the voice was male or female. It was a loud hoarse whisper. He thought of running into the house to safety.

"Over here!" the voice repeated. "Over here in the bushes behind the bus!"

He looked around for a bus. Finally, he saw not a bus, but the *shell* of a bus, half-burried in a patch of wild vines and bushes. It was on the other side of the fence, halfway between Mama Ray's house and the white house next door. There were no wheels underneath it. It seemed as if the shell had been removed and placed on the ground long before, and trees and bushes had grown up around it.

"Come here!" said the voice. "Don't be scared."

"No!" said Paul. "I ain't goin' over there." After a moment, he saw the bushes behind the bus shell begin to rustle, and the rustling started moving toward him. He thought again of bolting for the glass door, but he was petrified, as if he were glued to the swing set. The rustling kept coming closer. Suddenly a figure emerged.

"Hi, I'm Cindy," she said. Paul looked at her. He was relieved to see that it was just a girl, and not a monster. He couldn't tell how old the girl was, but she was older than him and not a grown-up yet. She had a cigarette in her hand.

"I'm Paul," he said, exhaling in relief.

Cindy laughed when she saw Paul's expression. "Was you scared?" she asked.

"No, I wasn't scared," Paul answered. He felt indignant. How dare she think that he had been scared!

"You was, too," Cindy said. "I seen it on your face."

"I was not," Paul said. "You don't know what you're talkin' about."

"It don't matter," Cindy said, looking Paul over. He seemed cuter and sweeter than he had the day before as she and her mother had watched him from their kitchen window. "I ain't got time to argue, anyhow. I ain't gonna hurt you. How old are you?"

"Seven," Paul answered. "How old are you?"

"I'm fifteen," Cindy answered. "I'm almost sixteen." She proudly took a drag off her cigarette. "Don't you tell my mother that I'm smokin'," she said. "She'll kick my ass."

"I ain't gonna say nothin'," Paul said.

"How do you like livin' with your old granny?" Cindy asked.

"I don't live here. I'm just stayin' for a while," Paul answered.

Cindy looked at him skeptically. "Hmph! Whatever," she said. "I wouldn't wanta live with that old bitch, neither," she added.

"She ain't a bitch!" Paul protested. "An' you watch your mouth when you talk about her."

"I'll say what I want to," Cindy said. "She ain't never been nice to me. Once time I went into that back yard just to play on that swing set an' smoke a cigarette. Your old granny came out with her broom an' started swingin' it at me, told me if I didn't get off her property she'd knock me cross-eyed and tell my mother that I was smokin'."

Paul couldn't imagine his grandmother doing that. She had been nothing but nice to him since he had arrived. "You probably just scared her," Paul said.

"Hell, she scared *me*," Cindy said. "Your old granny ain't scared of nobody. An' she's mean. I saw what she did this mornin'." She took one last drag off the cigarette and threw the butt over the fence into Mama Ray and Daddy C's yard.

Paul didn't know what to think. "What are you talkin' about?" he asked.

"I saw her kill that chicken."

"What chicken?" Paul asked.

"One of them chickens that they got in that yard." Cindy looked into the yard, searching for the chickens. "Where are they now?" she asked.

"They're takin' a nap," Paul answered. He really had no idea where the chickens were, as he hadn't seen them yet. However, he wanted Cindy to think that he knew what he was talking about. "She didn't kill no chicken," he added.

"Yes, she did," Cindy said, pulling her blond hair back behind her shoulders. "I seen it. I was out behind the bus smokin' when she did it. Her an' her fat old Mama. Her old Mama came out here doin' some kind of voodoo dance or somethin', an' then started to choke one of them chickens."

"You're crazy!" Paul said.

"No, I ain't. You don't have to believe me, but I know what I saw. Then they came back out, an' that chicken just fell over dead. They put some kind of spell on it."

Paul remembered the fried chicken they had eaten for lunch. His stomach started to tighten, and he suddenly felt sick. Could it really be true? Could Big Mama and Mama Ray really have murdered a chicken? He looked around and tried to see the hens, but they were not in sight.

"Don't you say nothin' to her about it," Cindy said. "I don't want her to do nothin' to me or my mama. I gotta go back in the house now, or my mama'll be out here lookin' for me. You wanna come over?"

"I can't," Paul said. "Mama Ray said not to leave the property."

"Where is she?" Cindy asked.

"She's takin' a nap with Daddy C."

"Well, you can come on over. It's just next door. Besides, my mama wants to meet you," Cindy said. "Come on, now."

Paul hesitated. He didn't want to get into trouble, but he was very curious. Cindy seemed nice, even though she had said those things about his Mama Ray, and had called Big Mama "fat." His curiosity got the best of him, and he jumped off the swing. He went over to the fence and opened the gate.

"You see that house right there?" Cindy pointed. It was an old white wooden house just on the other side of the bus shell, not far at all from Mama Ray and Daddy C's house. One could not really say that the house was white, but that it had once been white. Most of the paint had chipped away from its surface. "That's where we live," Cindy said. They walked together toward the house. As they passed the bus shell, Paul got an eerie feeling. It was covered in bushes and shadow.

They walked past the bus and into Cindy's home. The screen door made a loud thud that rattled the whole house as Cindy closed it.

The two stood in the kitchen, which was the first room in the house. It was small and tidy. The linoleum on the floor had turned brown, but the lemon yellow paint on the cupboards and the walls seemed new.

"Where've you been?" a voice yelled from the back of the house.

"Mom, we've got a visitor," Cindy yelled back.

Paul heard footsteps that made the walls shake as LaVelle walked into the kitchen. "Well, hello there!" LaVelle said, smiling widely. "We been waitin' for you. I'm LaVelle. I'm Cindy's mother."

Paul looked up at LaVelle. She was tall and skinny, but she was pretty. "I'm Paul," he said.

LaVelle put her hand on his shoulder and lookd down at him. "Paul, what a purty name," she said. "Has Cindy been out smokin' behind the bus again?"

Paul noticed that LaVelle herself was smoking a cigarette. He looked at Cindy, who looked sternly back at him. He remembered that Cindy had made him promise not to tell her mother that she had been smoking. "No," he said.

LaVelle smiled at Paul as if she knew the truth. She looked at Cindy, and her face turned serious. "Then she must have been out botherin' your poor old granny again." LaVelle went to the refrigerator and pulled out a pitcher of iced tea. She got an ashtray from the counter and put it on the table beside the tea pitcher.

"I ain't been around that old bitch!" Cindy protested.

LaVelle turned and chided her. "Watch your mouth around here, Missy Thang. You know we don't talk like that in this house. Cindy leaned against the sink, folded her arms, and made a sour face. "Now get a glass for you an' me an' Paul," LaVelle said.

Cindy unfolded her arms and got some glasses from the cupboard. She put them on the table. LaVelle laid her cigarette in the ashtray. She put ice cubes into the glasses and poured the tea.

"Have a seat, Paul," she said. He sat down. "I reckon you ain't hungry," LaVelle added. "Otherwise I'd offer you some pie."

"No, Ma'am, I ain't hungry. I done eat," Paul said.

"I bet your granny fed you real good. Did you like your great-granny's fried chicken?" LaVelle asked.

"Yes, ma'am," Paul answered. He wondered how LaVelle had known that the had eaten fried chicken for lunch. Then he remembered Cindy's story about Mama Ray and Big Mama in the back yard with the chickens. He wondered now if she had told the truth.

"Your great-granny was out here a few minutes ago for a visit," LaVelle said, noticing that Paul was uneasy. "That's how I knew that y'all ate fried chicken."

Paul felt relieved. Perhaps Cindy's story had been a lie, after all. "You know Big Mama?" he asked.

"Oh, yes," LaVelle said, smiling. "We're good friends. I don't know nobody who don't like your ol' great-granny. She's as sweet as they come. We've known each other for a long time. She's the salt of the earth."

"I told Paul about what his granny an' great granny done out there this mornin'," Cindy said, lifting her glass to drink some iced tea.

"They didn't do nothin' out there this mornin' that's any of your business," LaVelle said. She looked at Paul. "Don't believe her, Paul, she's got a vivid imagination." She turned to her daughter. "*Too* vivid," she added, blowing out a mouthful of smoke.

Paul didn't know what to think. He just sipped his iced tea quietly.

"It *is* my business, if I seen it with my own eyes," Cindy said.

"Were you out behind the bus smokin' again this mornin'?" LaVelle asked. Paul noticed the cigarette in her hand again.

"No, I was on my way to school, an' I saw 'em out there," Cindy said.

LaVelle gave Cindy a cross look. "Do you really think I believe you go to school?" she asked. "I ain't dumb, Missy Thang. I know you ain't been to school in a long time. You think I've forgotten? I don't forget that easily. My mind ain't gone yet. If you was out there, then you was out there doin' somethin' you wasn't supposed to be doin'. Now just be quiet an' stop tellin' lies about other people's business."

Cindy kept quiet. After a moment, she put her glass down, and said, "Paul, I gotta go get ready now. I got me a date tonight."

LaVelle rolled her eyes. "Yeah, go get yourself purtied up for your big date," she said. Cindy got up and left the kitchen.

Paul remained quiet as LaVelle looked across the table at him. "What's your granny doin'?" she asked.

"She was takin' a nap when I left," Paul answered.

"Well, you better get on back to the house. We don't want her to get worried when she wakes up. I know what it's like not to know where your kids are," she said, nodding her head back toward the bathroom, where Cindy was making herself beautiful. "You don't have to finish that tea if you don't want to," LaVelle added.

Paul put his glass down and got up from the table. "Thank you for the tea. It was nice to meet you an' Cindy," he said.

LaVelle looked him over. "You sure are a cute little booger," she said. "I know your grandparents an' your Big Mama are real proud of you. You be nice to them."

"I will," he said.

"An' you come back an' see us real often," LaVelle added.

"I will." Paul opened the screen door. As he stepped out the door, he turned to LaVelle again. "'Bye," he said. He heard the house shake again as the screen door slammed behind him.

"'Bye," LaVelle yelled as Paul was walking down the steps.

When Paul got back to the house, Mama Ray, Daddy C, and Baby Doll were all still in bed asleep. He sat down in Mama Ray's Lay-Z-Boy and watched *Wheel of Fortune* with little interest. He didn't like game shows very much. When *Wheel of Fortune* went to commercials, he got up and flipped through the channels again to see if he could find something else. There was nothing on but news, which he hated even worse than game shows. He decided to explore the living room.

In the living room Paul walked over to the plastic electric organ in the corner and thought of playing it. He noticed that the cord was not plugged in, and, as he bent over to connect it, he decided not to. He didn't want to wake his grandparents. He saw his mother's photo on the wall when he turned around. Connie looked very young in the photo, which had been taken in the late sixties. It was a black and white photograph, but his mother seemed to have had brown hair at the time it was taken, in contrast to the blond color which Paul had known all his life. She must have bleached it at some point after the photo had been taken.

Paul thought briefly of LaVelle. Both she and Connie were tall and thin, but Connie was much prettier than LaVelle, with fair skin, beautiful brown eyes which Paul had also inherited, and a perfect clear complexion. She looked so happy in the photo, smiling widely toward the camera lens. He looked at his brother's photo, and longed for Frank to be there. He wanted to tell him about Cindy, the girl he had met smoking behind the bus. He thought Frank would like her, and that maybe the three of them could have fun together. He skipped past his own photograph and saw that Jennifer's photo had been removed. He had seen it there just the day before, as they had arrived. Daddy C must have noticed that he was looking at it, and taken it down. Paul wondered why they would have taken her picture down.

Suddenly he felt the need to see that picture again. He wanted to see her again in his mind as she had been in that photograph — taken before she could even walk — smiling innocently with mouth open and spittle on her tongue. He tried to recreate that image in his imagination, but he could only see her on that last day, water dripping from her body as she lay in Connie's arms.

Paul was overcome with grief. His heart began to beat faster, and he sat down. He started to breath heavily. He had been sad since the day it had happened, but this time it was worse, like something that had been simmering inside him was now boiling over. It wasn't guilt right now that overcame him. It was sadness. He felt his skin go hot. He tried to fight it and stand up, but he couldn't. He missed Jennifer. The thought came to him that he would never see her again. He had known this before, but now the realization was inside him, had penetrated his heart, and he was aware, really *aware* that she was gone forever.

He could remember when his mother and new father had come home with her. He had been so happy to have a baby sister, so proud the first time he had fed her with a bottle, and when his mother had let him mix the sugar-water for her to drink. He had held her many times and rocked her to sleep. Now he would never see her again. Tears rolled down his hot cheeks. He tried to stop crying, but the tears kept pouring and he began to sob convulsively.

Paul had never felt so much pain before. He cried for a long time. He thought about his mother and how he missed her. Would he ever get to see her again? Would she ever welcome him back into the house and let things be the way the had been before, or would he always be a reminder of what had happened that day, of the pain he had caused everyone? Where had his sweet sister gone? Maybe it was right for him to be all alone now without his mother. He was older than Jennifer, and she was alone now, too. Was she scared? The thoughts flooded his mind. At first it hurt terribly, but, just as quickly as they came, the thoughts seemed to vanish in the flow of his tears. It was as if the hurt were somehow washing out of him the longer he cried. He lay back on the sofa and curled up, putting his arms around his knees. He rocked back and forth, and this movement began to soothe him.

"Paul?" The door opened. Paul didn't look up as Mama Ray came in and sat beside him. She opened her mouth to speak, but then decided to stay silent. She put her hand on her grandson's back and stroked him gently.

Paul eventually stopped crying. "I'm sorry," he said. He didn't look up, but he was glad that Mama Ray was there with him.

"Don't be sorry, Honey," she said. "You cry all you want." She looked at the photos on the wall as she continued rubbing her grandson's back. She, too, noticed that the picture of Jennifer had been removed, and she wondered if Paul had taken it down. She felt an overwhelming sadness, not just from Paul, and not just within herself. It was as if the sorrow had come to life, and it moved inside them and through the entire room. She fought hard to fight her own tears back, to be strong for Paul, but soon she was sobbing with him.

That evening Paul had dinner in the kitchen with Mama Ray and Daddy C. At bedtime both his grandparents went into Paul's room together to tuck him into bed, and they left his door open so that they could hear him if he started to cry again. Paul didn't cry, though. He was very tired that night, but he felt relieved. It didn't even worry him that Baby Doll hadn't woken up the whole day. After all, it was not the first time that Baby Doll had stopped speaking. He just cuddled up next to her and went very quickly to sleep.

The next morning around ten-thirty, Mama Ray went into Paul's room to ask him if he wanted to go to the grocery store with her. He was still sleeping. She wanted to go to the Piggly Wiggly store before noon, while the summer sun was still not so hot. She didn't want to leave Paul alone, however, and Daddy C had already left early with the dogs to make his rounds. She went into the den and began to watch *The Price is Right* on television.

From her Lay-Z-Boy she could see the chickens through the glass door. They were still pecking at the feed that she had put out for them earlier that morning. Even though she did not like the chickens, she didn't want to make them suffer, and so she had gone to the garage and dipped out a ration of chicken feed for them.

She wondered how long it would take until Daddy C noticed that one of them was missing, but the thought of his reaction didn't really bother her anymore. The deed had already been done, after all. The chicken had been eaten, and the garbage collectors had already been by that morning to haul the remains away. It was the law of nature for that chicken to be eaten, anyway. They were not made to be pets, and she would never have a lovely lawn if they remained.

Now she would have to think of a way to get rid of the other five chickens. If she couldn't convince Daddy C to let her fry up the rest of them, or to sell them, then she would have to think of another way to get them out of her back yard. Maybe she would have to "accidentally" leave the gate open so that they would escape. But they had probably grown so attached to the place that they would never leave, even if they had the chance. She thought of chasing them away with the broom, but, with her luck, they would turn around and attack her.

Mama Ray gave up scheming for the moment, and decided to go to the grocery store after all, before it got too hot outside.

Of course, she wouldn't leave her little grandson alone. She would call Big Mama to come and watch him until she returned. She got out of her chair and went to the telephone.

"Hello?" Big Mama answered.

"Mama, it's me," Mama Ray said.

"Well, good mornin', Wanda Ray," Big Mama said into the phone. "What're you callin' for, Honey? I don't live but just next door. Didn't wanna walk all the way over here?"

"It's just that I don't wanna leave little Paul alone," Mama Ray answered.

"We gonna get another chicken today?" her mother asked with a chuckle.

"No, Mama," Mama Ray answered. "I just wanna go to the grocery store, an' little Paul's still asleep. He had a real rough night yesterday."

"It all come up, didn't it?" Big Mama said.

"Yeah, I guess so," Mama Ray replied.

"Well, it had to happen sooner or later," her mother said. "It'll probably happen again, too. You want me to go over there an' sit with him?"

"Yeah, that'd be real nice," Mama Ray said.

"Okay, I'll be right over."

Paul woke up from his long sleep disoriented. He didn't know where he was. As he opened his eyes, he expected to see his room in Kingsland, Texas. Instead, he saw white walls, paintings, and furniture that were not familiar to him. He looked around to find something that he could recognize. Where was he? He felt Baby Doll beside him and he held her up. Her eyes were open wide, but he knew that she was still asleep. Suddenly it occurred to him that he was at his grandparent's house and not in Kingsland with his family. A feeling of relief came to him. He wanted to be in Kingsland, but at least that bedroom in his grandparents' house was a place that he knew. He put Baby Doll on the other bed — the one his brother Frank had slept in — and made his bed. He didn't know what time it was; but the sun was shining brightly through the curtains of his bedroom, and so he thought that it must be pretty late. He wondered why no one had woken him. He walked through the doorway of his bedroom and into the hall. He was still in his pajamas. He wanted to find Mama Ray and Daddy C. As he entered the hallway, he heard a strange voice that he didn't understand.

"Ja, klar ist es gut gewesen. Alles wird schon. Wir machen uns keine Gedanken drüber. Nein, hat er nicht. Jetzt ist es noch zu früh. Moment...hörst Du das? Der Kleine kommt gerade. Na, gut, mach' ich. Tschüß, Mutter."

The voice was coming from the den. Paul was not sure if he should enter.

"Come on in here, Sugar Pud," the voice said, louder. Paul knew now that it was Big Mama's voice. He continued down the hall and saw Big Mama seated on the couch. She was sewing something.

"Was that you talkin'?" He asked.

"Well, good mornin'," Big Mama said cheerfully. "Or, better yet, good afternoon. You sure was sound asleep, little boy."

"I heard a voice," Paul said. "Was that you?"

"Yeah, that was me, I guess," Big Mama said, looking down at her sewing. "Come on in here an' love your great granny's neck." Paul walked over and hugged his Big Mama.

"Oooh, boy! You sure do give good sugar!" she said, squeezing him. "That was even better than yesterday." It was true. Paul felt more comfortable around Big Mama, and reciprocated the hug this time, whereas, the day before, he had simply obliged her and let her squeeze on him a little. This time, he was not afraid of suffocating in her bosom. "I bet you're hungry, ain't ya?" Big Mama said.

"A little bit," he answered. He did feel a little hungry. It seemed that it had been a long time since he had eaten.

"Well, I'd fix ya somethin' to eat, but your granny's gonna be back soon from the grocery store. I guess we'll all eat together. You want me ta fix ya somethin' little to tide you over?" she asked as she continued with her sewing.

"No, that's all right. I can wait. I ain't that hungry," Paul answered. "Who were you talkin' to?" he asked.

Big Mama was still worried about what was happening with Mama Ray, and she knew that her daughter would have her hide if she got wind that she had been talking to Paul about the spirit world. She decided to avoid the topic. "Aw, I was just a talkin' to myself, I guess," she said.

"But you wasn't talkin' in English, was you?" Paul asked. "I didn't understand what you was sayin', but it didn't sound like English to me." He had the feeling that his great-grandmother was hiding something, and his curiosity wanted to get to the bottom of it.

Big Mama smiled. "No, Honey, it wasn't English," she said. "Now let me get back to my sewin'. You can watch TV if you want. I can't stand it myself." Paul noticed that the TV wasn't on. Big Mama pulled the needle through the material that she was working on.

"What language was you speakin', then?" he persisted.

Big Mama looked up at him with a stern face. She saw innocence in his expression, and she could not get cross with him. It was natural that he was curious. Perhaps he would understand when she told him. After all, he was still very young and his heart had not yet closed up with scabs to protect him from what adults called the real world.

She smiled again and shook her head. "You ain't gonna give up, are ya?" She put her sewing down. "Come here an' sit down next to me." Paul sat down next to her on the couch. "Well, if you're so curious, then I guess that means you're ready," she said. "Now, I ain't gonna tell you to keep no secrets from Mama Ray, but if you don't tell her this, then I'll know I can trust you. An' if I can trust you, then I can tell you more later."

"I won't say nothin' to Mama Ray," Paul assured her.

"Well, I know you probably won't," said Big Mama. "But I gotta be sure, you see?" She put her hand on Paul's knee. "Your Mama Ray don't like to hear about this stuff, an' she just thinks I'm crazy. But that's okay, 'cause I know I ain't crazy. She can believe what she wants to. Folks only believe what the wanna believe anyway. She can listen to her preacher on TV all she wants, and he can tell her what she wants to hear. But I know somethin' they don't know, an' I don't need to go to church to prove it."

It seemed to Big Mama that the biggest travesty was that parents made their children suffer, when suffering was the last thing that they wanted for their children. They set boundaries on what was real and not, training them to prepare them for reality — *their* version of reality — and destroying the possibilities that lay in their hearts. Of course, she had done the same thing when Mama Ray had been a child, defining the same limits for her that she had grown up with, in hopes that her daughter would have a happier life than she had experienced. Now it seemed ridiculous to her that parents try to make their children grow up happy by making them afraid of life and the unknown, when, in reality, young children are happier than most parents are. She was suffering the consequences now, because those original definitions apparently were still held firmly by her daughter, even though Big Mama herself had changed. It seemed difficult now to kill the weeds in her daughter's mind, and Big Mama knew that she herself had been largely responsible for their planting. She thought they all could learn a lot from Paul. Perhaps, if Mama Ray would listen, she could learn from him not to be afraid of life.

"What do you know?" Paul said. He had no idea what Big Mama was talking about, but his interest was certainly piqued.

"I know a lot of things," she said. "But that don't mean nothin'.." She laughed. "Ha! We all think we know a lot of things, don't we? But that ain't what you wanted to hear. You asked me who I was talkin' to, didn't you?" She looked into Paul's eyes as he looked back at her. Through her glasses he saw big brown eyes which were the same as his.

"Yes, Ma'am," he said. "Who were you talkin' to?" he repeated.

Big Mama looked out the glass door, but her glance seemed to look far past the back yard. "I was talkin' to my mother," she said. "I talk to her a lot."

"Is she here?" Paul asked. He hadn't seen anyone else in the house, and he had always thought that Big Mama's mother was dead.

"No, she ain't here," Big Mama said. "She done left just before you come in the room. She said to tell you howdy, though. I wasn't goin' to, but, since you asked." She looked at Paul again. "Now, don't you tell your granny about that."

Paul was confused. He couldn't imagine why Mama Ray would get angry about Big Mama talking to her own mother. And, if the woman was Big Mama's mother, then that would make her Mama Ray's grandmother. What would Mama Ray have against her own grandmother? "Why don't you want Mama Ray to know?" he asked. "Don't she like your mother?"

Big Mama laughed heartily. "Oh, boy!" she said. "It ain't that simple. My Mama's done passed away, you see. A long time ago." She looked at Paul to see how he would react to what she had just said. She knew that it wouldn't be easy for him to understand, at first; but, she believed he would soon be able to accept it. Maybe she would even eventually introduce him to his great-great-grandmother. Big Mama knew that her mother would love to meet him.

Paul was surprised. He knew that "passed away" was a polite way to say that someone had died. "You mean she's dead?" Paul asked. Suddenly he began to feel scared. He looked around to see if he could find a ghost.

"Don't start gettin' scared, now," Big Mama said. "Ain't nothin' gonna happen to you. Come sit closer to me." He scooted closer to his great-grandmother and she took him in her arm. "There ain't nothin' to be scared about. Besides, I didn't say she was *dead*," she added. "I said she had passed away. That just means that she ain't here anymore. At least not the way she used to be. But that don't mean nothin'."

Paul's eyes widened. "Is she a ghost?" He still felt scared. Big Mama laughed again.

"Well, boy howdy!" Big Mama said. "Ha ha! Honey, there ain't no such thing as ghosts. Ghosts is somethin' out of story books an' television. She ain't no ghost."

"Well, where is she then, if she ain't no ghost?" Paul asked. He had seen ghost stories on television, and had heard stories from his brother Frank and the other children at school. His brother had once told him of a woman who had been decapitated in a car accident. After that she walked headless from house to house, cutting off the heads of each person she encountered. She would put each severed head upon her neck, and toss it away when it didn't fit her. Paul hadn't been able to sleep the night his brother had told him about that woman. Every noise outside had seemed to him to be that woman's footsteps, stumbling slowly toward the house in search of a head that suited her. Even though his mother had told him that there was no such thing as ghosts, there was still some primal part of him that believed in the possibility.

"I can't explain to you where my mother is," Big Mama said. "That'll have to come later. I'll just say that she *is* here, but she *ain't here*. I know that don't help you, but she don't have the same rules that people do. That'll have to do for now." Big Mama patted Paul on the head and picked up her sewing again. As she pulled the needle through the cloth, she added, "Now, remember, if you tell that to Mama Ray, we won't be able to talk about it again. And don't start scarin' yourself. There ain't no ghosts around here."

"I won't tell her," Paul said. He was thinking: if Big Mama could talk to her mother, who had passed on, then perhaps she talk to others, too. Could she talk to Jennifer? The thought sent a chill over him. He was frightened by the idea, but he had to know. If she could talk to Jennifer, then maybe Big Mama could tell her that he was sorry for what had happened. And she could tell him where his sister was, and whether she was alone and sad. "Can you talk to Jennifer, too?" he asked.

Big Mama stopped sewing and looked up, but not at Paul. She grinned contentedly. Her great-grandson was curious, and he was making progress. He was asking the right questions. She decided to grant him an answer, but not too much. Not yet. "Yes, Honey. I already have talked to her."

Paul felt a lump in his throat. Big Mama had talked to his sister! "You have?" he asked. He felt excited and frightened at the same time.

"Yes, Honey," Big Mama answered.

"Is she okay? Is she lonely? Does she hate me for what happened?" He could not hide his excitement.

Big Mama had been a little apprehensive that this would happen. She knew that he would want to know more. She remained calm. He would have to wait for some of the answers. "She's fine. Don't you worry about that. Look at me, son," she said. Paul looked at her, into her deep brown eyes beneath the horn-rimmed glasses.

Big Mama smiled. She spoke slowly and clearly. "She don't blame you. An' she ain't sad at all. She's surrounded by people who love her, and they're takin' good care of her. She don't miss nobody, an' you don't need to miss her. She's happy, an' you should be too."

"Did you really talk to her?" Paul didn't mean to sound as if he didn't believe Big Mama. He just needed her to reassure him. It was all so difficult to believe, but he *wanted* to believe her.

"Yes, Honey. I done talked to her, an' I seen her, too. She's happier than she's ever been. Don't you worry about her. She told me to tell you that. She don't need a thing from you right now. She loves you, an' she knows you love her, but she's happy where she is."

"Is she with angels?" Paul asked. He had heard about angels in Sunday school. They lived with people in Heaven.

Big Mama thought a moment, and closed her eyes. "Yes, Honey. You could say that she's with angels, an' they're takin' real good care of her. An' she's just fine." As she said this, they heard the garage door open, and Big Mama opened her eyes. "Now, remember what I told you about Mama Ray. We can talk more about this later, but only if she don't find out," she said. "Now go on in your room an' get dressed, Honey," she added, and continued with her sewing. As Paul walked out of the den, Big Mama could not help but smile. She was proud of her great-grandson, and her plan was working.

Mama Ray had pulled her car up into the garage, and was retrieving the bags of groceries that she had bought at the Piggly Wiggly. Although it was dark inside the garage, she was still wearing the big black sun glasses her doctor had prescribed to her for her glaucoma. There had not been many people she knew at the grocery store. There had only been one person, an old acquaintance from the school days of Lorene and Connie, with whom Mama Ray had served on the Sulphur Springs PTA. They said hello to each other, but, aside from that, there hadn't been anything to say. Mama Ray had barely recognized the woman, anyway, and she certainly couldn't remember her name. So many years had passed since her daughters' school days.

It seemed that Mama Ray met fewer and fewer people in the Piggly Wiggly that she had known before. She supposed that was the price of staying home and out of sight from the rest of the world, except for that one weekly trip into town. She didn't mind the anonymity, though. It came as a relief, in fact. She had lived her whole life in a small town where everybody had known her. She had often longed for a sense of privacy which small town life had never afforded.

Around the time that she had first developed diabetes, her blood pressure would suddenly drop down to nothing and she would faint in the middle of whatever she was doing. Her doctor hadn't known what was wrong with her, but it was clear that she was dropping rapidly in weight. She had fainted almost everywhere: at work; at home; and even in church. She hated the fact that everyone knew about, and had even witnessed, her inexplicable condition.

Mama Ray had never been so weak before that. She had always done her part in community events, and had always been able to hold her head up high in public. Even when Connie got pregnant in high school, Mama Ray had been able to console herself with the fact that she herself had led a good life devoted to community service and church activities.

When she had first been diagnosed with diabetes and started to suffer from complications that the doctors themselves could not explain, she hadn't wanted people to know that she needed to inject herself daily with insulin, or that her body was no longer even strong enough to carry itself on two feet like a real human being. She had appreciated all the cards and visitors to the hospital, in a way. But they all knew that she was ill, and it made her angry that she didn't even have the right to conceal this very intimate fact about her health. She couldn't stand to have visitors as she lay there in the hospital, hooked up to a catheter and IV. She knew that those sympathy cards and well-wishing visits were really laced with pity, anyway, and she didn't want their pity, nor did she want them to help her.

Mama Ray was a tall woman, and she had rapidly gotten down to less than 80 pounds, but the doctors still couldn't understand what was causing her problem. There she was, a skeleton, lying in the hospital bed, having to smile at the people who dropped by and pretend that she was strong. She hadn't even been able to go to the bathroom on her own. She had lain there in a diaper on that hard hospital bed, and couldn't control her most intimate bodily functions. She had cried at the thought of the upstanding community members coming in and smelling what she smelled. The nurses came in to change her diaper a few times a day, but, to her at least, that odor never really seemed to go away.

Since the doctors had released her from the hospital, Mama Ray had been reclusive. At first, she had still been ashamed of the spectacle she had been in the hospital. Also, she still had feared the possibility that she would faint again with no warning, suddenly falling over in front of passersby and urinating on herself.

With time, however, her physical condition had improved greatly. Big Mama moved into the house next to them and stayed with her every day to nurse her. Mama Ray's weight came back, and she began to look healthy again. Her recovered strength gave her a new sense of freedom. It was no longer shame that kept her away from society, but a desire to maintain the liberty that she had finally found in the beginning of her self-exile. She didn't want to go back to donning that social mask that she had worn, to pretending that she cared about trivialities like raising money to buy a star for the courthouse Christmas tree or bake sales for the Lion's Club. Her illness had given her the perfect excuse to slip away from the community.

During her stay at the hospital, her neighbors and acquaintances in town had already made their obligatory visits. They had done it mostly out of pity and a sense of civic and religious duty, she knew. After these obligations had been met, most of the townspeople had not been particularly keen on repeating their penitence, and so Mama Ray's seclusion wasn't met with too many objections. Perhaps some people had felt betrayed by her recoil from social funcitons; but they all had lives of their own, after all, and they had better things to do than to twist her arm to attend Ladies' Auxiliary meetings if she wasn't feeling up to it.

She had even stopped going to church services, eventually. Her Pastor, Brother Hansen, initially paid visits to the house in order to convince her to go rejoin his congregation. Mama Ray assured him that she was reading her Bible regularly, and that it was better for her to stay at home due to her health. She had wanted to continue going to church, at first. She got so used to being at home, however, that the thought of having to leave her comfortable house on Sunday to go to church became unthinkable.

Although she had stopped attending the church services in person, she still watched Brother Hansen's sermons, which were broadcast live every Sunday on the local television station. Also, she still set aside some money from her social security check to make a monthly donation to the First Baptist Church of Sulphur Springs.

Mama Ray pulled two bags of groceries out of the car and went into the house with them. She saw Big Mama, who was still on the couch sewing. "Paul ain't still asleep, is he?" Mama Ray asked. She put the grocery bags on the table and walked back toward the door to the garage.

"Naw, he's gettin' dressed," her mother answered. "Need help with them groceries?"

"No, you just keep on sewin'," Mama Ray replied. "Whatcha makin'?"

"It's a surprise for Paul. I don't wanna say it too loud, 'cause these walls seem to have little ears all over 'em." She laughed, thinking of Paul and his curiosity.

Mama Ray looked closer at the material that her mother was sewing. It looked like a little dress. She guessed that Big Mama was making clothes for Baby Doll. "Well, I'm gonna get these other groceries out," she said finally.

When all the groceries were put away, Big Mama and Mama Ray started making lunch. Paul went into the kitchen to sit with them, but their grown-up conversation didn't interest him much. He went out to swing. Before he knew it, the bushes behind the old bus shell were rustling again, and the rustling was moving toward him. Cindy, he thought, and he had to smile.

"Well, hi there!" Cindy said, as she emerged from the bushes with cigarette in hand. "Did you survive another day with your old granny?" She walked up to the fence and took a drag off her cigarette.

"Why do you smoke?" Paul asked. He had never seen another young person smoke before. His mother had told him that smoking was trashy behavior, like putting one's elbows on the table during dinner, and so he was pretty sure his mother wouldn't approve of Cindy. But his mother wasn't there, and he liked Cindy okay.

"There ain't nothin' else to do. I might as well smoke," she said. She put her hand on her hip. "I tried to take up swingin' like you're doin' now, but your old granny done run me off with that broom," she added.

"Well, she probably thought you was gonna break the swing," Paul laughed.

"You tryin' to say I'm fat?" Cindy asked.

Paul looked at her. She was a little chubby, but he hadn't wanted to imply that she was too fat to be on the swing set. He just wanted to say that she was too *big*. In his mind, a swing set was for little kids. "No," Paul said. "I didn't mean that. You're just a little old for swingin', ain't you?"

Cindy looked at him cynically. "I ain't too old for nothin'," she said. "You're granny's too old to catch me. I outran her easy," she said. "I know you think I'm fat."

"No, I don't. You ain't fat. Just a little chubby, that's all," Paul said. He wanted to make her feel better.

"Well, I still can get boys," she said. "I had me a date last night with a boy. He loves me, too," she assured him. She smiled and took another drag.

"You in love?" Paul asked. He had never been in love. He didn't understand why people acted the way they did when they were in love. It seemed strange to him that two people would just pair off and ignore everybody else around them. And they did unpleasant things like stick their tongues in each other's mouth. One time a little girl in pre-school had been in love with Paul. She had also tried to stick her tongue in his mouth. When her mouth had gotten close to him, he smelled her sour breath and gagged. He thought it was one of the dirtiest things imaginable, for somebody to stick their nasty old tongue into someone else's mouth.

"I don't know if I'm in love," Cindy said. "But he's a good kisser, an' he's on the football team at school," she added. Her face turned dreamy. "An' he's *so* cute."

"Does your mama know about him?" Paul asked, remembering LaVelle. He wondered what LaVelle would think about her daughter sticking her tongue in a boy's mouth. He figured that she probably wouldn't like it, even if the boy was on the football team.

"She knows I been to the movies with him," Cindy said. "But I don't have to tell her everything, and *you* better not, either," she added. "I don't know why I told you, anyway. You wouldn't understand it."

"I do, too!" Paul said. He didn't like being accused of ignorance.

"Oh yeah?" Cindy said as she blew smoke out her nose. "You done been in love?" She smiled at the thought of little Paul catching the love bug.

"No, but I know all about it. My brother Frank was in love one time," he said.

Cindy looked curious. "Oh, yeah?" she said. "I didn't know you had a brother."

"Yeah," Paul said. "He's older than me, but a little younger than you. He's fifteen."

Cindy perked up at the new prospect. "Where is he, then?" she asked. She didn't mind dating younger men.

Paul looked at his feet, scooting along the dirt below the swing. "He's at home with my mama an' my step-daddy."

Cindy looked sad. "Oh," she said. "I bet you miss him."

"Yeah," Paul said. "A little." He lied. He didn't miss his brother *a little*. He missed him terribly. He had thought of him often since he had arrived in Sulphur Springs.

"Well," Cindy said. She dropped her cigarette onto the ground and put it out with her foot. This time she chose not to throw it into Mama Ray's yard. Perhaps she wasn't feeling as brave as she had been the day before. "Maybe he'll come an' visit. Besides, I'd like to meet him, too. I bet he's real cute if he looks anything like you." She smiled. "Paul, I have to go now. But you come an' visit whenever you want, now."

She had lost the defensive pose that she had adopted before, and she seemed really genuine. "Okay," Paul said.

"Come by tomorrow," Cindy said. "If you can get away from your old granny."

"I will," he said. He looked forward to visiting her and LaVelle again. Cindy walked away, disappearing into the bushes behind the bus shell. As Paul resumed his swinging, he looked around at the other houses. Their yards seemed neatly kept, covered in bright green St. Augustine grass. It was a sharp contrast to the chicken-ravaged, barren yard of his grandparents. He looked around and still didn't see the hens. He felt at ease somehow, without dogs and chickens around to have to worry about. After a while, he grew tired of swinging and went inside.

Daddy C had come back home while Paul had been swinging, and was sitting in his Lay-Z-Boy with Buster. Mama Ray was in the recliner next to him, with Dawn and Tinker on either side. All the dogs had been fast asleep until Paul opened the sliding door. They were so tired when they heard the door open that they did nothing more than perk their ears up and then relax them again.

Big Mama was sitting on the couch, and a man whom Paul didn't know was sitting next to her. The man was old and gaunt, with thin white hair combed back across his head. They all looked at Paul when he entered, and he wondered if he had done something wrong.

"Well, there he is!" said the man, smiling. "Come on in here an' let me get a good look at you."

Paul stood in front of the closed glass door. He wasn't sure where he should go, as the seats in the den were taken. He looked at Big Mama, who was facing him. She noticed Paul's apprehension. "Come on over here an' sit in my lap, son," she said, beckoning him in her direction. He moved slowly toward her. "This is your great-uncle Norbert," she added. Paul moved cautiously past the man, who followed him with his eyes as he moved toward Big Mama. Paul felt nervous. "Come on, now, he ain't gonna bite you," she said.

"Well, if I do, it won't hurt none with these false teeth I got," Uncle Norbert joked. Big Mama, Mama Ray, and Daddy C all laughed.

Paul sat down in Big Mama's lap, and she put her arm around his waist.

"Uncle Norbert is Big Mama's uncle," Mama Ray said. "He's my great-uncle, 'course he's more like my uncle, 'cause he ain't no older than Big Mama," she added.

"I thought he was Big Mama's *cousin*," Daddy C said. "Now you got me all confused."

"No, he's my mama's little brother," Big Mama said. "But he ain't but three years older than I am."

Now Paul was confused. They said he was Big Mama's uncle, but he was only three years older than she was. Paul thought somehow that a person had to be old enough to have babies to be an uncle or an aunt. "How did that happen?" Paul asked.

"How did what happen?" Big Mama asked. Now *she* was confused.

Paul tried to clarify his question. "How come he's your uncle if he ain't no older than you are?"

"Well, he's my mama's baby brother," Big Mama said.

"Course my mama an' daddy had thirteen kids," Norbert said. "An' thirteen is just the ones that survived. Your Big Mama's mother, Gertrude, now she was a lot older than me. She an' her husband came over here to Texas 'fore I was even born. That was a long time ago."

"Where'd they come over from?" Paul asked.

"Germany," Mama Ray said, turning her head in the Lay-Z-Boy so that she could join the conversation. "But you know that already, son. Both my grandparents came from Germany, an' Big Mama was the first in the family born here in Texas."

Paul remembered that his great-great grandparents had come from another country, but he had never met them, and so he had never really paid any attention to the name of the country. Besides, America, or, more specifically, Texas, was the only place that he had ever known. He didn't really know what Germany was. His mother had explained to them that Germany was in a place called Europe, and that they spoke

another language there. Another language called German. He
remembered that he had heard Big Mama speaking another
language that morning. It occured to him in that moment that
she must have been speaking German when he had heard her
from the hall.

Paul looked up at Big Mama. "Do you speak German?" he
asked.

Big Mama smiled. "I used to could. It was the first
language I learned, growin' up in the country with just my
mama an' daddy an' brothers an' sisters around. We couldn't
speak no English till we started school. My daddy learned to
speak English like we did, but my mama, she never did learn.
My daddy *had* to learn to speak it, 'cause he had to work. But
my mama didn't have much of a chance to out there takin' care
of the farm. 'Course I never did learn proper German. I
couldn't imagine ever speakin' it to nobody except my daddy
or my mama." She winked at little Paul and squeezed him
gleefully. "Uncle Norbert can speak real good German, can't
ya, Uncle Norbert?" she added.

Uncle Norbert laughed. "He he. I think I done forgot just
about all of it by now. I been livin' here for over sixty years
now." He looked at Paul. "I was real young when I come over
an' your Big Mama's parents helped me to get started. I used
to sleep in the same bed with Big Mama's brothers. You
remember that, Martha?"

"I sure do," Big Mama said. "Till you got it in your head
that you was too good for country life an' moved away to work
in the coal mines," she teased him. "We sure did miss you
when you went away. But we understood. Didn't nobody
wanna stick around there too long, out in the country away
from what most folks like to think of as civilization. But, even
so, it was just like losin' a brother when you left."

"How long you gonna stay, Norbert?" Daddy C asked as he
stroked Buster's coat.

"Not long, Calvin. I gotta get goin' in a few minutes, as a
matter a fact," Norbert said.

"You'll do no such thang, Uncle Norbert," Mama Ray said.

"Naw, you gotta stay a little longer," Daddy C agreed.

"Amen to that," Big Mama added.

"We're just about to eat, an we got plenty of food there, Uncle Norbert," Mama Ray said. "An' it's good down-home cookin', too. I bet they ain't got food like that in DEE-troit." Uncle Norbert had moved to Detroit to work in an automobile plant many years before. "I won't hear of you takin' off without gettin' your belly full of mine an' Big Mama's cookin'."

"No, sir, we won't hear of that!" Big Mama seconded.

"Well, y'all don't have to twist my arm to get me to stay for your good cookin'," Uncle Norbert said. "I was kinda hopin' you'd invite me," he admitted with a smile.

"It'll be ready in a minute. Just give me two shakes," Mama Ray said. She disturbed Tinker's slumber as she got up from her Lay-Z-Boy. Tinker, disoriented, growled at Mama Ray. Mama Ray, in turned, slapped the little chihuaha on the side of her head. "Shut up, you ungrateful thing! Quit your growlin'." Tinker, surprised, quit her growling. Paul was amused. As Mama Ray's tactic seemed to have worked, he thought that he would try it the next time he had an encounter with the dogs. It might not work for him like it had just worked for Mama Ray, but the idea of slapping Tinker upside the head made him smile.

"Y'all get your hands washed," Mama Ray said to everyone. "Big Mama, will you come an' help me get it served?"

Big Mama tapped Paul on the arm. "Let me up, kiddo," she said. "We gotta get the show on the road." Paul got off her lap, and she pushed herself up from the couch and followed Mama Ray into the kitchen.

Paul went into his bedroom to check on Baby Doll. "Well, hello there!" He said. Baby Doll was lying on the bed facing him. "You sure did sleep a long time. I thought you wasn't ever gonna talk to me again."

"Yeah, they got a visitor."

"Big Mama's uncle."

"Uncle Norbert."

"No, he's just gonna stay for lunch. You wanna come eat with us?"

"Okay. I'll be back later."

Paul went into the bathroom and washed his hands. He was happy that he had finally heard from Baby Doll again. He knew that Baby Doll didn't actually speak to him, that it was just make-believe. He didn't hear her like he heard real people, but he *felt* her speaking to him, somehow. She didn't speak to him in words, exactly, but in thoughts that came to him in his mind. It just seemed natural to talk to her, like Mama Ray talked to Dawn and Tinker, or like someone might talk to a house plant.

After he had dried his hands, Paul went into the kitchen and sat at the table next to Daddy C. Uncle Norbert sat down across from them, and Big Mama and Mama Ray put the dishes on the table.

"Dig in!" Big Mama said as she sat down next to Uncle Norbert.

"Wait, we gotta say the blessin'," Mama Ray said. Normally, she wasn't too strict about saying the blessing before meals. She mostly just contented herself by saying a silent prayer before she ate, since Daddy C and Big Mama — the only two people who regularly ate with her — were heathens. It did no good to pretend to herself nor to God that Big Mama and Daddy C took the blessing seriously. However, she did like to say the blessing when there were guests around. If she had to live with two heathens and could no longer uphold the standards of Christianity in her house, then at least she liked to maintain the *appearance* of Christian values whenever she had guests. "Bow your heads, everybody. Paul, you wanna say it?"

Paul had never been asked to say the blessing before. He didn't know how to do it. He knew that, during the blessing, somebody had to thank God for the food and the weather; but he had never really paid attention to how it actually was said. He had just always lowered his head and closed his eyes, trying hard to control his desire to sneak a bite while the others were lost in prayer. "I can't do it," he said.

"Uncle Norbert, you're the guest. You go ahead an' say it," Daddy C offered.

Uncle Norbert looked up. He had been eyeing the food, and didn't seem too keen on saying the blessing, either. "Well, I don't wanna steal your fanfare, Calvin. Why don't you say it?"

"No, you say it, Uncle Norbert. That's a good idea," Mama Ray agreed. "Bow your head, Mama." She looked at her mother to make sure that she heeded her command.

Big Mama looked up with her eyes sealed shut, making a show. "I got my eyes closed," she said. "Ain't that enough?"

Mama Ray scowled. "No, Mama, you gotta bow your head. Now stop showin' out."

Big Mama thought it best to do as her daughter had asked. The sooner the blessings were over, the sooner she could eat. She bowed her head.

"Paul, you got your head bowed?" Mama Ray asked.

"Yes, Ma'am," Paul answered as he looked down at his hands.

"Go ahead, Uncle Norbert," Mama Ray said, finally satisfied.

"Well, all right," Uncle Norbert said. "I ain't said the blessin' in a long time." He bowed his head. "Dear Lord," he said, and then he paused. "Dear Lord, bless this food, an' these fine people." He searched for more words. "Bless this food," he repeated. "Bless Ronald Reagan an' the Republicans, an' God bless America." Big Mama exploded in laughter, chuckling so hard that she bumped the table. Everyone looked up at her. Paul started to laugh, too, but he stopped when

Mama Ray looked over at him. Uncle Norbert stopped the blessing again to check whether he had forgotten anything. "Thank you, an' Amen," he concluded.

"Through the lips an' over the gums. Look out stomach, here it comes!" said Big Mama. "He he!" She helped herself to a pork chop.

Daddy C had barely been able to control himself since Uncle Norbert had included Ronald Reagan and the Republicans in his rendering of the blessing. Daddy C was hungry, but it did not seem right to eat food that had been blessed by a Republican. "What was that crack about the Republicans, Norbert?" he asked.

Mama Ray, who was serving food on their plates, paused. She was on the alert, and didn't want to let the conversation get out of hand.

Uncle Norbert smiled shyly and looked at Daddy C, who didn't seem at all amused. "Oh, I'm sorry, Calvin. I didn't know y'all was Democrats." He laughed nervously.

"Hell, them Yankees up there in Dee-troit musta had a bad influence on you, Norbert," Daddy C said. "Since when have you been a Republican?"

Big Mama laughed. She liked it when men got bent out of shape over trivial things like politics. To her it was a testament to the size of their egos. They became heated and would often start to argue, as if they were powerful enough to change anything. She was sort of hoping that one or both would lose their tempers and make the meal more interesting.

Little Paul didn't know what Republicans and Democrats were, but he had heard the words somewhere before. It was the first time that he had heard one of them mentioned in the blessing, however.

Uncle Norbert decided it would be best to back down. He was a guest, after all, and didn't want to wear out his welcome. At least not before he had finished his dessert. "Aw, Calvin, I ain't a real Republican. I just was just jokin'." He hoped that would be enough to satisfy Daddy C so that he could eat his pork chop in peace and then be on the road.

"A joke is usually funny," Daddy C said. He was not going to let Uncle Norbert off the hook. "I didn't see no humor in puttin' Ronald Reagan in the blessin'," he added. "That son-of-a-bitch ain't nothin' but a…."

Mama Ray beat her fist against the table. "That's enough!" she said. She had already had too many dinners ruined by politics in her lifetime. "Everybody's got the right to his opinion," she continued. "What are you gonna do, Calvin? Teach little Paul here that two grown men can't get along because of some dumb President?" Mama Ray didn't particularly like Ronald Reagan as a President, either, but at least he was a Christian.

"He ain't dumb!" Uncle Norbert protested. He couldn't help himself. He had to stand up for Ronald Reagan, who wasn't there to defend himself.

Mama Ray became flustered. "Oh, Uncle Norbert, I didn't mean that. I like Ronald Reagan," she lied. As she said this, Daddy C opened his mouth to speak, but Mama Ray kicked him from under the table. Daddy C did not say anything.

"My Daddy always used to tell me that if you wanna keep a friendship, don't ever talk about religion or politics," Big Mama said. She saw the serious expressions on the faces of the other adults, and it made her laugh again. "Now, we're all kin folks here," she said between laughs. "An' lets just get along. We don't get to see one another but once in a great while. We better enjoy it."

"That's right," Mama Ray said. She handed Uncle Norbert a plate of food. Paul and Big Mama had already filled their plates and were eating contentedly. When Uncle Norbert saw the food, he immediately stopped thinking about the discussion. He was too old to hold grudges for too long anymore, and the food looked appetizing. Besides, he didn't want to let the pork chops get cold.

Daddy C soon got over his indignation and filled his plate as well. He liked Uncle Norbert and forgave him, even though he had shown his ugly Republican skin.

"Mmm, mmm!" said Uncle Norbert. "I ain't had such good pork chops in a long time. You don't get good ol' down home cookin' like this in Detroit," he added. "I sure did miss it."

"We thought you would," Mama Ray smiled. She hadn't received many guests since she had left society, and she liked it when her food was complimented.

"We'll give you a bag to take some with you," Big Mama said. "If there's any left."

"Well, that sure is kind of you," Uncle Norbert replied.

Daddy C looked up from his plate with his mouth full. "Where you headed, Norbert?"

"Well, I got me some business to take care of in Waxahachee. Then I'm headin' up to see some old friends in Branson, Missouri, then back on up to Detroit," Uncle Norbert said.

Daddy C swallowed his food. "Well, you oughta take in a show while you're in Branson. They got a good ol' opry house up there. I ain't been up thataway in a while, but Wanda Ray an' me used to go down to the ol' opry house when we was goin' through thataway. It was a lotta fun."

"They probably don't have that ol' opry house no more," Mama Ray said. "That was a long time ago when we was up there," she added. The thought of the old opry house in Branson, Missouri, brought back fond memories. She and Calvin had travelled frequently together before Connie was born. They would often take Lorene with them, but sometimes they would leave her with Calvin's mother. They had gone all around the country together to pick up and deliver produce. That was back in the days when Daddy C actually made a profit from selling produce, back before the big super markets had come into fashion.

Mama Ray and Daddy C didn't have a lot of money even back then, but Mama Ray had enjoyed the trips, even when they would just pull over and sleep beside the road. They had made love many times in the cab of that pickup when Lorene wasn't with them. Every trip had been like a new honeymoon. Of course, after Connie was born, Mama Ray began to stay at home and take care of their daughters full-time. By the time Connie and Lorene were both attending school, Mama Ray had to get a job at the blouse factory to make ends meet, as the profits from the produce had already begun to dwindle. With both of them working and trying to support a family, the time for romance and second honeymoons already seemed to have withered away.

Daddy C shook his head. "I bet they still do have that old opry house up there. Don't everything change," he said.

"Well, I'll look for it when I'm up there," Uncle Norbert said. "These taters sure are good. Ain't had taters like this in dog years."

"It's been a lot of dog years, too, Uncle Norbert," Big Mama said.

"What's a dog year?" Paul asked.

"It's about seven years, Doll," Daddy C said.

"You ain't got but about one dog year on you," Mama Ray added. Paul still didn't really understand. Why was a dog year seven years? Did they live by a time schedule that was different to that of humans?

After lunch, Mama Ray and Big Mama packed some leftovers for Uncle Norbert to carry with him on the road. Daddy C went into the den and reclined in his Lay-Z-Boy to watch the news. He unzipped his pants to give his stomach room to breathe. Paul sat in Mama Ray's Lay-Z-Boy next to him. From his chair Paul could see the back yard, but he still didn't see those chickens. He wondered whether he would ever lay his eyes on them.

Mama Ray and Big Mama went into the den. "Well, here's them leftovers, Uncle Norbert," Mama Ray said, handing him a paper grocery sack. "They ain't much, 'cause y'all done eat most of it." She giggled.

"I sure do 'preciate it. It was real good to sit an' visit with y'all, an' eat your down home cookin'," Uncle Norbert said.

"It was our pleasure," Big Mama said.

"It sure was," Mama Ray agreed. "You come back an' see us again real soon," she added.

"Mama Ray?" Paul said. "Where are them chickens?

Mama Ray was surprised by her grandson's question. She wasn't sure whether she had understood correctly. "What?" she asked.

"Where are them chickens?" he repeated.

"What chickens, Doll?" Daddy C asked.

Paul pointed toward the glass door. "The ones in the back yard. You said I should hit 'em with a broom if they came after me."

Mama Ray couldn't understand why Paul was asking about chickens. "Honey, we ain't got no chickens," she said.

Now Paul was confused. "You do, too. You told me yesterday to be careful about those chickens."

Big Mama watched with keen interest to see her daughter's reaction. She hoped that Mama Ray would remember the chickens and bring them back. Paul had already heard her talking about them, and it was therefore better for them to stay. Would Mama Ray remember? Her memory had been very fragile since just before the funeral.

"Honey, there ain't nothin' out there in that yard but a bunch of dirt an' dog turds," Mama Ray said. "We ain't had no chickens in years." She was getting frustrated. She had been worried for a while already that Paul was regressing into fantasy. First he had been playing with a doll, and now he was imagining chickens in the back yard.

"I remember them chickens," Daddy C told Paul. "They was just like pets. Seems like I got 'em from tradin' at a flea market when your mother was just a baby."

"Seems I remember y'all havin' chickens," Uncle Norbert chimed in. "A whole slew of 'em, too. Whatever happened to 'em?" he asked.

"One of the girls left the gate open an' they ran away," Mama Ray lied. She had always felt guilty for having blamed the incident on her daughters, when actually she was the one who had deliberately opened the gate and run the chickens out with her broomstick, one day while her daughters were at school and Daddy C was on the road. But she had already told the lie, and it was too late to change the story now after so many years had passed. She had not been able to tolerate those horrible hens, leaving chicken droppings all over the place and pecking her grass away.

"That's right," Daddy C said. "I was always tellin' 'em not to leave that gate open, but I might as well have said it to Buster here." Buster's head bolted up from Daddy C's lap to see who had said his name, and, satisfied at seeing Daddy C, he lay his head back down. "They never did listen," Daddy C added.

Paul couldn't believe what he was hearing. Mama Ray had just been talking about the chickens the day before, and now she was telling him that he was lying. He was confused and angry. He remembered Cindy, and what she had said about Big Mama and Mama Ray killing a chicken in the back yard. He had promised her that he wouldn't tell, but he couldn't help himself. "Y'all are lyin'!" he shouted.

Mama Ray and Daddy C were shocked. They had never heard their grandson speak like that. "Watch your little mouth, Mister!" Mama Ray said.

"Ain't nothin' to get upset over," Daddy C said.

"Y'all are lyin'!" Paul repeated. He looked at Mama Ray. "Cindy said that you an' Big Mama was out there yesterday an' killed a chicken. An' you was talkin' about the chickens yesterday, so don't tell me there ain't no chickens out there!" He was so angry that he felt the blood rush to his head. How could his grandparents lie to him about some stupid chickens?

He remembered that he himself had never actually seen the chickens. Maybe there were no chickens out there in the back yard. But if his grandparents were telling the truth now about there being no chickens, then that meant that they had been lying to him the day before. It seemed to him a stupid thing to lie about.

Mama Ray was mortified. How could he accuse her of killing a chicken? She hadn't killed a chicken since just before she let the other chickens out the gate many years before. She had wrung one's neck and served it to Lorene, Connie, and herself for Sunday dinner. Did he know something about that? Who was "Cindy"?

"Just who is Cindy?" she asked.

"Nobody," Paul answered. At that point he was so angry that he didn't care about protecting Cindy's identity, but he also didn't want to give his grandmother the satisfaction of knowing who she was.

"Well, it sounds like 'Nobody' has got a big mouth an' don't know what she's talkin' about. She better be careful, too, if she knows what's good for her," Mama Ray threatened. She too was feeling angry and defensive now, since she had been reminded of the chickens. She remembered the doll that Paul had brought with him and kept in his room. "I guess Cindy is what you call that little doll of yours," she added. "I done heard you talkin' to her. If she's a answerin' you back, then you got some problems. We all have."

"Y'all cut that out, now!" Big Mama said. "Quit your arguin'. We got a guest in the house."

"I don't talk to that doll!" Paul protested. He was embarrassed for the others to know that he talked to Baby Doll. It was just a game. He didn't want anyone to think that he was crazy. "You're the one who talks to yourself," he told Mama Ray. "I heard you talkin' while you was sleepin' the other day." It was true. He had woken up in the middle of the night and had heard Mama Ray talking to herself. His brother Frank had often talked in his sleep at home, and so he hadn't thought anything of it when he had heard his grandmother doing it; however, now seemed like the perfect opportunity to use it against her.

"Well!" Mama Ray said. "I guess we're all crazy, then."

"Ain't nobody crazy around here," Daddy C said. "Except maybe Uncle Norbert. He's a Republican, after all." He laughed. "But we love you anyway, Norbert."

Uncle Norbert laughed, too. "Ha ha!" His laugh sounded like Big Mama's. "Well, Calvin, the Democrats ain't all so bad, neither."

Paul, disgusted by the whole thing, ran into his room. Mama Ray started to cool down. She satisfied herself that there was no way Paul could have known about the chickens. It was just his imagination. And, what did it matter if he knew about what she had done to Daddy C's chickens, anyway? Those hens had been gone for years. She supposed that the person named Cindy was just a figment of his imagination as well, as she couldn't recall having heard the name.

Uncle Norbert stood up. "Well, I gotta be on the road."

"Well, you don't have to rush," Big Mama said. "We got plenty of room here if you wanna stay the night."

"Yeah," Mama Ray said, as she looked out the glass door into the yard.

"We sure do, Norbert," Daddy C said. "You could sleep in Connie's old room." They had moved into the house after Lorene, six years older than Connie, had already left for college. Connie had slept in her own room, and the room that Paul was sleeping in had originally been used as a guest room.

"Naw," said Uncle Norbert. "I gotta get on the road if I'm gonna get to Waxahachie 'fore dark." He picked up his cowboy hat. He had lived for many years in Detroit, but he still wore his cowboy hat when he came back to Texas. "I sure did enjoy the visit, though," he added.

The adults followed him outside to his pickup. "Tell little Paul I said ''Bye,'" he said. "I sure did enjoy seein' him. Don't y'all worry about him. He's just havin' a hard time of it."

"Will do," Daddy C said.

"You be careful, Uncle Norbert," Mama Ray said.

"An' watch out for them highway patrolemen," Big Mama warned. "They's a lot of 'em out there on the road to

Waxahachie, an' they ain't got nothin' better to do than to give out tickets." Big Mama had gotten plenty of speeding tickets in her driving days. She had always just laughed about them, though. One of her cousins had been the county judge during that time, and he had always let her off without paying them.

"Don't y'all worry," Uncle Norbert said. "I still know these roads like the back of my hand." He shut the door of his pickup and backed out of the drive as Mama Ray, Big Mama, and Daddy C waved good-bye.

When they went back into the house, Mama Ray went to clean the kitchen and Daddy C lay down to take a nap. Big Mama, however, went into Paul's room. He was lying on his bed holding Baby Doll. "That's a pretty little doll," she said. "Can I hold her?"

Paul, still angry, was holding Baby Doll tightly to him. He didn't want to give her to his great-grandmother. "She's asleep," he said.

Bid Mama sat down on the bed next to Paul. "I won't wake her up," she said as she reached down and gently put her hands on the doll. Paul let his great-grandmother take her. "Uh-oh," Big Mama said. "You see that?"

Paul turned over and looked at Big Mama and Baby Doll. He didn't see anything. "What?" he asked.

"She opened her eyes," Big Mama said. "I woke her up." She smiled, but Paul didn't react. Baby Doll's eyes were always open, and Paul knew that his great-grandmother was just trying to get his attention. "Were you a sleepin', Sweety?" Big Mama asked Baby Doll. "I'm sorry," she continued; then she put the doll in her lap and held her like she would have held a real baby. "What's your name, Honey?" she asked.

"Baby Doll," Paul answered.

"I know. She told me," Big Mama said, smiling. She looked at Paul. "I'm just jokin', Sweety. This doll ain't got nothin' to say to me. I just wanted to get you to talk to me."

She put her hand on Paul's stomach. "Paul, I know this don't make no sense right now, but there ain't no chickens here."

"But Mama Ray said there was chickens," Paul said.

Big Mama nodded. "I know she did. But she's old, an' she ain't always in her right mind. You gotta understand that. Sometimes she forgets what's goin' on. You gotta forget about those chickens, an' about what she said to you in the den. She didn't mean it. She was just mad when you called her a liar."

"But, she *did* lie!" Paul said.

"I know," said Big Mama. "But she didn't know that she was lyin'. Just forget about them chickens, an' about what Cindy told you, an' don't take anything that your Mama Ray says too seriously."

It was true that Mama Ray had cried a lot since she and Daddy C had arrived in Kingsland to get Paul. He had assumed that it was because of what had happened to Jennifer. Was something else bothering her?

"An' don't pay no attention to what Cindy tells you about your Mama Ray," Big Mama said. "She don't know what she's talkin' about. Her mother'll tell you that."

Paul wondered how Big Mama knew about Cindy and LaVelle, and then he remembered that LaVelle had told him that she and Big Mama were good friends. He wondered whether Mama Ray knew that Big Mama talked to them.

"Promise me you'll try to do what I said, Honey," Big Mama said.

Paul nodded. "Ok."

"Promise me, Honey," she repeated.

"I promise."

Big Mama patted his tummy. "Good boy," she said as she put Baby Doll back in his arms. "Now, bring Baby Doll over to see me tomorrow after you get back from visitin' with Cindy an' LaVelle. Don't let Mama Ray know that you're over there. She won't like it. If you need to, you can tell her that you're comin' to my house. It won't be a lie, exactly, 'cause you'll be comin' over to see me afterwards. I got a present for you an' your little dolly."

Paul was surprised that Big Mama was suddenly helping him to conspire in deceiving Mama Ray. He felt somehow like he had an ally, and he liked that feeling. "Okay," he said. "I'll come after lunch tomorrow."

"Good," Big Mama said. She got up from the bed and started toward the door. "Now I gotta go back to my house. You gonna stay in here?"

Paul was tired and actually felt like taking a nap. "Yeah," he said.

"I'll see you tomorrow, then," she said.

"I love you," Paul said, turning to her.

Big Mama turned to her great-grandson. "I love you, too, Honey." She left the room and went back to her house.

About an hour later, after waking up from his nap, Paul went into the den and found Mama Ray and Daddy C still sitting in their recliners and watching television. Mama Ray looked up from the program. Dawn and Tinker were in her lap. "I'm sorry I called you a liar," Paul said.

"It's all right," Mama Ray answered. "I done forgot all about it." She reached her arm out. "Now come over here an' give me some sugar." As Paul approached, Tinker began to growl. Mama Ray popped her on the head. "Stop growlin' at my grandson," she said. Paul hugged her, keeping one eye on Tinker and Dawn, but they didn't dare to bother him. Paul loved Mama Ray.

"You wanna watch TV?" Daddy C asked.

"Yeah," Paul answered. He sat down on the couch near his grandparents and the dogs.

That night, as Mama Ray lay in bed, she was awakened by a noise. It was the same sound that she had heard only a day before: that of a little girl crying. It didn't sound like crying, exactly, but was more like a soft whimpering. She tried to discern where the sound was coming from. As she looked around the bedroom, she saw that Daddy C and the dogs were sound asleep. She decided not to wake Daddy C, but instead got up to explore the noise herself. Sitting up in her bed, she put on her slippers and got up. The noise had seemed to be in the hallway, but, as she walked into the hall, she noticed that the noise seemed to have somehow moved into Paul's room. Still half asleep, Mama Ray scooted her house shoes along the floor. The door to Paul's bedroom was open. She could see him easily in the soft glow of the night light. He was cuddled up with his doll and appeared to be fast asleep. Mama Ray noticed that the whimpering sound had stopped, but she stood in the doorway for a moment to be sure that Paul was really sleeping. He didn't stir. Puzzled, she dragged her feet back down the hall and went to bed again, wondering if she had been dreaming.

Across the country, in Detroit, Michigan, Norbert Mueller was waking from a dream of his beloved Texas, of dear and long-forgotten kinfolks, and a delicious down-home meal. Refreshed and nostalgic, he sprang into the shower and prepared himself for a new day.

Runny Joe and Cowboy were sitting outside the fruit stand. They were playing checkers on top of a cardboard box, and Runny Joe was winning. "You can't jump me, Runny Joe. It's my turn," Cowboy protested.

"You take too long," Runny Joe replied. He was frustrated that Cowboy had noticed that he had played out of turn. He had become impatient waiting for Cowboy to make his move, and so he decided to go himself, knocking off two of cowboy's checkers in the process. They had been playing the game for years, but Cowboy had never really caught on. He was making progress, though. Before, he had never noticed when Runny Joe had cheated. And Runny Joe cheated whenever he got a chance. For him, it was the most exciting way to win.

"Put 'em back," Cowboy said.

Runny Joe groaned. He was getting tired of playing checkers with Cowboy. It was boring to always win, especially if Cowboy wasn't going to let him cheat in the process. Reluctantly, he put Cowboy's checkers back on the board. "There, you happy now?" he said.

Cowboy shook his head. "That wasn't where they was," he said, noticing that Runny Joe had put the checkers back in the wrong position. "Put 'em back like they was."

"Damn," Runny Joe said as he put the checkers back.

"That's better," Cowboy said, finally satisfied. "Now, watch this, you old buzzard." Cowboy took his red checker and knocked off three of Runny Joe's black ones. "Now crown me, damn it," he said. Runny Joe was shocked, as Cowboy had never gotten crowned before.

Runny Joe scratched his head. "How'd you do that?" he asked.

"You didn't think I had it in me, did ya?" Cowboy said. "I ain't as dumb as people think."

"Ain't nobody said you was dumb, Cowboy. Just stupid." Runny Joe laughed and put a crown on Cowboy's checker.

Cowboy didn't get offended. He was used to being teased about his intellectual inequities. He was just happy to have wiped out three of Runny Joe's checkers. "At least I ain't ugly," he said.

"Who you callin' ugly?" Runny Joe asked.

"I ain't callin' nobody ugly," Cowboy replied. "If you're ugly, you oughta know it. I don't have to tell you," he added with a laugh.

Paul and Daddy C drove up with the dogs. They had gone to Dallas earlier that morning to get a fresh load of produce. Paul was munching on a banana as they turned into the short driveway. Runny Joe and cowboy stood up from their game, and Runny Joe walked toward the pickup. Daddy C and Paul got out, and Dawn, Tinker, and Buster followed.

"Sure looks like a lotta work," Runny Joe said, looking at the load of produce in the back end of the pickup. He had been enjoying beating Cowboy at checkers — even if Cowboy hadn't let him cheat this time — and he didn't like the thought of having to stop his game to unload produce in the hot summer sun. Cowboy walked up next to him, also eyeing the pickup. He wasn't too keen on unloading, either.

"It ain't that much," Paul said. "I helped 'em load it," he added proudly. He had been around Runny Joe and Cowboy often in the two weeks following his arrival in Sulphur Springs. He had gotten used to the two, and had even learned to like them.

"Well, good," Cowboy said. "Then you can help us to unload it, too."

"Y'all go ahead," Runny Joe said. "I been down in my back lately."

"You're always down in your back when I got a load of produce, Runny Joe," Daddy C said. "What do I pay you for? Lord knows it ain't for your excellent customer service." Daddy C didn't really pay Runny Joe and Cowboy much money. They just got a little pocket change, a roof over their heads, a place to play checkers, and somewhere to drink Wild

Turkey in the evenings. They didn't really *work* for Daddy C. It was more like they lived there, and they just watched the produce and took the people's money when they came by to buy their fruits and vegetables. It was a small way of earning their keep. They ate their share of produce, but neither of them was really cut out to be vegetarian, and so daily they would make off to the Super Handy down the street to buy a package of wieners and some bread. Other than the wieners, bread, and alcohol, they didn't have any expenses, since Daddy C paid the rent and utilities. "Get crackin'," Daddy C said. "Let's get them boxes down."

They all went to the back of the pickup and started to unload the produce. Runny Joe had exaggerated when he had said that it looked like a lot of work. Daddy C never brought in a lot of produce. The fruit stand wasn't big enough to hold much, and about half of it was used as Cowboy and Runny Joe's living quarters. Within ten minutes they had unloaded the entire stock and put the produce out on display.

"These watermelons sure do look good an' juicy," Cowboy said.

"They oughta be," Daddy C replied. "They's high dollar ones, but I got a real good deal on 'em." He picked up a watermelon and thumped it. "Let's cut one," he said.

Runny Joe pulled out his pocketknife. "You ain't gonna use that old nasty thang to cut that watermelon," Cowboy said.

"Hell, my knife ain't nasty," Runny Joe argued.

"The hell it ain't," Cowboy said. "I seen you usin' it this mornin' to clean out your toenails."

"Hell, Cowboy," Runny Joe said. "That was this mo-nin'. I done washed it since then."

"Watch y'all's mouths around little Paul," Daddy C warned.

Paul stopped arranging the golden delicious apples and looked at Runny Joe's knife. He didn't like the thought of eating a watermelon that had been cut by a knife which Runny Joe had used to clean out his toenails. He didn't really believe that Runny Joe had washed his knife since that morning, and he thought that he surely wouldn't eat the watermelon if Runny Joe used the knife to cut it.

Daddy C seemed to be of the same opinion. "Cowboy, go get a clean knife. And make sure it's really *clean*," he said. "Runny Joe, put that dirty ol' knife away." Cowboy went to the back as Runny Joe put the knife away. Buster followed Cowboy to the back, but Tinker and Dawn stayed at Daddy C's feet. Paul, Runny Joe, and Daddy C heard a lot of scuffling in the back as Cowboy searched through boxes for a knife. Soon he came back to the front, and the others noticed that he was carrying a saw.

"What you gonna do with that saw?" Runny Joe asked, incredulous.

"Ain't no knives back there that's good for nothin' 'cept spreadin' butter," Cowboy said. "This saw is clean."

"Ain't never heard of sawin' up no watermelon," Runny Joe said.

"Let me look at it," Daddy C said. Cowboy handed him the saw, and he examined it. "Well, it looks clean to me," he said. "Paul, you wanna cut it up, Doll?"

"*Saw* it up is mo' like it," Runny Joe said.

"No, you can do it," Paul said. He wasn't interested in cutting up the watermelon; he just wanted to eat it.

Daddy C sawed into the watermelon, cutting it into big chunks. Inside the meat was yellow.

"What's that?" Paul asked. He had never seen a yellow-meated watermelon before. The only ones he had eaten had been red inside. He thought it was rotten.

"What's what?" Daddy C asked as he handed Paul a chunk. Paul took the piece, but looked at it uncertainly. It did not look right to him.

"It don't look like no watermelon," he said. "It's yellow."

Daddy C, Cowboy, and Runny Joe all chuckled. "You ain't never seen a yellow-meated watermelon before, have you?" Daddy C said.

"No," Paul answered.

"Go ahead, taste it," Cowboy encouraged.

"It's better than the other watermelons," Daddy C said. "Sweeter."

Paul looked at the chunk again, and then cautiously bit into it. Daddy C was right. It was sweet and warm. It seemed to melt on his tongue. Paul noticed that the others were looking at him, waiting for his reaction. "It's good," he said. The others, satisfied, began to eat theirs as well.

Paul looked around at the fruits and vegetables which they had just put on display. They were bright and vivid. He felt as if he were sitting in a garden and having a picnic with his grandfather, Cowboy, and Runny Joe. The shapes and colors of the produce decorated the inside of the old washateria, giving it a glow and sense of life.

The four of them ate heartily. Runny Joe licked his hands as the juice ran down them, and Cowboy grunted and slurped a time or two. Daddy C and Paul also enjoyed the watermelon as Buster, Dawn, and Tinker sniffed out the fruit stand.

Daddy C dropped Paul off at home to have lunch with Mama Ray. He told Paul that they would have to eat without him because he had business to take care of. From his driver's seat, Daddy C made sure that Paul got into the house, and then he backed his pickup out of the driveway. Paul walked through the living room and into the den.

Mama Ray was sitting in her Lay-Z-Boy staring at the television. It was not turned on. When Paul shut the door, she looked up. Paul noticed that her eyes were red through her glasses. She looked as if she had been crying. "Well, hello, there, Sugar Pud," she said, managing a smile. "I been a waitin' for you. I bet you're hungry, ain't ya?"

Paul felt insecure. He could tell that Mama Ray was sad, and he wasn't used to grown-ups crying. They had always been there to comfort him when he was sad. He wanted to say something to Mama Ray to make her feel better, but he wasn't sure what would work with an adult. His mother had sometimes offered him cookies when she knew that he was sad, or after she had yelled at him when it wasn't his fault. He didn't think that a cookie would work with Mama Ray, however. He knew that she couldn't eat them because of her diabetes, anyway. "Do you want me to turn on the TV?" he asked, thinking that maybe it would help if she had something to entertain her.

"No, honey," she answered. "I just wanted to sit still for a little while. I didn't get around to cookin' nothin' for lunch. I thought I would, but I just didn't feel up to it. You want a ham sandwich?"

Paul shook his head. "No, Ma'am, I ain't that hungry. We ate a watermelon at the fruit stand. A yellow-meated one."

"Well, I bet that was real good," Mama Ray said.

"Yeah, it was," Paul agreed. He wanted to break the silence that he sensed around them. Even though they were talking, there still seemed to be an awkwardness in the room. It was too quiet. He wanted to turn on the television, but Mama Ray had said that she didn't want it on. "What's wrong?" He asked finally, although he wasn't sure that he wanted her to give him an answer. What would he do with it?

"Oh, nothin', really," Mama Ray said. "You ever have a dream that seemed real to you? That you could swear that it was really happenin'?"

Paul thought about the question. He had dreamed many things before, but he couldn't normally remember his dreams. His favorite dreams were those in which he could fly, floating over land and water like a cloud or an angel. It seemed to him that in his flying dreams, he always knew that he was dreaming, and so he never had felt as if it were real. "I don't know," he said.

"Well, I guess I just had one of 'em," Mama Ray said. She stared again at the television.

"What'd you dream about?" Paul asked.

"My first husband," she said. "Lorene's daddy. I was back in the little house we was buyin' on Locust Street before he got sent off to the war." She paused and looked around for the dogs. "Did Daddy C take the dogs with him?" she asked.

"I guess so," Paul said. He hadn't thought about the dogs, but he remembered that they had stayed with Daddy C in the pickup as he had dropped Paul off.

"Well, I wonder why he did that," Mama Ray said. Paul sat down in Daddy C's recliner next to his grandmother.

"What was you doin' in your old house?" he asked. He was curious now, and he wanted her to continue telling him about her dream.

"I was just sittin' there, it seems like," Mama Ray said. "But it was so real. I felt like I was really there, an' I could see my hands an' my body, an' I was a movin' my arms, just like right now." As she said this, she put her hands into her view and she began to examine them. "But they was young hands, just like when me an' Johnny was married. I wasn't no more than 15 years old when we moved into that ol' house. I was just sittin' there, an' then the door opened, an' Johnny walked in in his uniform, just like the day he left. He didn't have a scratch on him."

Mama Rays eyes welled up with tears. She paused again, and wiped her eyes with a tissue. "He didn't know where he'd been. I had to tell him that he'd been in the army before he could remember it. Then I remembered the letter I'd wrote him to tell him that I was expectin' Lorene. He didn't even know I was pregnant when he left to the army." She stopped and looked over at Paul. "I'd wrote him a letter to tell him I was gonna have a baby, an' I never knew whether he'd got it or not. He told me he already knew, an' he even knew that Lorene had growed up an' had kids of her own. He didn't tell me, but I knew that he also knew that I'd gone an' married Calvin. He an' Calvin was best friends when they was growin' up, right up till they both joined the service. I didn't tell him that we'd got married, but somehow I knew that he already knew an' that he was happy about it."

Mama Ray started to sob, clenching the tissue in her fist against her chest. She continued to speak, but now it was more difficult through her sobs. "He just came over an' hugged me for a long time, an' we kissed like we done when we was married. I could feel that he still loved me. He looked just like he did the day he left, hadn't changed one bit. Then I remembered the letter I'd wrote him, an' I went into the other room to get it so that he could read it." She hit her hand against her chest, and began to sob more loudly. She looked at Paul and tried to continue. "When I came back, he was gone. He didn't even say goodbye."

Paul didn't know what to say. He wanted to tell her that it was just a dream, that she shouldn't worry. He had dreamed about many strange things in his life, and it was nothing to worry about. When he had had bad dreams, his mother always told him not to worry, that it was just a dream. Somehow, he didn't think he should tell Mama Ray that. He decided not to say anything at all.

After a few moments, it was Mama Ray who broke the silence. "If you don't want a ham sandwich, you can go on out an' swing, or go an' play with your Baby Doll," she said. "I'll make us a good supper tonight. We can invite Big Mama over to keep us company."

"When's Daddy C gettin' back?" Paul asked. His grandfather hadn't told him where he was going.

"He ain't comin' back tonight," Mama Ray answered. "He'll be back tomorrow."

"Where'd he go?" Paul asked. Daddy C had always come back home to have supper with them.

"He went to pick up a surprise for us," Mama Ray said. "You'll find out tomorrow."

Paul had begun to like surprises. Back in Kingsland, his mother and step-father had never given him many surprises. Only at Christmas and on his Birthday. Maybe they had had too many children to worry about. Since he had arrived in Sulphur Springs, his grandparents and Big Mama had given him many surprises. A few days after his arrival, Big Mama had given him a dress which she had sewn for Baby Doll. Baby Doll had worn the dress ever since then. And, just a few hours earlier, he had gotten to eat a yellow-meated watermelon for lunch. He would never have been able to do that in Kingsland. He wanted to ask what the surprise was that Daddy C was bringing back, but he knew already that Mama Ray wouldn't tell him.

"You go on, now, an' play," Mama Ray said. "But be careful."

Paul decided not to look in on Baby Doll. He had begun to play with her less and less in the past couple of weeks. She seemed to almost always be sleeping, anyway. Instead, he decided to go swing. Of course, he wasn't really going to go swing, but to run across the yard to visit Cindy and LaVelle. He had seen a lot of them lately, and had grown very fond of the two.

"I'll go an' swing," he told Mama Ray.

"Okay," she said. "But don't let them dogs get out."

"The dogs are with Daddy C," Paul said.

"Oh, yeah," Mama Ray said. "You see how my mind's goin'?" She added. Sometimes she surprised herself with her own forgetfulness. It seemed that so many things were slipping from her mind lately. "Well, be careful," she said. "I'm gonna go an' lay back down, see if I can ease my head."

"I hope you feel better," Paul said. He went out the glass door and headed for the swingset. He swung for a few minutes until he decided it was safe to make a getaway to LaVelle's house.

"Well, hi, Honey!" LaVelle said as she answered the door. "Come on in. We was just talkin' about you." Paul followed LaVelle into the living room. The walls of the house creaked as they walked down the short hallway. When they got to the living room, Paul saw Big Mama seated in a purple upholstered chair in front of the window. The tops of her hose were exposed under her dressline. Her walking cane was resting on the arm of the chair.

"Howdy, Dumplin,'" Big Mama said. "Where's your Mama Ray?"

"She's takin' a nap," Paul answered. He sat down on the couch, facing his great-grandmother. LaVelle sat down in another chair near Big Mama.

"How's she doin'?" Big Mama asked.

"I don't know," Paul answered. "She had a bad dream."

"'Bout what?" Big Mama asked.

"'Bout her first husband, Lorene's daddy," Paul said.

"Oh." Big Mama looked pensive for a moment. "Well," she said, "that's normal, I guess. She sure did love him. When he died, we didn't think she'd make it, thought she'd die of a broken heart. It was all we could do to get her to eat. It's a wonder she didn't lose that baby, she got down so skinny. She wasn't nothin' but a kid herself. 'Bout Cindy's age, I'd reckon. 'Course, that was a long time ago."

"Time don't really matter with somethin' like that," LaVelle said. "Poor thang, I don't know what I'd do if my husband had died on me. I guess it was better that he lived. It gave me enough time to get fed up with him an' get a divorce," she added.

"Yeah, I guess Calvin ain't her perfect love 'cause he made the mistake of livin' long enough for her to get used to lovin' him," Big Mama agreed. "But they've held up longer than I ever did with my marriages."

"I guess love gets old after a while," LaVelle said.

"Hell, I loved ever one of my husbands," Big Mama said. "All four of 'em. I still do love 'em. I just couldn't stand to live with 'em any longer. It ain't got nothin' to do with love."

"I never thought of it that way," LaVelle said.

"You can love everybody, but that don't mean you gotta live with 'em. Sometimes you just need your own space," Big Mama said.

"Maybe that's true," LaVelle said. "Maybe I started hatin' Joe Bob 'cause I thought that hatin' him was the only way I could bring myself to leave him," she added. "But that was a long time ago, too. I guess he wasn't all that bad, when I think about him now. We just needed to go our separate ways."

"Yeah, it's a shame people have to always hate each other when they split apart," Big Mama said. "I think they expect too much out of the other person, an' then they just end up hatin' 'em 'cause they don't get what they wanted. Everybody should just learn to stop wantin' from other people what they should be givin' to themselves. Then they wouldn't need nothin' from nobody, an' they'd be happy about what the got."

"That's right," LaVelle agreed. "They say that people in Hell want ice water, but that don't mean they get it." She smiled. "Imagine how disappointed those poor people are if they go around expectin' what they ain't never gonna get." LaVelle winked at Paul, and she laughed.

Paul was confused by the adult talk. He gathered that they were talking about love. He had never been in love. He had never asked his parents to love him. They had just done it. He hadn't expected the surprises they had given him, either. Maybe that was why he had been so happy when he had gotten them. He remembered the surprise that Daddy C was bringing, and then he tried not to think about it.

Paul sort of wished that Big Mama was not there. He loved to be with her, but he was not used to mixing the company of the two women. He was used to being the focus of the two's attention, and, now that they were together, they wanted to talk about adult things that he didn't really understand. He thought that maybe he should have stayed on the swings.

Big Mama looked at Paul. "Did your Mama Ray tell you about the surprise?" she asked.

"Yeah," Paul said.

"Did she tell you what it is, too?" Big Mama said.

"No, she just said that Daddy C was bringin' it."

"Well, that's no wonder," Big Mama said. "She didn't tell me, neither." She grinned wryly. "I had to used other ways to get the information." Big Mama turned to LaVelle. She picked up her cane and used it to point across the room to a desk that stood against the wall. "Bring that board out, LaVelle," she said, still pointing with her cane. "We can show it to little Paul. He won't tell nobody. I done tested him."

LaVelle got up from her chair and walked across the living room to the desk. The furniture in the room seemed even older than Mama Ray's. The living room walls were covered with old paintings that looked like they could have been painted by a child. It had surprised Paul to see such decorations, because LaVelle was closer to his mother, Connie's, age, than to Mama Ray's. He had wondered why a relatively young woman would have such old furniture in her house. His mother had put only the most modern furniture in their house in Kingsland. He supposed that LaVelle must not have much money, and then he had felt bad for having secretly criticized her furniture. However, after the first visit, he had stopped noticing the difference and had gotten used to the decoration. LaVelle pulled out a board from behind the desk, and she placed it on the brown plastic coffee table in front of the couch. On top of the board she put a piece of plastic that was shaped like a leaf.

"What's that?" Paul asked. He had never seen anything like it. He saw that the alphabet and some symbols were painted on the board.

LaVelle simply smiled and sat down next to him.

"It's a Ouija board," Big Mama said. "Don't tell nobody that you saw it here," she added.

Paul had grown to like keeping Big Mama's secrets. It intrigued him somehow to hide so many things from his grandmother. At first he had felt guilty, like he was lying. But he trusted Big Mama, and now he liked the thought of conspiring in her secrets.

"I won't tell nobody," Paul said. "But what's a Ouija board?"

"It ain't much, really," Big Mama said. "It's just a piece of plastic. But sometimes it's a good way to get information when nobody around wants to tell the truth."

"Huh?" Paul said. How could Big Mama get answers from a piece of plastic? Was she crazy, too, like Mama Ray was? Or, was Mama Ray the sane one? He was completely confused.

LaVelle took the piece of plastic that looked like a leaf in her hand and gave it to Paul. "Look at that," she said.

"What is it?" Paul asked.

"It's an oracle," LaVelle said. "It shows you the answers." She took the oracle from Paul's hand and put it back on the board.

"How does it show you the answers?" Paul asked.

"It points to 'em," LaVelle said.

Paul looked at the board. He noticed that the oracle was pointing to the letter "R." He wondered if "R" was the answer to her question. "What does "R" mean?" he asked.

"What?" LaVelle said.

Big Mama leaned forward to look at the board. She squinted through her glasses, but could not get a good look at it from where she was seated. She wiggled forward, until she finally was able to see it clearly.

"The plastic's pointin' to the "R" on the board," Paul said.

Both Big Mama and LaVelle laughed. "No, you gotta move it, Honey," LaVelle said.

"Well, if you move it, then you can just get your own answers," Paul replied. He didn't see the point of spelling out the answers. He thought LaVelle meant that one had to spell out the answers after they had already thought of them. Paul reached down to put his hand on the oracle.

"Don't do that!" Big Mama said. She tapped her cane loudly on the floor, causing the walls to shake. It startled Paul. "LaVelle, get that oracle away from him." LaVelle slid the oracle away from Paul's grasp, and Big Mama leaned her cane back against the arm of the chair. "Paul, Honey, don't ever try to use that thing by yourself. It ain't a toy to play with, an' it can be dangerous if you don't know what you're doin'," she said.

Paul didn't understand how a piece of plastic could be dangerous. After all, it was just a bunch of letters. "How is it dangerous?" he asked.

"It's to talk to spirits," LaVelle said. "They ain't all nice, you know."

Paul knew that "spirit" was another word for "ghost." "You said there wasn't no such thing as ghosts," Paul said.

"There ain't," Big Mama said. "Not the way that you think of 'em." She searched her mind for the right words to explain. She didn't want to scare her great-grandson, but she wanted him to understand. "We don't talk to no ghosts. A ghost is somethin' out of them TV movies covered in sheets a draggin' a chain behind it. Ghosts is somethin' that's died an' wants to come back an' hurt people. Don't believe in none of that. Don't nobody wanna hurt you, Honey. We been talkin' to spirit guides. These ones we been talkin' to ain't even been alive in a regular body like you an' me."

"How do you know?" Paul asked.

"They done told me," Big Mama replied.

Paul remembered that Big Mama had been talking to her mother a couple of weeks before, the day before she had given him the dress for Baby Doll. "Were you talkin' to your mother?" he asked.

Big Mama smiled. "Yeah, I talked to her this morin', but not with that Ouija board. I don't need a Ouija board to talk to her. She's the one who told me about the secret surprise. She knows your Mama Ray pretty well, an' knows what's goin' on with her most of the time. She's her grandmother, you know."

"What was the secret surprise?" Paul asked. Somehow, it seemed normal to him by now to hear Big Mama speak about communicating with her mother.

Big Mama had known that Paul would get used to the idea much faster than the adults. He was still very young and open to the possibility that reality was much more than most people chose to recognize. It would make his training much easier. She was still worried about Mama Ray, though. In her daughter's fragile condition, she could easily counteract any progress that Big Mama might make with Paul. She would have to start working on her daughter, too, especially now that they were all going to receive a visitor. Matters were becoming crucial.

"Your mother is coming to visit us for a while," she said. She saw Paul's eyes widen in excitement. Big Mama had needed the Ouija board to connect with Connie's guides. Only they could give her the specific answers that she had needed. She had to understand exactly why Connie was coming. She didn't expect to ever hear it from Mama Ray, who often covered up the truth, adorned it with white lies in order to create a better image of herself and those she loved. Gertrud, Big Mama's mother, had been able to tell her that Connie would come, but she had been unable to explain why.

"My Mama's comin'?" Paul repeated. He could hardly contain his excitement. He had wanted to see her so badly since he had been taken away to stay with his grandparents. "Is she gonna live here?"

Big Mama frowned. She needed to be very careful not to get Paul's hopes up. She knew that the visit would be short, that Connie couldn't stay with them for very long. Perhaps she would be there for a few days, at most. Big Mama wanted Paul to be prepared for the shortness of the visit, so that he wouldn't be crushed when his mother had to leave again. "No, she ain't gonna live with us, Honey. She's just gonna be here for a little while, but—"

"Is she gonna take me back with her?" Paul asked.

"Wait, Honey," Big Mama said. She wanted to make sure that Paul listened to her carefully. It was crucial that he understand that his mother's condition would be very fragile when she would arrive. The spirit guide had explained to Big Mama that Connie was recovering from an overdose of barbiturates which she had taken. It seemed that the grief of loss had been too much for her. Connie had been depressed most of her life, and she hadn't been able to cope with everything that had happened. One evening, already drunk on bourbon and Coke, she had taken one-too-many tranquilizers and ended up in the intensive care unit with her stomach pumped and her urine drained.

"Honey, your mother is comin' to stay with us 'cause she's sick," Big Mama said. "She's been in the hospital. She had an accident."

"What kind of accident?" Paul asked.

Big Mama didn't know how to mention the topic of the drugs and the overdose, nor did she think it was necessary. How could Paul understand that someone could put so much poison in her body to make herself feel better? She decided to avoid the subject and to address a more important issue. "Honey, she's sick, that's all. Remember what I told you about Mama Ray, about how she forgets things from time to time, an' don't always remember what's goin' on around her?"

"Yeah, but what's that got to do with my Mama?" Paul asked.

"Well," Big Mama said. "Your Mama is a lot like that right now. She had an accident that made her forget some things, an' she needs to stay with us for a while to get better. We gotta be real careful around her, just like with Mama Ray. Don't tell her nothin' about the Ouija board or nothin'."

"Are Frank an' my Step-daddy comin', too?" Paul asked.

"No, Honey," Big Mama said. "Your brother has gotta go to summer school, an' your Step-daddy's gotta work. Your

Mama's gonna be here for a little while for us to take care of her. But you gotta be real strong for her, an' don't talk about your sister. Can you promise me that?"

"Why can't I talk about Jennifer? Is Mama still mad at me?" Paul asked.

"No, Honey," Big Mama answered. "I don't know if she even remembers. Like I told you, her mind is real bad right now. You shouldn't even mention none of that to her, 'cause it'll upset her an' she won't get better. You want her to get better, don't you?" Big Mama looked her great-grandson directly in the eyes.

Paul noticed the intensity of Big Mama's stare. He felt that she had seized him somehow, and he couldn't turn away. "Yes, I want her to get better, but—"

"Then don't say nothin' about it, Honey," Big Mama said. "You gotta trust me. Have I lied to you yet?" She was still looking directly into him.

"You do what your great-granny says, Honey," LaVelle said. "It took me a long time, but I finally learned that she knows what she's talkin' about." LaVelle winked at Big Mama as she took the Ouija board and put it back behind the desk.

Paul thought for a moment about Big Mama's question. He had only really known his great-grandmother for a few weeks, but he couldn't think of a time when she had lied to him. At the same time, he couldn't be sure that anything had actually been *true*. How could he know for sure that she had actually talked to spirits.

Big Mama nodded her head. She had sensed what he was thinking. "You're a smart boy," she said. "You shouldn't believe nothin' just 'cause I tell you it's true." She thought a moment. "Let's make a deal," she said.

"What kind of deal?" Paul asked.

"If your mother comes tomorrow, then you'll know that I ain't lyin', won't you?" Big Mama said.

LaVelle came back to the couch and sat down beside Paul.

Paul thought over what his great-grandmother had said. As far as he knew, Big Mama hadn't spoken to Mama Ray that morning. But, what if Mama Ray had told her about the surprise while Paul had been at the fruit stand with Daddy C. He didn't want to distrust Big Mama, but he had to be sure. He would ask Mama Ray when he saw her. Then he could be sure that Big Mama was telling the truth. But, if Mama Ray *had not* told Big Mama about the surprise, then what if Big Mama was wrong about the surprise altogether? What if his mother was not really coming to visit them?

Big Mama closed her eyes and smiled. "You ask your granny if she told me," she said. "Then you'll know that I didn't find it out from her. An' when your mother comes tomorrow, then you'll know that you can believe me." She looked at Paul again. "An' if everything I said is true, then do you promise not to say nothin' about your sister to your mother?"

Paul nodded. "I promise," he said.

"Good," Big Mama said. "Then it's settled. Now let's go for a walk."

"But y'all just got here," LaVelle protested. "Sit down an' stay a while," she added, disregarding the fact that both Paul and his great-grandmother were already sitting.

Big Mama shook her head. "No, Honey, I think little Paul here oughta check in with his Mama Ray. She'll be lookin' for him 'fore too long. Then we're gonna go for a walk."

LaVelle got up from the couch. "Well, I hate to see y'all go," she said. "I was enjoyin' the company, an' Lord knows where Cindy is. You didn't see her out behind the bus smokin', did you, Paul?" she asked as she lit a cigarette for herself.

Paul remembered his promise to Cindy. It seemed that everyone was asking him to keep secrets from the people they loved most. Why couldn't they just tell the truth? He was too young to understand that they didn't tell the truth *because* they wanted the others to love them, that they wanted to be accepted, and that this was their way of maintaining peace in their relationships. How could a child, who loves unconditionally, understand the intolerance that people develop as they become more sophisticated? He was also puzzled about Cindy's insistence on hiding the fact that she smoked from LaVelle, when LaVelle seemed to already know that her daughter smoked. And, if LaVelle already knew that her daughter smoked, then why was she always asking him about it? It was all too complicated for Paul to grasp, but, luckily, this time he didn't have to lie. He hadn't seen Cindy on his way to their house. He simply shook his head, confident that he was neither lying to, nor betraying, anybody. "I ain't seen her," he said.

"Well, I know she ain't at school," LaVelle said. "She tries to pull that one on me from time to time. She thinks I'm losin' my mind like your granny." She stopped herself. "I'm sorry, Honey," she said. "I didn't mean that the way it sounded. Your granny's a good woman. Don't pay no attention to me."

Big Mama wiggled forward in the chair and pushed herself up with the help of her cane. "Let's get crackin'," she said.

"Where we goin'?" Paul asked.

"To visit an old friend," Big Mama answered. She turned to LaVelle. "If we see Cindy out, we'll send her your way," she said.

"You do that," LaVelle said. "An' any good-lookin' men you come across, too. Lord knows, I could use one," she added.

Big Mama laughed. "He he! Well, I wouldn't mind a couple myself, even at my old age." She winked at LaVelle. "Ain't never too old for good company." Big Mama started out the living room and down the hall. Paul and LaVelle followed her.

Big Mama and Paul went into Mama Ray and Daddy C's house through the glass door that led to the backyard. Mama Ray was still sitting in the recliner. "Look who I found a swingin'," Big Mama said. She patted Paul on the shoulder.

Mama Ray turned and looked at the two. "Where was you?" she asked Paul. "I looked out there a few minutes ago an' couldn't find you. I just about called the law. I was worried."

Paul didn't know what to say. He didn't want Mama Ray to be angry with him for having gone to LaVelle's house.

Big Mama stepped in. "I found him out there an' asked him to come an' help me put up a picture," she said. "I didn't tell you, 'cause I didn't think we'd be at it but just a few minutes. Then we come back up here to check on you."

"Well, I was just takin' a nap till a few minutes ago," Mama Ray said. "I got a headache, an' can't seem to get rid of it."

"Did you take an aspirin?" Big Mama asked.

"No," Mama Ray answered.

"Maybe your blood sugar's a little low," Big Mama suggested.

"No, I done checked it. It's about normal."

Big Mama walked up to Mama Ray's chair and put her hand on her forehead. "You ain't got a fever," she said. "You been havin' them dreams again?"

Mama Ray looked at Paul. She seemed suspicious. Had he told Big Mama about her dream? Then she decided that it didn't matter. It was not a secret that she had loved her first husband, and why should she be ashamed of dreaming of him? "Yeah, I guess," she said. "But I keep dreamin' that I hear a little baby cryin'. I don't know why, but I could swear I keep hearin' it. Why would I dream somethin' like that?" she asked.

Big Mama shrugged her shoulders. She had learned not to give Mama Ray her real opinions. Her daughter had always rejected them in the past. "Don't pay too much attention to what you dream," she said. "Just ask yourself what it means to you in your life, an' take it with a grain of salt."

"I'd rather take it with a good dose of somethin' stronger," Mama Ray said. "Maybe then I'd stop dreamin'," she added.

Big Mama laughed. "Well, just take some aspirin, an' your headache will go away," she said. "Me an' little Paul are goin' for a walk."

"Where are y'all goin' to?" Mama Ray asked. She started to rub her temples.

"We're just goin' down to the cemetery," Big Mama said. "I wanna put some fresh flowers on your daddy's grave."

"Well, y'all be careful," Mama Ray said. "An' don't y'all be gone too long. I thought we'd have supper together. Calvin ain't gonna be here till tomorrow."

"Oh, where'd he go off to?" Big Mama asked. She nudged Paul.

"He just went to see about gettin' some more vegetables, an' he's gonna sleep over at a friend's house, 'cause it's too long to make the drive back in one day," Mama Ray said.

Paul looked at Big Mama. She winked at him in return. He realized that Mama Ray hadn't told Big Mama about the surprise after all. But, it still remained to be seen whether what Big Mama had said about his mother was true. Would she really be coming back the next day with Daddy C? He felt a knot of excitement in his stomach.

"We'll be back in a couple of hours," Big Mama said. "I'll help you fix dinner."

"Okay," Mama Ray said, and then she repeated, "Y'all be careful, now."

"We will," Big Mama said. "An' you go an' take an aspirin for that headache." She and Paul went out through the living room.

When Paul and Big Mama left, Mama Ray continued to sit in her Lay-Z-boy. Maybe Big Mama had been right about her diabetes. Maybe it was causing her to hallucinate. She had told her grandson earlier about her dream. But, while she was dreaming, it had seemed real to her, as if she had actually been with her first husband in their old house. She could see her own arms, young and smooth, caressing Johnny. She could remember the smell of his cologne as he brushed his chin against her neck, the taste and texture of his tongue inside her lips. When she had woken, she had felt disoriented.

She had expected to still be inside that old house, waiting for Johnny to come home again. But her skin was no longer young, and the smell of Johnny's cologne had vanished, but somehow she had still been able taste his breath faintly on her lips. She had begun to cry when she saw that she was back in that house on Bellview Street, the one she had started her second life in, with Calvin's empty bed next to her and her insulin bag and arthritis cream beside her on the night stand.

Somehow, the dream of Johnny had seemed more real to her than where she was now. Sitting in her recliner and staring at the blank television screen as other people lived their lives in other houses, Mama Ray reviewed the dream in her mind. It was not as clear to her as it had been before, but she could see her first husband's sweet face, young and smiling, just as he had been in her dream. She might have thought that she was dreaming at that very moment, if she hadn't had a headache as a painful reminder to her that she was awake. Soon, her first husband's image began to dissolve in her mind just as quickly as it came.

Mama Ray went into the kitchen to get some aspirin from the cupboard. As she pulled the bottle of tablets out, she realized that her headache was already gone. Puzzled, she shrugged her shoulders and put the bottle back without opening it. She went back to her recliner and turned on the television. She wondered if Johnny knew that she had been thinking of him.

Outside, Paul realized that Big Mama could get around pretty fast. She trodded forward, using her cane to mark her pace. It was all that Paul could do to keep up with her. He had never seen the town on foot before. The streets were lined with many houses of different colors, some brick and some wooden. The whole town seemed to be sleeping after lunchtime. Occasionally, they walked by a house with a dog or two in the back yard, but even the dogs seemed too lazy to move in the heat. After a while, Paul realized that they had walked a long way in a relatively short time. He didn't know where they were.

"It sure is hot," Big Mama said, wiping her forehead with a handkerchief that she pulled out from the pocket of her dress. "Ain't many people dumb enough to go out a walkin' in heat like this, he he!" She put her arm around Paul. "You wanna stop an' get a soda pop?" She asked.

Paul *was* getting thirsty. He hadn't really noticed it until Big Mama had mentioned the soda pop. He wondered where they could stop to get one. He didn't see anything but houses. "Is there a store around here?" he asked.

"Sure," Big Mama said. She pointed to a small white wooden house with blue trimming. "Right up yonder."

"That don't look like a store," Paul said.

"Well, it is," Big Mama answered.

They were already approaching it. When they got up to it, Paul noticed the sign on the front: "Super Handy." He also saw the Slushy logo over the window. Suddenly his mouth watered for a Slushy. "Come on in," said Big Mama. She held the door open for him.

"Well, hello, there, Martha," the woman behind the counter said to Big Mama.

"Well, howdy do, Helen," Big Mama said. "How's everything?"

Helen shrugged her shoulders from behind the counter. "You know how it is. Same ol' same ol'. Ain't nothin' new to complain about." She laughed.

"Helen, have you ever met my little great-grandson Paul?" Big Mama asked. She took Paul, who was digging through a box of bubble gum, by the arm and pulled him up next to her. She ruffled his hair.

Helen squinted down at Paul through glasses that were hooked around her neck by a chain. "I don't know," she said. "Is that one of Lorene's?"

Big Mama shook her head. "No," she said. "He's Connie's little boy. He's here with us, now."

Helen frowned a little. She, too, had heard the news a few weeks before. "Well, I hope he likes it here," she said. She looked at Paul. "It might take you a little time to get used to the folks around here, but we ain't so bad, once you get to know us." Helen grinned.

"I ain't gonna be here too long," Paul said. It seemed to Helen that she had also heard that Mama Ray and Daddy C had brought back their grandson with them, but she had been told that the situation would last longer. She looked at Big Mama for a clue, but she did not return her glance.

"Big Mama, can I get a Slushy?" Paul asked, pointing to the Slushy machine. He hadn't had a cherry Slushy in a long time, and it seemed the perfect companion for their walk in the heat together.

"Sure you can," Big Mama said. "But, why don't you let Helen help you with it, so we don't make a big mess for her to have to clean up?"

"You go ahead, Paul," Helen said. "Help yourself." She looked at Big Mama. "Kids love to fill up them Slushys themselves. It's a lot of fun for 'em." She went over to the machine and handed Paul the largest cup. Paul took the cup and pulled the lever on the machine, filling the cup with cherry Slushy. "Now drink that down," Helen said. "And then fill your cup some more. It's hot out there."

Paul was delighted. No one had ever let him drink a Slushy and then fill the cup again. He decided that Helen was a nice lady as he started to gulp down the Slushy.

"Don't drink that too fast, Honey," Big Mama said. "You won't like that Slushy no more when you start to pukin' out there in the heat," she added.

Big Mama was right. One summer, Paul had been playing soccer with his brother Frank. Afterwards, they had both drunk three bottles of Coca Cola each. The colas tasted good going down, but when they had emptied the bottles, they had never felt sicker. He decided to stop drinking. He filled his cup up again and put the lid on it.

"The straws are on your left," Helen said.

"You go an' grab some candy, Paul," Big Mama said. "I saw you a eyein' it before. We don't want you to starve before we get back to Mama Ray's." She giggled.

Paul grabbed a handful of Double Bubble and a package of *Dukes of Hazard* playing cards. He put them on the counter with his Slushy. Big Mama took a bouquet of cut flowers from a cooler near the motor oil. She put the flowers on the counter next to the Slushy and candies. "I wanted to pick some flowers on the way, but it looks like there ain't nothin' growin' out here in this heat but broomweed," she said.

"Y'all goin' out to the cemetery?" Helen asked. It seemed that the only reason people bought flowers from her was to go to the cemetery.

"Yeah, I thought I'd show little Paul where some of his kinfolks is buried. What do we owe you, Helen?" Big Mama asked. She unpinned some folded money from inside her dress and pulled it out.

"I ain't gonna charge you for the Slushy," she said. "It's hot out there, an' a kid has got to drink. Besides, we wanna welcome little Paul here to Sulphur Springs," she added, smiling at Paul.

"Well, that sure is nice of you," Big Mama said.

"Ain't you gonna get nothin' to drink?" Helen asked. "You'll parch out there."

"No, I don't need nothin'. I kinda store water like a camel at my age." Big Mama patted her belly, and Paul, who was standing next to her, could hear it jiggle. He laughed despite himself. "I could use your toilet, though," Big Mama added.

"Well, you know where it is," Helen said. Big Mama paid her. She put her cane on the counter and scooted off to the toilet. Soon, the two were on the road again.

After a while, Paul and Big Mama reached the outside of town. There were no more city houses, only farmhouses that were spread few and far between. Eventually they turned onto a dirt road. Big Mama was using her cane, and carrying the bouquet of flowers in her other hand. Paul was carrying his Slushy, still trying to sip conservatively. It was difficult not to just gulp it down, because he loved the taste of cherry Slushys and it really was hot outside on the road. "Is it much farther?" he asked. He had never been to a cemetery before, and he was excited about going to a place where dead bodies were buried.

"We still got a little ways," Big Mama said. "But it ain't too far. You just keep a suckin' on that Slushy, an' you'll be all right." Paul started to think about the dead bodies in the cemetery. He wondered what happened to their bodies after they were buried. "Why do they put dead people in the ground?" he asked.

They continued walking as Big Mama answered. "They don't always put 'em in the ground," she said. "Sometimes they put 'em in concrete above the ground. They do that in New Orleans so they don't wash away. In some countries they used to wrap 'em up in bandages an' put 'em in the walls of temples."

Paul didn't know what a temple was. "Why do they wrap 'em up?" he asked.

"Oh, I don't know. It seems like I heard they thought it would keep their bodies in good condition in case they needed it in the afterlife. 'Course that ain't true. A body ain't good for nothin' when you don't use it no more. It don't really matter what they do to it," she said. She thought a moment, then added, "It's mostly important for the families that wanna have a place to go back to an' say hello. 'Course, they don't realize that all they gotta do is talk to 'em in their hearts."

"How can you talk to a dead person in your heart?" Paul asked.

"You just do it. If you listen, they'll talk to you," Big Mama said. She looked at Paul. "But only when *you're* ready to hear it," she added.

"Is that the way you talk to your Mama?" Paul asked.

"Yeah, that's how I talked to her in the beginning," Big Mama answered. "It didn't really start that way, though. I didn't wanna hear nothin' 'bout spirits an' all that stuff neither, just like your Mama Ray don't. But she started comin' to me in dreams. That's how it really started, I guess." Big Mama paused. "'Course I didn't think nothin' of it, 'cause we dream all kinds of crazy things. But then I started to hear a voice in me that told me when things was gonna happen, even when I wasn't sleepin'. I didn't believe it at first, but then things kept a happenin' just like the voice was tellin' me they would. I just thought they was coincidences."

"What's a coincidence?" Paul asked. He had heard the word before, but had never really learned what it meant.

Big Mama thought a moment. How could she explain that to her little great-grandson? "A coincidence is when two things happen that seem related, but don't have nothin' to do with one another, if you can understand that, he he!"

"I don't think I understand it," Paul said.

Big Mama wanted to make it very simple for Paul to understand. "For example, when we went into the Super Handy. You was thirsty, an' I had been a lookin' for some flowers to take to the cemetery. We went into the store, an' I found flowers, an' you got yourself a Slushy."

Perhaps the example was too simple. From the example Big Mama used, Paul began to think that "coincidence" was a very big word used to describe nothing special. It was normal to find Slushys and flowers in a convenience store.

Big Mama continued, "Now a lot of people think that ain't related, an' they would say that it's a conicidence. But I learned a long time ago that there ain't no such thing as coincidences. Everything we get, an' everything we do is made by magic, 'cause it wasn't there before."

"Huh?" Paul asked. He had never heard anything like that before. His mother had always told him that magic, like ghosts, didn't exist.

"You went to Sunday school an' church, didn't you?" Big Mama asked.

He had gone many times to Sunday school and church. They had never talked about magic, though, as far as he could remember. "Yes, Ma'am," he answered.

"Well, think of it this way," Big Mama said. "When God put us here on this earth, Adam an' Eve didn't have nothin' but the skin on their backs an' each other. But then they started creatin' things like their two boys, Cane an' Able, an' then houses to live in, an' big buildings, an' later on cars, an' airplanes, an' movies, an' telephones, an' fancy computers, an' all kinds of crazy machines. They made all that out of nothin', an' that's *magic*, Paul. They didn't do it alone, neither. God gave 'em everything they needed to make magic. An' they didn't need nothin' else but the desire to do it."

Paul thought about it. He had never heard it put that way before. He still wasn't really sure that he understood the explanation, but he had secretly always wanted to believe in magic. "Can you make magic?" he asked.

Big Mama laughed. "He he! Well, sure I can. That makes me a magician," she said. She had never used that word to describe herself, but somehow she liked the way it sounded. "You remember that dress I made for your sweet little baby doll?" she asked.

"Yeah," Paul answered. "I remember. She's wearin' it right now."

"Well, I made that thing out of a couple of rags an' some thread," Big Mama said. "I didn't make the rags, but I could have made them, too, if I'd a wanted to. I turned those rags into a pretty little dress for your baby doll. That's just the basic kind of magic. I can do a lot more than that, the kind that your Mama Ray don't wanna hear nothin' about. But I made that dress for your Baby Doll with my own hands, and I did it with love, too. An' that's the best kind of magic there is, the kind that's made with love."

"Can you make magic without love, too?" Paul asked.

"You sure can. That's called black magic, an' there's plenty of that around nowadays. Too much, if you ask me."

"Can you teach me how to make magic?" Paul asked. He wanted to be a magician, too.

"You already can make magic," Big Mama said. "I done seen you do it. What I can do is teach you to recognize that you can make magic, an' then you'll get even better at it. But you gotta always do it with love, though, or else it's black magic, an' you'll end up hurtin' a lot of people. Most of all, yourself. People who make black magic can't never be really happy, an' we don't want that to happen to you."

Paul thought about all the people he knew. Some of the other children at school had been really mean to him. One boy, Tommy Owens, had pushed him out of the swing and made him scrape his knee badly. Paul wondered if Tommy was a black magician.

"Do you know any people who make black magic?" he asked.

Big Mama laughed again. "Oh, Lordy," she said. "I know lots of people who make black magic, Honey. I've made my share, myself. Most people don't realize that they make magic, an' that's why they ain't careful with the kind of magic they're makin'."

"How can you know if you ain't makin' black magic, then?" He didn't want to be a black magician.

"Anything you do or say that don't come from love is black magic, Honey. People don't realize the power that they have over others, an' they go around hurtin' other people more than they know. I guess that's the real power of black magic. People don't believe in it. They think that they're helpless, that they ain't nothin', but they're powerful enough to go around hurtin' others an' hurtin' themselves, just the same. I done hurt a lot of people in my life by doin' things that didn't come from love," she said.

"Why did you wanna hurt people?" Paul asked. He couldn't imagine that his great-grandmother would ever hurt anyone. She had always been very kind to him since he had met her.

"Honey, I didn't wanna hurt 'em. Most of the time they was people I loved a whole lot. I sure didn't wanna do nothin' bad to 'em. But I wasn't always careful with what I said an' done. I'd lose my temper an' say things, or gossip about people. I never thought about what it might do to 'em."

"Did you ever hurt Mama Ray?" Paul asked. He knew that Big Mama loved her daughter very much.

"I'm sure I did, Honey," she said. She thought a moment. "I'm sure I hurt her plenty of times, but I didn't mean to." She smiled. "I wasn't smart enough then to realize the power I had over the people I love." She put her arm around Paul's shoulders and added, "That all changed when I started talkin' to my Mama again. She taught me things I never would have believed before."

"What kind of things?" Paul asked. By now, the idea of Big Mama talking to her dead mother had become almost normal to him.

"Oh, lots of things," Big Mama said, as they continued walking down the dirt road. "Like I was tellin' you, at first I didn't believe those voices was nothin' but coincidences when the things they told me would come true. But then they started to happen more often, an' I got to wonderin' if they wasn't more than coincidences. Then, one day, I was in the kitchen washin' dishes, an' I saw my Mama sittin' there in the rockin' chair just like I can see you here beside me." Big Mama looked at Paul. "But she didn't look like she did before. There was light all around her, an' I could feel—" Big Mama stopped. She tried to find the words. "I could feel her inside me." She stopped again. "Well, not exactly inside me, but all around my body. An' I felt somethin' like a chill, but it wasn't like a chill, it was more like there was love all around me, an' I felt her happiness, how glad she was to see me." Big Mama looked at Paul again. Paul noticed that her face was glowing somehow, and that there were tears welling up behind her horn-rimmed glasses. They both stopped walking, and stood beside the dirt road.

Big Mama smiled, and she squeezed Paul's shoulder. As she squeezed him, Paul himself noticed a chill move through him. It felt like an electrical surge moving circularly from his head to his feet. Suddenly, he felt a strange sensation of pressure between his eyes. "Do you feel that, Honey?" Big Mama asked.

"Yeah," Paul said. "What is it?" He began to shiver. He had never felt anything like it before. He thought he might fall over.

"Don't be scared, Honey," Big Mama said. "That's just my Mama sayin' hello. That's what I felt when it first started, when she was sittin' there in my kitchen. Except, then, it was even stronger. I felt my head open up, an' it felt like my head was gonna split in two. It didn't hurt, but it sure wasn't nothin' I was used to. I was scared, too, but she told me not to worry, that wasn't nothin' gonna happen to me. Now, all I gotta do is think about her, an' she's there, just like right now." She looked at Paul and smiled as tears rolled gently down her cheeks. "An' now you feel it, too, don't you?"

Paul nodded. He did feel it. He didn't know what *it* was, but it was something, and it felt as if it was somehow touching his forehead and his shoulders. He thought that maybe it was just a coincidence, that maybe he had drunk his Slushy too fast, or that he had been walking too long. Suddenly, the sensations went away, just as quickly as they had come. Paul felt relieved, yet at the same time a little disappointed. "It's gone now," he said.

Big Mama smiled. "Don't worry, Honey," she said. "She wants to tell you howdy, but she ain't gonna bother you till you're ready for it." She planted her cane firmly on the ground and said, "Let's get crackin'. We don't wanna be late for supper, an' we ain't even got to the cemetery yet."

Soon Big Mama and Paul arrived at the Wind Creek Cemetery. In front of the cemetery gates, before the chain-linked fence surrounding the graves, was a small white wooden church. Next to the church was an even smaller wooden building that looked like a tool shed. Big Mama motioned for Paul to follow her as she walked toward the shed. "Let's see if ol' Mr. Watkins is home," she said. She walked up to the shed and knocked on the screen door. Paul looked in through the screen. He could see a bed and a chair next to it. There seemed to be another room off to the right, but it was hidden in shadow. Paul had never imagined that someone could actually live in something so small. Big Mama knocked again, and the screen door creaked open.

A very old man with short white whiskers opened the door. He was wearing old blue denim overalls with a long-sleeve shirt underneath. Paul noticed that the old man didn't have much hair, but what he did have was very messy. The old man looked at the two of them with a puzzled look on his face.

"It's me, Hurlis," Big Mama said, smiling and waving. "Martha Hathaway."

The old man's puzzled expression turned immediately into a smile. He waved excitedly at both Big Mama and Paul, and motioned for them to go into the small house.

"No, Hurlis," Big Mama said. "We don't have time to stay too long. We just wanted to come out an' say howdy."

The old man, Hurlis Watkins, pointed to the boy next to Big Mama and again formed an inquisitive expression.

"That's my great-grandson, Paul," Big Mama said. The old man nodded. "Paul, say hello to Mr. Watkins," Big Mama said.

"Hello," Paul said. He expected the old man to answer, but instead Mr. Watkins just smiled tenderly and waved. Noticing Paul's confusion, the old man pointed to his throat and shook his head.

"He can't talk, Honey," Big Mama said.

"Oh," Paul said. For some reason, he felt a little embarrassed, but he didn't know why.

"Mr. Watkins takes care of the cemetery," Big Mama said. She took the bouquet of flowers in her hands and put them in front of Mr. Watkins. "These are for you, Hurlis," she said. "I wanted to pick you some fresh ones, but they're all dried up in this heat. I didn't think you'd like a tumbleweed." She laughed.

Mr. Watkins smiled so widely that all eleven of his teeth shone as he took the flowers. He put the bouquet over his heart and feigned a bow to both Big Mama and her great-grandson.

"I hope you like 'em," Big Mama said.

Mr. Watkins nodded profusely as he put the flowers to his nose and inhaled deeply.

"Well, say good-bye to Mr. Watkins, Paul," she said.

Paul said good-bye, and Mr. Watkins waved to both of them in return. Big Mama and Paul headed toward the cemetery gate.

"I thought you was gonna put those flowers on a grave," Paul said. "Ain't you got family out here?"

"I sure do, but I ain't gonna waste no pretty flowers on a bunch of rotten bodies, Honey," she said. "They don't need 'em. That poor old man lives out here all alone an' ain't even got a dog to keep him company. He appreciates those pretty flowers a lot more than anything that's buried out here. I guarantee it."

Paul decided that she was right. The old man had seemed really nice, even though he had seemed a little spooky with his dirty overalls and messy hair.

As they walked through the cemetery, Paul wondered for a moment whether Mr. Watkins might be Big Mama's boyfriend, but then the thought seemed foolish to him. Maybe Big Mama had just wanted to do something nice for the old man. Then he remembered what she had said about white magic, and he couldn't help but smile to himself. It suddenly occurred to him that his great-grandmother was teaching him how to be a white magician.

As they stood in the center of the cemetery, Paul looked around and estimated that there were about a hundred headstones on the lot. He wondered how old the cemetery was. Big Mama said, "I knew just about everybody buried here in this cemetery, an' about half of these people went out way before they ever expected to." She looked at Paul and added, "Let that be a lesson to you."

"A lesson about what?" Paul asked.

"Don't no one know when their time is up. Some people die a lot sooner than they think, an' some of 'em a lot later. It ain't for us to decide. But, the one thing we can choose is to enjoy what time we got, 'cause we don't never know who's gonna be next."

Big Mama pointed to a grave in front of her. "You see that one there?" she said. Paul saw the headstone, but the letters were so worn that he couldn't make them out.

"Yeah, I see it," he said. He followed his great-grandmother over to the grave that she had pointed out.

"That was one of my old school teachers," she said. "She told us for years how one summer she was gonna take off an' visit her kin folks in Holland, but she never got around to it. An' you see where she is now. I don't guess she'll be seein' Holland any time soon. At least not in that body." She took a penny from her pocket and put it on the headstone.

"What's that for?" Paul asked.

"I don't know," Big Mama said. "I just wanted to contribute to her fund. Maybe she'll finally make it to Holland some day." She turned and walked away from the grave. She and Paul continued further to the back row of the cemetery, and they stopped at another grave in the center of the row.

"Who's that?" Paul asked. Again, the letters on the headstone were too worn to be legible.

Big Mama smiled. "You know her already. Take a wild guess." She pulled Paul close to her.

Just from seeing Big Mama smile, he knew who was buried there. "Your mama," he said.

"Very good," Big Mama replied. "Look how them tombstone's are just a wearin' away. That one right there on the right is where my daddy's buried. Right next to my mama. An' that one on the left was my brother, Otto. I never did meet him. He was just two days old when he died before I was born."

Paul remembered that Big Mama had had many siblings. "Where are all your other brothers an' sisters?" he asked. He could only see three tombstones in the cluster.

"Oh, they're all over," Big Mama said. "My mama an' daddy came over to Texas from Germany, an' raised us all here, but then we just kinda all spread out. Some of 'em's dead an' buried in other parts with their husbands an' wives. But my brother Michael is still a livin'. He's up north in Minnesota with his wife an' family. I don't know why he wanted to live in such a cold place." Big Mama wiped her face with her handkerchief, and added, "But I guess this heat ain't for everybody." She chuckled and slowly put the handkerchief back into her pocket.

"Do you feel it now, Honey?" Big Mama asked.

Paul knew that Big Mama was asking about what he had felt on the road, that strange electrical sensation that had almost overwhelmed him. "No, I don't feel nothin'," he said.

Big Mama smiled. "That's 'cause she ain't here," she said. "When she comes to visit, she comes to my heart, an' not to some old graveyard. She can be just about anywhere she wants to be, an' the last thing she wants to do is hang around her ol' rotten bones out here in the cemetery." She paused for a moment. "My daddy ain't here, neither. There ain't nothin' here in this cemetery but sweet ol' Mr. Wilkins and a bunch of bones an' weeds. That oughta prove to you that I don't go around talkin' to ghosts. He he!"

In films and the stories Paul had heard from his school friends, sometimes ghosts could be found in cemeteries, lurking around their own dead corpses. But, if Big Mama's mother, his great-great grandmother, was not lurking in the cemetery, then where was she? It was too hot, and, although he was still curious, Paul had heard too much talk of spirits for one day. He chugged down the last few drops of his Slushy and squashed the paper cup in his fist.

"There's a trash can out at the front," Big Mama said, noticing that his cup was empty. "We'll get you another one on the way back, if you want. Let's get truckin' before your Mama Ray gets excited."

As they left the cemetery, Paul tossed his Slushy cup into the trashcan beside the gate. Paul thought that the way home seemed shorter. This was partly because the weather was cooling as the sun moved down the horizon, but it was also because the roads had already become familiar to him.

When Big Mama and Paul returned to Mama Ray and Daddy C's home, they heard loud noises coming from somewhere in the back of the house. It sounded as if things were being thrown across the room. They looked around for Mama Ray but didn't find her. They followed the noises to the back, and saw that the light was on in Paul's bedroom. The door was half-open. Within the bedroom, something crashed onto the floor with a loud thud. Big Mama opened the door the rest of the way and they saw Mama Ray. She was dragging something out of the closet. The two twin beds, the floor and dresser were all covered with boxes and clothes.

"What are you doing?" Big Mama asked.

Mama Ray looked up. Her hair was stuck to her sweaty face. She raised up and pulled her hair out of her eyes. Her glasses were steamed up. She exhaled loudly. "I think we got a possum in here," she said. "I done pulled out all these boxes an' put 'em back in here twice. This is the third time." She looked around. "I can't find nothin'. Every time I put everything back up, I hear it bellowin' again. Sounds like a little girl a cryin'," she said.

"You sure it was a possum?" Big Mama asked, looking at the mess. "How would a possum get into the house?"

"I don't know," Mama Ray said. "But I heard it. Don't they sometimes sound like a little kid cryin'?" she asked.

Big Mama shrugged her shoulders. "I don't know," she said. "I guess they can, if they're hurt or somethin'. How long you been hearin' it?"

Mama Ray thought a moment. "Several days now," she said. Then she remembered. The noises had become more frequent for the last several days, but it seemed that she had heard them before. They had started a few weeks before. She remembered that the first time she had heard the noises was the day after Paul had arrived. "It must've got in while we was at the funeral, 'cause I heard it the first time the day after we come back. You heard it, too, didn't you Paul? You must have. It's in your room."

Paul shook his head. He hadn't heard anything, except for the occasional sounds of Mama Ray and Daddy C snoring in their bedroom. One time he had heard one of them pass gas very loudly while he was lying in bed, and he hadn't been able to control his laughter. He hadn't heard anything that sounded like crying, however. "No, Ma'am. I ain't heard nothin'," he said.

"Well, it must of gone out an' come back in just today, 'cause I've heard it several times today already," Mama Ray said. She looked around. "It sure does hide good, 'cause I can't find it nowhere."

Big Mama shook her head. She didn't really believe that there was an opossum in Paul's bedroom. She began to think that it was time to really start worrying about her daughter. She needed to bring her back to reality. She was afraid that Mama Ray was becoming hysterical, and that her hysteria would destroy all the work that needed to be done when Connie arrived. "Honey, you go on into the kitchen an' get supper ready. Paul an' I will look for that darned possum, an' we'll plug all the holes up with steel wool."

Mama Ray pulled her hair back from her eyes again. She was tired of looking for that opossum, and also fed up with moving all the boxes from the closet. She decided that it was a good idea to go into the kitchen and let her mother and grandson take care of the problem. "Well, okay," she said. She put her hand on her back. "How was the walk? Y'all sure was gone an awful long time."

"It was great," Big Mama said. "I took little Paul to see where his great-great grandparents are buried."

"Well, that was nice," Mama Ray said. "I bet he enjoyed that." She looked at her grandson and tried to smile, but she couldn't hide her frustration. "Did you have fun, Paul?"

"Yeah," he said. "It was real nice."

Mama Ray tried to smile again. "Well, I bet they appreciated the chance to see you, too," she said. She looked at Big Mama. "There's steel wool in the broom closet," she added. She left the bedroom and went into the kitchen.

From inside the bedroom, Big Mama quietly closed the door. "Will you help me get this mess cleaned up, Honey?" she asked Paul. She scooted a box into the closet

"Ain't we gonna look for a possum?" Paul had never seen an opossum before, and he was a little excited about the prospect of finding one in his bedroom, although he didn't like the idea of sleeping with it in close proximity.

Big Mama shook her head. "No, Honey. There ain't no possum. Let's just get these things put away," she said.

If there was no opossum, then why had Mama Ray been in there digging through his things? Had she been snooping? Had she thought that Paul had taken something from her? "Why was she in here, then?" Paul asked.

"I don't know," Big Mama said, shaking her head. She was still very worried about her daughter. She would have to do something about the problem fast. It just wouldn't do to have two ill people in the house when Connie arrived. She had taken care of sick people in her time, but she didn't want that responsibility now. She was making so much progress with Paul, and she didn't want to waste her time feeding the illusions of someone who seemed to be going mad.

"I guess she thinks she heard somethin' cryin' in here, an' the only rational way she can explain it is to say it was a possum." Big Mama looked at Baby Doll, who was lying on the bed, her face peering out from under a jacket which Mama Ray had haphazardly thrown on top of her. She picked Baby Doll up. "Your little dolly don't cry, does she?"

Paul looked at Baby Doll. He had never thought that Mama Ray might have heard her. "No, she don't cry. She just talks a little if you pull her string. There on the back," he said, pointing to Baby Doll's back.

Big Mama turned the doll over. She put her hand under the dress which she had sewn, and she pulled the string that came out of the doll's back.

"It's my birthday! Do you want to play with me?" Baby Doll said.

Mama Ray pulled the string again. "Help me blow out the candles. Hee hee hee!"

Big Mama looked at Paul. "Have you been pulling on her string?" she asked.

Paul shook his head. He had gotten tired of her real speaking voice a long time before. She always repeated the same things, and he didn't like to pretend that it was her birthday every day. "I haven't played with her in a long time," he said. It was true. In the beginning, he had somehow found comfort in holding her, but he had really outgrown dolls. His mother had given Baby Doll to him on his fourth birthday, and he had put her in the closet when he was five. When his grandparents had helped him pack to go with them to Sulphur Springs, he had taken her out. He didn't have any stuffed animals, and he had wanted something to hold. He hadn't pulled her string, though.

The truth was that Baby Doll's recorded voice annoyed him. He had preferred to invent a voice for her in his head, a voice that was much prettier and less artificial. In his imagination she could talk to him about anything, not just about blowing out birthday candles.

"Well," Big Mama said. "I got an idea. We're gonna tell your Mama Ray that what she heard was this little dolly laughin'." She looked Paul in the eyes. "Now, I know it ain't true, but at this point what's true don't really matter to her anyway."

"Why do you always wanna lie to Mama Ray?" Paul asked. It didn't seem right to him to lie to people. His mother had always told him to tell the truth. It seemed that some of the things his great-grandmother was teaching him were not very nice. Why should they tell Mama Ray that she had heard Baby

Doll laughing? Maybe there really *was* an opossum in the room.

"Honey, I know it's hard to understand," Big Mama said, "but she wouldn't believe us if we told her there wasn't no possum in here unless we can find some other explanation for the noises she's been hearin'." She put Baby Doll down onto the bed. "Have you ever heard any noises in here?" she asked. "You told Mama Ray that you haven't," she added.

"I haven't," he said. "I wasn't lyin'."

"Honey, I didn't think you was lyin'," Big Mama said. "But that's just my point. You done told her the truth. There ain't nothin' in here. Anything that's in here is just what she's hearin' in her mind. If she'd heard a possum in here or somethin' cryin', Honey, then you'd of heard it, too. Wouldn't you?"

Paul thought about it a moment. Mama Ray had said that she had heard the noise while he had been in his room. She had even accused *him* of crying. At that moment, Paul himself had thought that his grandmother must have been hallucinating, because he had not been crying, and he hadn't heard anyone else. He had never heard anyone crying, except when he himself had been crying in the living room. He started to think again that maybe Big Mama was right. Maybe Mama Ray was hearing things that weren't real. "I guess I would have heard it if somethin' had been cryin'," he said. "But I ain't heard nothin'."

"You see?" Big Mama said. "You can tell her till you're blue in the face that there ain't no possums or nothin' in here, but she ain't gonna believe you. We gotta find a reason for the noise or she'll come in here again tomorrow an' do the same thing she done today." She pointed to the mess around the room. "I don't wanna have to come in here every day an' clean this mess up. Do you?"

"No," Paul said. He didn't want to have to clean up all the things that Mama Ray had scattered around the room in the first place. He thought that if lying was the price to pay in order to prevent her coming back in and making a mess again, then it was only a small price. He surely didn't want to have to clean up another mess.

"Well, good, then," Big Mama said. "So we'll tell her that she must have heard your Baby Doll in here a laughin'. The batteries must have been runnin' down on it," she added, winking at Paul.

Paul thought that Big Mama was a really good liar, for a white magician. He wondered what a black magician would have done in the situation.

"It's gonna take us a long time to put this junk back up," Paul said.

"Maybe not," Big Mama said. She smiled at Paul. "Paul, Honey, this'll be the biggest secret yet." She moved a box from the bed and sat down on it. "How long it takes to clean this mess up is gonna depend on you," she added.

"How?" Paul asked.

Big Mama motioned for her great-grandson to come to her. "Come sit on my lap," she said. Paul did as she said. Her lap felt soft and comfortable after their long walk.

"Good, now that's better," Big Mama said. "We done had a real long walk today, an' I don't wanna clean this mess up, neither. Remember what I told you about white magic earlier today?"

"Yes," Paul said.

"Well, you love your Mama Ray a whole bunch, don't you?" she asked.

Paul nodded. He did love his grandmother. She had taken him in when no one had seemed to want him.

"Good, an' she knows you love her, too," Big Mama said. "I want you to think about how much you love her. Close your eyes if you need to."

Paul closed his eyes. He didn't know how to think about how much he loved someone. He had always just known that he loved Mama Ray. "I can't," he said.

"Sure you can," Big Mama responded. "Just think about how it feels when you hug her. What it feels like in your heart."

Paul thought about hugging Mama Ray. He had never noticed it before, but it was true that it made his heart feel warm. Somehow this feeling came back to him. His heart seemed to glow with this warm feeling, and it became stronger. Suddenly he felt an electrical sensation around him similar to the one he had experienced earlier that day. This time he was not frightened. The feeling in his heart felt too good to be scary.

"Now, keep your eyes closed," Big Mama said. "an' think of why we're cleanin' up this room. Who are we doin' it for?"

Paul thought about it. They were going to clean up the room because Mama Ray had made a mess. Paul wanted it clean also because he would have to sleep in it. But Mama Ray had been there when they had come in, and she had been planning to clean it up herself. She had looked very tired, and Big Mama had told her to go into the kitchen so she wouldn't have to worry about the mess anymore. Suddenly, he understood. "We're doin' it for Mama Ray," he said.

"Good," Big Mama said. "An' why are we doin' it for your Mama Ray?" she asked.

"Because we love her," Paul answered.

"Now use that feeling in your heart that comes from love." She looked at Paul. "Keep your eyes closed, an' imagine that that love in your heart is puttin' everything back in its place. Just imagine what your room looks like when it's spic an' span."

Paul imagined his room perfectly clean. In his imagination, there were no boxes or suitcases out of place, and all the clothes were hanging in the closet where they should be.

"Now, imagine that your heart has the power to do that, just 'cause you love her an' want her to be happy," Big Mama said.

As Paul imagined this, he felt a stronger sensation in his heart. He didn't feel like a little boy, but like a giant. He was stronger than anyone else in the world. He felt at this moment that anything was possible.

"Now, open your eyes, Honey," Big Mama said.

Paul was a little afraid to open his eyes. He still felt the pounding sensation in his heart, and he liked it so much that he didn't want it to go away. He did open his eyes, however. He looked at the room. It was the same as before, with boxes and clothes scattered all over. He felt disappointed because he had wanted to clean up the room for Mama Ray and he had failed.

Paul started to speak, but suddenly, his vision became distorted. The colors and shapes in the room blurred and mixed together. He felt scared; he thought that he was going to lose his vision. Big Mama was still holding him. He blinked his eyes, trying to get his vision back, but all he saw were different shades of color and light. "I can't see," he said. "What's wrong?"

"Just relax, Honey," Big Mama said. "Ain't nothin' gonna happen. Now, close your eyes again."

Paul closed his eyes. He felt better, but, even with his eyes closed, he could tell that his vision was still somehow distorted. He saw flashes of light through the inside of his eyelids.

"Now, tell me how you want the room to look when you open your eyes," Big Mama said.

"I want it to be clean," he said.

"Where do you want the boxes to be?" she asked.

"In the closet."

"An' the clothes?" she asked. "Where should they be?"

"Hangin' on the rack in the closet," Paul answered.

"Now, tell me that everything is gonna look the way you want it to look when you open your eyes," Big Mama said.

"It's all gonna be clean," Paul said.

"Do you believe it?" she asked. "You have to believe it, or it won't happen."

"I believe it," Paul said. He did believe it. His heart was still pulsating, and something deep inside it told him it was true.

"Now, open your eyes again," Big Mama said.

Paul opened his eyes. This time the colors and shapes had returned to their normal forms. His mouth gaped open as his vision focused and he saw that his room was spotless. All the boxes and clothes were back where they were supposed to be, exactly where he had imagined them. He felt a feeling of excitement like nothing he had ever felt before. He also felt powerful. He had become a white magician.

"You sure did a good job of cleanin' up your room, he he!" Big Mama said. She kissed Paul on the cheek and nudged him. "Now, let me up. Let's see if supper's almost ready."

Paul was still stunned. He was so surprised by what had just happened, and especially by the fact that he had done it himself.

He was happy and proud of what he had just been able to do.

"How did I do that?" Paul asked.

Big Mama laughed. "It's real simple," she answered. "You did it just like everything else in the world gets done."

"How's that?" Pauls asked.

"Well, Honey, there's three rules of white magic. First, you gotta want somethin' to happen. Second, you gotta believe that it's possible an' that you deserve it. An', finally, you gotta use all the will in your heart to make it happen."

"That's easy," Paul said. It sounded to him like making magic was a piece of cake.

"Well, I guess it ain't as easy as it sounds, or other people would be doin' it more often," Big Mama said. "The trouble is, lots of folks want lots of things, but they don't believe it's possible for them to have it. An' even if they do believe it's possible, they don't think they deserve to have nothin' good happen to 'em. An', if they don't believe it's possible or that they deserve it, they think why should they even try for it, if it's out of their reach to begin with." Big Mama patted Paul's stomach. "You're still young," she said, "an' you don't have as many limits in your mind as other people do. It would of taken Mama Ray another hour to clean this mess, an' all you had to do was close your eyes an' make it go away. Now, let your great-granny up, an' let's go eat. I'm hungry."

Paul got off Big Mama's lap. He turned to her and offered her his hand to help her up.

"Well, thank you," Big Mama said, surprised by Paul's unexpected gesture.

"Thank *you*," Paul said. He really liked white magic, and he was grateful to his grandmother for bringing it to him. He wanted to practice it more often.

"Now take them batteries out of your Baby Doll," Big Mama said. She winked slyly at her great-grandson. "We don't want her to start a cryin' again."

Mama Ray was in the kitchen. Big Mama grabbed her cane from where she had laid it on the couch, and she and Paul went into the kitchen to join Mama Ray. "I hope you don't need no help," Big Mama said. "We're done pooped out."

"Naw, I'm just finishin' up in here," Mama Ray said. "I hope y'all don't expect no culinary masterpiece tonight. I'm about wiped out myself, an' I didn't get to watch Julia Child today, so I don't know what was on the menu. I just made some beans an' cornbread, with some collard greens."

"Well, that's just what I wanted," Big Mama said. "We'll be makin' some fine music in the mornin', he he!" She sat down in Daddy C's chair at the table. Paul sat down across from her, so that Mama Ray would be in the center.

"I guess that's right," Mama Ray said. "But I put ginger in 'em, an' that oughta tone 'em down a bit." She laughed. "Y'all didn't find a possum in there, did ya?" she asked.

"No, we didn't find no possum, but we figured out what was makin' that noise," Big Mama said.

"What was that?" Mama Ray asked.

"It was a little girl," Big Mama said. "But she wasn't cryin', she was laughin'." She tapped Paul's leg with her foot from under the table and winked at him.

Paul giggled. He had never seen Big Mama tease Mama Ray before.

Mama Ray turned around from the stove. "What do you mean, a little girl?" she asked. "What'd you find in there?" She had the suspicion that her mother was playing one of her pranks, but she wasn't sure where this one would lead.

Big Mama laughed. "Yeah, she was a loud one," she said. "Wouldn't shut up for nothin'. Just kept on a laughin' like she didn't have no sense."

Mama Ray was getting impatient. She had put up with her mother's jokes many times, and often had even found them funny. But she had been racking her brains trying to find the source of that noise, which she had thought was something crying. This time she had no patience. "Mama, cut it out," she said. "Tell me what in the world you're talkin' about."

She started putting the food on the table. Then she thought of the girl that lived next door. One day she had found her in the back yard smoking on a swing. When she had told the girl to leave and go home — where she should have been in the first place — the little girl had begun to curse at her. Mama Ray had been forced to chase her off the place with a broom. She thought that perhaps that little girl had been playing a trick on her to get revenge. "Was it that little brat that lives next door?" she asked.

Big Mama and Paul both shook their heads. "No, it wasn't Cindy," Paul said.

Mama Ray wondered how Paul knew the little girl's name. Then, she remembered that he had mentioned the name "Cindy" before, when he had been talking about those damned chickens. At the moment, however, she didn't care about that little girl who lived next door. She had more important issues to address. "What was it, then?" she asked.

Big Mama and Paul grabbed chunks of cornbread and started filling their plates with food. Mama Ray sat down at the head of the table to join them.

"Oh, Wanda Ray, it wasn't nothin', Honey," Big Mama said. "We was in little Paul's room a cleanin' up, an' all of a sudden we heard somebody talkin' an' then a laughin' like crazy. It like to scared us both to death. Didn't it, Paul?"

Paul looked at Big Mama. His great-grandmother's face had turned serious. Paul thought that Big Mama actually seemed to believe the story she was telling. He decided to cooperate with her, even though he knew that she was telling a lie. He looked at Mama Ray and nodded his head. "It scared me so bad I almost peed my pants," Paul said. He liked the extra detail about peeing in his pants, but, after saying it, he wondered if he had gone over the top. Big Mama simply nodded in agreement. Paul thought he saw a grin almost form on her face.

Mama Ray didn't seem affected by the detail of Paul almost peeing. She simply wanted to find out what had been making the noise. "What was it?" she asked. Her impatience with the two was growing.

"Well, we looked around an' we couldn't figure it out neither, at first," Big Mama said. True to her slow, southern style, she didn't like to get to the point of a story too quickly. She believed that the art of telling lay in the detail, even if her daughter had to suffer a little in the process. It was all in the name of good fun, after all. "So, we kept a lookin', an' we couldn't find nothin'. Just like it happened to you. We heard it, but it stopped just as fast as it had started." She shrugged her shoulders in mock-frustration.

Mama Ray shook her head. "That's just what happened to me," she agreed. "I would hear somethin' cryin', an' then I would go in there, an' it would stop. I looked all over for what was makin' that noise, but I didn't find a durned thang."

"Mmm hmm," Big Mama nodded. Her mouth was full of cornbread and beans. "That's just what happened to us, Honey." She pushed some food back into her mouth that had begun to leak out a corner. "But we kept on a lookin' till we heard it again," she added. She decided to finish chewing before she finished her story. Her daughter could wait. "These beans sure are good," she said as she swallowed.

Mama Ray beat her fist on the table. "Durn it, Mama! Tell me what it was. I don't want none of your games right now. Now, what was it?"

Big Mama looked at Paul. "Tell her, Paul," she said.

Paul put down his cornbread and looked at Mama Ray. "It was Baby Doll," he said.

Mama Ray looked bewildered. "What do you mean? That doll was cryin'?" she asked.

Big Mama nodded her head. "Yep," she said. "It must have had real old batteries in it, 'cause it would just start talkin' up a storm, an' laughin' for no reason." She looked at Paul intensely. "When it laughed, it sounded like a little girl cryin', didn't it, Paul Honey?"

Paul nodded. "Yep," he answered. He looked with an earnest face at Mama Ray. "Like I said, I almost peed my pants." Miraculously keeping a straight face, he resumed eating his cornbread.

"Well, my Word," Mama Ray said, shaking her head. "That thing like to drove me crazy." She shook her head again. "I never thought about that doll." She looked at her mother. "Did y'all take the batteries out?" she asked.

Big Mama nodded. "Yeah, we done took care of it. She won't be sayin' nothin' for a while. We threw them batteries away, didn't we, Paul?"

"Yep," Paul said.

"Well, good," Mama Ray said. She was relieved to know that the problem was solved. She could eat her beans and collard greens in peace now that she no longer had to worry about that sound of a little girl crying. "I thought I was about to lose my mind," she said. "I started to think that maybe we had a ghost in there or somethin'." She shook her head. "Now, isn't that somethin'?"

Big Mama grinned. "Now, why on Earth would you think somethin' like that?" She put a forkful of greens in her mouth. "You know that there ain't no such thing as ghosts," she added as she chewed.

"Well, you know how the mind starts to wander, an' the crazy things it can think up when it don't have a rational explanation for what's goin on," Mama Ray said. She looked at Paul. "Don't worry, Honey," she said. "We'll get you some new batteries as soon as I go to the grocery store."

"Okay," Paul said. He didn't care whether Baby Doll had batteries or not. He felt like he was outgrowing her again. Besides, he had so many people to talk to now.

"When are we gonna start preparin' for Paul's birthday party?" Big Mama asked. She loved parties. "His birthday ain't but about a week away."

Mama Ray had forgotten about Paul's birthday. She became worried now that it might not be such a good idea to have a birthday party. "Well," Mama Ray said. "I guess we'll start gettin' ready for it in a few days. All I gotta do is go to the grocery store an' buy a few things." She thought a moment as she chewed her food. "Maybe we can have it at Mrs. Celecia's," she said. "Then she can invite her little granddaughter that Daddy C was talkin' about. What's her name again?"

"I think she said Daniela," Paul said.

Big Mama nodded her approval. "That's a good idea," she said. "I ain't seen ol' Marie in years. An' it'd be good for Paul to meet somebody his age. It ain't good for him to always be around a bunch of old people."

"Well, we'll get Calvin to talk to Marie when he gets back tomorrow." Suddenly Mama Ray felt a worry come over her. How would they get along with a sick person in the house? And what would it do to Paul?

After supper Big Mama went home. She wanted to talk to her mother, who was surely happy about the progress Paul had made that day. She also needed to find some way to deal with her daughter's slipping memory. She needed Mama Ray to be strong when Connie arrived, because she would play a decisive role in the outcome of her visit. Big Mama had tried to be gentle with her daughter to pull her back to reality. She had thought that the episode with the chickens might bring her back to them, but it had only seemed to send her further back into fantasy.

She thought now that she would have to become more aggressive in her approach with Mama Ray. It was a difficult matter, however, and the last thing she wanted to do was to hurt her own daughter. Perhaps she would have to influence Mama Ray's dreams to remind her of who she was. She would also have to address an additional problem before a solution could be found. She would have to investigate the sounds of a little girl crying.

The next morning Paul got up bright and early. He had lain in bed, waiting for the sun to shine through his window. He couldn't wait to see his mother. Half of him believed that what Big Mama had told him was true, that his mother Connie would arrive with Daddy C today. This was the half that had woken him up before sunrise. In spite of the fact that everything else that Big Mama had told him had been true, there was still doubt in his mind. This doubt told him that he had just imagined everything that had happened the day before. His rational side told him that he had not cleaned his room by the sheer power of his will, because that was impossible. That rational side of him aslo told him that he had not felt the presence of Big Mama's mother around him. Those strange sensations he had experienced were caused by that cold Slushy that he had drunk too fast in the blistering sun. It was the only way that rationality could find to explain what had happened.

As soon as Paul saw the first hint of sun show through the curtains, he got up and left his room on tiptoes. He looked into Mama Ray and Daddy C's bedroom. Mama Ray was snoring peacefully, and Daddy C's bed was empty. Paul walked down the long corridor to the back bedroom where his mother and step-father had always slept when they had visited on holidays. The hallway was always dark, because there were no windows. Paul didn't want to turn the light on, since Mama Ray was still sleeping. He made his way past the broom closet and an old sewing machine covered with boxes, and down to the door of his mother's bedroom.

Silently Paul turned the door handle. The door squeaked a little as he opened it. He cringed. He didn't want to wake Mama Ray. He looked inside the bedroom. The morning light shone through a big window onto the king-sized bed, which stood empty in the corner. Paul felt disappointed as he closed the door behind him. He passed Mama Ray's room again, and noticed that she was still sleeping as he went into the bathroom to take a shower.

After his shower, Paul didn't know what to do with himself. He couldn't go back to bed, because he was too excited. He thought of watching the Saturday morning cartoons, which would just be starting around that time, but the noise would disturb Mama Ray. He was surprised that she hadn't woken up during his shower. She seemed to hear everything.

Paul decided to go to LaVelle's house. He thought that maybe Cindy would still be there. Maybe he would find her out smoking behind the old bus shell. He went out the glass door, and through the back yard to the bus shell. The bushes and vines behind the bus shell were so thick that he couldn't see his way through them. It was also surrounded by trees, and what hints of morning sun shone through their shade seemed to be blocked by the masses of vines that loomed overhead. Paul wondered why Cindy chose it as her favorite smoking place. He assumed that it was the only place where she could really have privacy, since no one around could see what she was doing. He walked slowly through the high bushes, but he didn't see Cindy anywhere.

As he approached the bus, he saw an open space in the shell where the door had once been. It was now just a black hollow space, and the vines and bushes had also grown up around it. As Paul got closer, he heard a loud mechanical hum that seemed to come from within. As he walked closer to the entrance, the hum seemed to become louder. It began to hurt his ears. Paul tried to make his way through the bushes, but they seemed to get thicker as he walked. Convinced that Cindy was not there, and also frightened by the thought of being trapped alone in those bushes with snakes and that loud hum, Paul turned around and left the way he had entered. He ran out of the bushes and made his way to LaVelle and Cindy's house.

Paul knocked on the door. Normally the inside door was open, letting the breeze blow in through the screen door. This time, both doors were latched. Paul decided not to knock a second time. He didn't want to wake Cindy and LaVelle, in case they were still sleeping. As he turned to go back to Mama Ray and Daddy C's house, he heard the door unlatch from inside. He turned around and saw LaVelle's head peek through. Paul noticed that her head was wrapped in a towel.

"Good mornin', cutie," she said. "Did you come over for breakfast?"

Paul shook his head. He hadn't even thought about breakfast. He had been too nervous to think about food. "No," he said.

LaVelle opened the screen door. "Well, come in," she said.

Paul walked into the kitchen. LaVelle was in her bathrobe. She sat down at the end of the table in front of the refrigerator, and picked up her coffee and cigarette. "You sure are out an' about early today," she said.

"I couldn't sleep no more," Paul said. He walked up to the table and sat down. "Where's Cindy?" he asked.

LaVelle shook her head as she took a drag off her cigarette. "I ain't seen her," she said, "Not in several days." LaVelle looked at Paul. "You ain't seen her, have you?"

Paul shook his head. He could tell that LaVelle was worried about her daughter. He wanted to help, but he didn't know how.

LaVelle raised her head and looked Paul directly in the eyes. "You sure you ain't seen her out there smokin'?" she asked.

Paul wanted to look away from LaVelle, as her stare was so intense. He couldn't look away. "No, Ma'am," he said. "I done went out there this mornin' an' checked out behind the bus."

LaVelle shook her head. "Hmm," she said. "Well, you ought not to be goin' out there behind that bus. Haven't your grandparents done told you that it's dangerous? There's big snakes out there."

"They ain't told me nothin' about it," Paul said.

"Well, don't get it in your head to go out there diggin' around in that thing, just 'cause Cindy spends half her time out there," LaVelle said. "If you stick your hand inside there you're liable to draw back a nub." She looked at Paul intensely. "There's big snakes inside there," she repeated.

"I didn't go in there," he said. "What's that hummin' sound that's inside there?" he asked.

"I don't know," LaVelle said. "Ask your Big Mama to tell you about that." LaVelle sat quietly for a moment. Paul thought that she must be deep in thought. "I guess Cindy's at her daddy's house," she said finally. She took another swig of her coffee, and then she took the towel off her head, letting her dark brown hair fall onto her shoulders. She looked at Paul and smiled. Even though her smile was genuine, Paul could tell that she was still worried about Cindy. "You're excited about your Mama comin', ain't ya?" she said.

Paul shrugged his shoulders. "She ain't there yet. I don't know if she's really comin'," he said.

"Honey, if your Big Mama said she's comin', then she's comin'," LaVelle said. She took another swig of her coffee. "I didn't wanna believe none of that stuff at first, neither, but I learned that when she says somethin's true, then it's true," she added.

"I don't know," Paul said. "I ain't sure."

"Honey, she ain't told you nothin' yet that wasn't true, has she?" LaVelle asked.

Paul shrugged his shoulders again. How could he be sure that anything was true? The day before, he had been convinced of everything. He had believed that he had felt the presence of Big Mama's mother as they were walking to the cemetery. He had believed that magic was possible. He had even believed that *he* had made white magic. But, somehow, when he had woken up that morning, his rational mind had told him that it had all been an illusion, that it wasn't true. He had wanted to believe so strongly that he had created the magic in his mind. It had all just been his imagination.

"Big Mama lies to Mama Ray all the time," Paul said. "How can I know that she ain't lyin' to me?"

"Oh, boy!" LaVelle said. "It sure is early in the mornin' for this conversation." She took a drag off her cigarette and another swig of coffee. "Your great-granny was right about you. You're a smart one, especially for such a little boy. But that's a good thing. It's good that you don't believe everything that people tell you. It'll help you make your own decisions about the truth." LaVelle stopped talking and looked at Paul. She put her cigarette out in the ashtray. "Honey, I know this sounds crazy, but sometimes you have to tell a little white lie now an' then, just to help people out. You remember when you an' your Mama Ray had that fight about those chickens?"

Paul nodded. He still couldn't understand what had happened, and why Big Mama had told him to forget about it. He was sure that he had heard Mama Ray say that there were chickens in the back yard. In the end, it all seemed crazy to have argued over a bunch of chickens that didn't exist in the first place. "I remember," Paul said.

"Well, what would've happened if you'd a kept tellin' your Granny that she was lyin' about them chickens?" LaVelle asked.

"I don't know," Paul answered.

"Well, I bet you'd of both got real mad at each other an' never come to no agreement," LaVelle said. "You know you heard her talkin' about those chickens, an', in her mind, she knows she didn't never say nothin' about no chickens."

"But she *did* talk about 'em," Paul insisted.

"That ain't the point," LaVelle said. "You know that she talked about 'em, an' your Big Mama an' Grandpa know it, too." She shook her head. "The point is that your Granny forgot all about ever mentionin' 'em. In her mind she didn't never say nothin' about 'em. You could argue with her till the cows come home, an' she would just think that you're crazy."

"But I ain't crazy," Paul said.

"Well, in her mind, she ain't crazy, either," LaVelle said. "Imagine what would've happened in the end. You'd both end up thinkin' that the other was crazy, an' then you might end up not talkin' to each other. Honey, in a case like that, you've just got to have the sense to let your Granny believe what she wants to. You know the truth, an' it don't matter what she believes. You just have to let her believe what she wants to. That's the only way to get along in a case like that. You can believe what you want to, an' she can believe what she wants. Your Big Mama's done learned from experience."

"But it's still lyin'," Paul said.

"Honey, it ain't lyin' if it's the only way to get along," LaVelle replied.

Paul thought about what LaVelle had said. He remembered how angry Mama Ray had gotten when he had called her a liar, and how upset he had become when she had gotten angry with him. Perhaps it was best just to let everybody be right.

"But, how can I know that Big Mama ain't lyin' to me?" Paul asked.

LaVelle looked down at the ashtray and moved it to the side. "That's a good question," she said. "I guess you can't." She pulled out another cigarette from the packet and lit it. "You just have to believe what you want to believe, really. Just like your Mama Ray. Just like everybody, as a matter of fact. You just gotta ask yourself one question."

"What question?" Paul asked.

"A simple question," LaVelle said, smiling. "Just ask yourself if you like what you believe, if it makes you feel good."

Paul wasn't sure whether he understood what LaVelle was saying. He liked to believe Big Mama. He wanted to believe in magic, and to believe that she could speak to her mother. He also wanted to believe that his mother was coming. But it didn't seem to him to matter whether he liked to believe her or not, if what she had told him wasn't true.

LaVelle noticed that Paul was confused by what she said. "Honey, let me put it this way," she said. "You can believe whatever you want to. Just like your Mama Ray, an' just like anybody. When you understand that, then you know that you should only believe in things that make you feel good. If it don't make you feel good, then don't believe it. Who cares whether it's true or not for other people. It don't have to be true for you an' me."

It made sense. He had felt something as he had been walking to the cemetery with Big Mama. At that moment, he had believed that it was her mother. It had felt good to him, as if he had been surrounded by love. That night, as he had made magic in his room, he had felt better than he had ever felt before. Who cared whether anyone else believed him? And, who cared about those stupid old chickens, anyway? He had never seen them, and maybe he had even been wrong in the end. Maybe Mama Ray had never mentioned any chickens in the back yard. Maybe he had only imagined that she had talked about them. Whatever the case, it didn't matter anymore.

He remembered the strong sensation of love that he had felt for his grandmother as he had closed his eyes and cleaned up the room for her that evening. That sensation seemed to matter much more than who was right or wrong. Suddenly Paul felt happy again, and he decided to believe that Big Mama was right. It made him feel good to believe that his mother was coming. Even if Connie didn't come in the end, he could enjoy the feeling of anticipation that he had.

"Do you want some breakfast?" LaVelle asked.

Paul hesitated. He thought that perhaps he should eat breakfast with Mama Ray, but she was probably — hopefully — still sleeping, and he was starting to feel a bit hungry. He nodded his head.

"Good," LaVelle said. "I'm gettin' kinda hungry, too. I'll fry us up some bacon an' eggs. You wanna pour some orange juice, Honey?"

Paul poured some orange juice into glasses and sat down again as LaVelle cooked breakfast.

Mama Ray was lying in her bed, dreaming. She found herself back in the house on Locust Street. She was young and beautiful, and the healthiest she had ever been in her life. This time she was not waiting for Johnny to come home, because she knew that he was there. He was outside setting up the picnic table with his best friend, Calvin Sewell, whom Mama Ray — Wanda Ray Poindexter at that time — would later marry. Wanda Ray was in the kitchen with Big Mama, who was also much younger and thinner. They were gathering the potato salad and bread.

Calvin was outside with Johnny. He was at the grill, flipping hamburger patties. Wanda Ray carried the salad and bread outside, and the two men smiled at her. She could see in their eyes that they both loved her. Big Mama came out of the house and joined them. The four of them sat together and ate hamburgers, celebrating with hugs and laughter.

This time when Mama Ray woke from her dream, she didn't feel sad. She opened her eyes with a clarity that she hadn't felt in a long time. Even her vision was clearer. The white paint on the walls became more vivid. She looked out the window, and a smile formed on her lips as she welcomed the morning sun to shine upon her face. She could feel its warmth penetrate her skin, which no longer seemed old to her.

She decided not to check her blood sugar this morning. Instead, she took her entire insulin kit and tossed it into the trash can beside her bed. She would give herself no more injections. She felt healthier now than she had ever felt before. She looked at the jar of arthritis cream next to where her insulin bag had been, and she tossed it, too, into the trash can. Since she wouldn't need them anymore, she decided to make them disappear. She watched as the entire contents of the trash can faded into nothing. Out of sight, out of mind, she thought as she stood up from her bed feeling wonderful.

Mama Ray got dressed. She went into the den and called her mother on the telephone to ask her to come over. She wanted to make the biggest breakfast ever for the two of them. She hadn't felt so hungry in her life.

"Ooh, boy!" Big Mama said on the telephone. "I'll be over in a shake."

Big Mama came in through the glass door and found her daughter in the kitchen, cooking. Mama Ray stopped her work and walked over to her mother. Her eyes were welling up with tears, but she was smiling. "I remember everything now," she said. "I guess the funeral an' everything that happened was just too much for me. I don't really know what happened."

She hugged her mother for a long time.

Big Mama giggled. "Well, welcome back to the real world," she said. "We thought we'd lost you for a while there." She couldn't help but smile as she felt her daughter's love flow through her. After a while, the two separated.

"Where's Paul?" Big Mama asked.

"He's over at LaVelle's," Mama Ray said. She grinned widely. "But he don't know that I know it."

"We'll have to be real careful now when Connie comes," Big Mama said.

"I know," Mama Ray replied.

"Has that cryin' stopped?" Big Mama asked.

Mama Ray shook her head. "No, it ain't stopped, but Paul don't seem to hear it," she answered.

"It sure is strange that he don't hear the cryin'," Big Mama said, "but I guess he don't realize that he's been talkin' to his little sister all this time. We'll have to tell him soon."

"Do you think he's ready?" Mama Ray asked.

"Almost," Big Mama said. "It'll do him good to see his mother. But it might make it harder on him."

"It'll make it harder on all of us," Mama Ray said. "I sure do miss her."

"I know you do," Big Mama said. "But we'll have her here with us for a while. Paul knows she's comin'. I done told him, but I ain't sure if he believes his old kooky Great-granny."

Mama Ray laughed, but soon her laugh faded. "I guess she still hasn't forgiven me," she said.

"Oh, don't worry none about that," Big Mama said. "Situations like this one have a way of bringin' out forgiveness. I remember how you was when I first come back to take care of you. You didn't wanna have nothin' to do with me."

"Yeah, I guess I was still real pissed off, but that's because I didn't remember nothin' at the time," Mama Ray answered. "Do you think she'll remember?"

"I doubt it," Big Mama said. "Don't nobody usually know what's goin' on at first. Little Paul don't remember nothin', either. Poor thing." Big Mama looked at the counter. "Got any coffee?" she asked.

Mama Ray nodded and poured her mother a cup of coffee.

"When's Calvin comin' back with Connie?" Big Mama asked.

"I don't know," Mama Ray answered. "I guess they should be back any time now."

The two sat together and ate breakfast. Mama Ray chewed her food slowly, enjoying every bite. She couldn't remember a time when food had tasted better.

Big Mama and Mama Ray were finishing their breakfast when Paul came into the house through the back yard. "Well, howdy do, Sugar Pud," Mama Ray said through a bite of biscuit.

Paul looked into the kitchen and saw his grandmother and great-grandmother sitting together. He was surprised and felt guilty. He had stayed too long at LaVelle's house. He had no idea how long Mama Ray had been up, but he could see that she was already fully dressed and finishing with breakfast. "You been out at LaVelle's?" Mama Ray asked.

Paul didn't know what to say. Mama Ray had never officially told him not to go to LaVelle's house, but she *had* told him not to stray from the back yard.

"Come on in here," Big Mama said. With a piece of bacon in her hand, she motioned for Paul to join them. "You can tell her," Big Mama said. "She ain't got nothin' against LaVelle."

"Of course I ain't got nothin' against her," Mama Ray said. "We're friends, as far as I know." Mama Ray laughed. "Of course, that daughter of hers might not like me too much. What's her name? Cindy?"

Paul nodded his head. "She told me you tried to hit her with a broom," Paul admitted.

Both Big Mama and Mama Ray chuckled.

"That sounds about like your Mama Ray," Big Mama said.

"I bet she didn't tell you that she started to cussin' at me when I told her to go on home to her Mama, did she?" Mama Ray said.

Paul shook his head. "No, she didn't tell me that."

Mama Ray nodded. "I didn't figure she would," she said. "Her mama called me askin' if she was out there. I don't know why she didn't come out lookin' for her herself, seein' how we don't live but a few feet away. Anyhow, I went out there to tell her that her mama was lookin' for her, an' she just started a cussin' away, tellin' me how I needed to mind my own business."

Paul was surprised. It seemed like nobody told the truth, or at least they only remembered what they wanted to. He was beginning to wonder whether there was any such thing as the truth. He thought about what LaVelle had said. Maybe it really was true that people just believed whatever they wanted to believe. "She just said she was out there swingin' an' you came chasin' after her with a broom," he said.

"Ha ha!" Mama Ray laughed so hard that she dropped a chunk of biscuit from her mouth and onto the table. "Ha ha! I scared her, too," she said. "She went runnin' out of there like nine hunnerd, she was so scared. I bet she won't come a cussin' me again no time soon." Mama Ray picked the piece of biscuit up and put it back in her mouth.

"No, she won't," Paul said. He, too, laughed at the thought of his grandmother chasing Cindy out of the back yard with a broom. "She said she ain't gonna go near the place again," he added. "She just hides out behind the bus now." He wondered whether he should have kept Cindy's hiding place a secret.

"I know she does," Mama Ray said. "I done seen her. She goes out there smokin' just like she was doin' when I found her out on the swing. It ain't none of my business, an' I figure she can do what she wants to, as long as she don't start a cussin' at me." She took a drink of her iced tea. "She can come around here any time she wants to," Mama Ray said. "Her an' her mother, too. But I don't want her out here if she's gonna be a cussin' at me in my home."

Paul remembered what LaVelle had told him about the bus shell. He wondered why it was so dangerous. He remembered that, when he had asked LaVelle about that strange hum that he had heard, she had told him that he should asked Big Mama. "What's that humming sound in the bus shell?" he asked.

Big Mama and Mama Ray looked at each other. "Have you been out there in that old bus?" Big Mama asked.

Paul shook his head. "No, Ma'am," he said. "I was just out there in the back lookin' for Cindy?"

"Was she there?" Big Mama said.

"No, LaVelle said she ain't seen her for a couple of days," Paul answered.

"Poor LaVelle," Big Mama said.

Mama Ray nodded. "I guess it's still real hard for her not to get to see her all the time like before," she said.

Big Mama took a look at Paul. "Sit down, Honey," she said. Paul sat down across from Big Mama at the table. "Ain't you gonna have some breakfast?"

Paul shook his head. "No, I done eat with LaVelle," Paul said. There was no sense in keeping it a secret anymore, and

Paul somehow felt relieved that he didn't have to lie about having visited LaVelle and Cindy. He was confused about what Mama Ray had said about LaVelle not getting to see Cindy all the time. "I thought Cindy lived with LaVelle," Paul said.

"Well, she used to, but then LaVelle got real sick an' couldn't take care of her all the time," Big Mama answered. "She's been livin' with her father for several years now."

"Cindy never told me that," Paul said. "She told me that she lived there with her mother."

"Well, sometimes she does live there with LaVelle," Big Mama said. "Just not all the time. Sometimes she has to go back an' stay with her father." Big Mama took another bite of bacon and added, "But that ain't none of our business. An' you oughta stay away from that ol' bus. It's dangerous out there. There ain't no tellin' what might come out an' get you. It's been out there since the beginnin' of time an' it's probably got snakes an' black widows an' no tellin' what else inside it."

"That's right," Mama Ray agreed. "We don't wanna have to run you over to the hospital because you was playin' in that nasty old bus."

"I just went behind it to see if Cindy was there," Paul insisted. He had had many experiences with snakes and black widows from living out on the lake in Kingsland. He knew how dangerous they were, and what they could do to someone who came into contact with them. "I wasn't playin' in it," he added.

"Honey, we know you wasn't," Big Mama said. "We just don't want you to get hurt, is all. It's just best for you to stay away from it, even if you see Cindy out there."

"Well, that was nice of LaVelle to feed you breakfast," Mama Ray said, trying to change the subject. She figured that the point had already been made about the danger of the bus shell, and she didn't want Paul to start asking more questions about it. "I'd invite her an' Cindy both to come over an' have dinner with us, but we're already expectin' company." She looked at Big Mama. "But, I guess Big Mama already told you that your mama's comin', didn't she?"

He was surprised by Mama Ray's question and didn't know how to answer. Big Mama had said that it was a secret. He looked at Big Mama. She nodded her head to let him know that Mama Ray already knew. He looked at Mama Ray. "Is it true?" he asked.

Mama Ray nodded. "Yeah, it's true," she said. "I didn't wanna tell you before because I didn't wanna worry you none. I guess Big Mama also told you that she's sick, huh?" Mama Ray asked.

"Yeah," Paul answered. "What's wrong with her?"

"Well, Honey," Mama Ray said, "that ain't easy to explain. I don't really understand it too well myself."

"Is she gonna die?" Paul asked.

"No, Honey, she ain't gonna die," Mama Ray said. "She just needs to sleep a lot an' get better. She's been real sad since what happened that day, just like we all have. Of course, it's different for a mother."

Paul felt sad again. He was reminded again that it was his fault that his mother was sad. He didn't know how to face her. He wanted to tell her that he was sorry about what happened, but Big Mama had told him not to talk about his sister with Connie. Would it make his mother sad again to see him? Would he remind her of what he had done to Jennifer? Did she still hate him? Now he wasn't sure whether he was excited about her coming. A sense of anxiety came over him. He suddenly felt like he wanted to disappear so that he wouldn't have to face his mother when she arrived.

Big Mama looked Paul in the eyes. "Don't worry about it, Honey," she said. "She ain't gonna remember nothin' about what happened. The poor thang ain't really in her right mind right now."

At that moment, they heard the outside garage door begin to rise. Paul felt a lump of anxiety in his throat. He could sense that his mother was coming.

The door that connected the kitchen to the garage opened. Daddy C came in and held the door. Connie walked in behind him. She was wearing dark sunglasses and holding Tinker in her arm. Buster and Dawn trotted in behind them.

Paul looked up. He was stunned. He didn't know what to say. Mama Ray got up from her chair. "Well, howdy do," she said from the kitchen.

Connie looked toward the kitchen and dropped Tinker nonchalantly onto the chair next to the door. She took her dark glasses off and squinted toward them, trying to focus her eyes. "Well, hello, everybody," she said faintly. She stumbled a little as she walked toward the kitchen table. She stopped and put her arm against the washing machine to hold herself up.

Paul noticed that his mother looked different from when he had last seen her. She had always been thin, but this time she was much thinner. Her skin was pale and her dark brown eyes were puffy. Her frosted blond hair looked as if it hadn't been washed, and she wasn't wearing makeup. She had always worn makeup when she had gone on trips before.

Connie looked at Paul. She pushed herself away from the washing machine and stumbled over to his chair. "Paul, aren't you gonna hug your Mama, Baby?" she asked. She put out her arms and bent down to him. Paul stood up to hug her, and when they hugged, he felt all her weight against him. Suddenly, his mother grabbed the table to push herself back up. As she pushed, the table scooted back against Big Mama, who was still seated on the other side.

"I'm sorry," Connie said, trying to adjust her weight and stand erect. Her body started to sway. "I don't know what kind of drugs they've got me on." She was mumbling. She put her hand on Paul's shoulder and braced herself against a chair. "I think I need to lay down for a while," she said. "Hi, Big Mama."

Big Mama pushed the table back and smiled at Connie. "Hi, there, Little Breeches," she said. "We sure are glad to have you here."

"They say I tried to kill myself," Connie mumbled. She looked around the kitchen, her head swaying. "That's a bunch of horseshit, if I ever heard any. If I'd have wanted to kill myself, then I'd have done it right." She looked at Paul again and smiled. "You know your Mama's a smart old gal, don't you?"

Paul was shocked. He had never seen his mother in such a state.

"Sure you do, Baby," Connie continued, still looking at Paul and smiling absently. She looked at Mama Ray. Her head was still swaying, and she was unable to keep her eyes focused. "Has that old bitch been treatin' you right?" she asked. Connie's head swung back toward the ceiling, and she collapsed onto the floor.

Paul got up from his chair. Tinker and Dawn ran up to Connie and began to lick her. Paul got down on his knees and, as he reached toward his mother, Tinker snapped at his hand. He slapped her squarely on the jaw, and she flew backward across the floor. Frightened, the little Chihuahua ran into the den, and Dawn followed her. Paul scooted forward and put his mother's head in his lap.

Connie opened her eyes and looked at Paul. Her eyes opened wide, but they were not focused. "I'm okay, Baby," she said. "I'm just gonna sleep here for a while." She closed her eyes again and tried to fall asleep right there on the kitchen floor. Daddy C had come up to see what the matter was. He and Mama Ray lifted Connie out of Paul's arms and pulled her up. Together, each holding one of their daughter's arms, Mama Ray and Daddy C helped Connie to her bedroom in the back of the house.

Paul and Big Mama walked behind them, but, this time, the dogs didn't dare to follow. Mama Ray and Daddy C put their daughter onto the bed, and Connie fell asleep as soon as her head fell against the old, familiar pillow.

Paul, Mama Ray, Daddy C, and Big Mama were sitting in the den. *Hee Haw* was on television. The dogs were outside in the back yard. It seemed to Paul that hours had passed since his mother had gone to sleep in her bed. After seeing how bad she looked and hearing her fragile voice, he was no longer afraid to have her there. He was worried about her, because he could tell just by looking at her that she was sick. He had never seen his mother look so frail. She had always seemed strong to him. She had always been there when he had been afraid or sick. He had never imagined that something like what had happened in the kitchen was possible. How could his mother ever be so weak that she would fall over in front of him?

"When is she gonna wake up?" Paul asked.

"Don't worry about her, Doll," Daddy C said. "They gave her some medicine at the hospital so she'd be okay to make the drive out here. It made her real sleepy. That's all it is."

"But why does she need to sleep so much?" Paul asked.

"Just 'cause of that medication, Honey," Big Mama said. "She said they doped her up out of her mind. I guess that sleepin' will help her get better."

"She'll be okay," Mama Ray said. "I remember when I had to have surgery on my gall bladder, an' they doped me up like that. I could've slept for days." She looked at Paul, who was sitting with Big Mama on the couch. "She'll be okay. We'll just let her sleep it off a while."

Paul had come to hate the phrase "a while." Everything seemed to last "a while." They had told him that he would have to stay there in Sulphur Springs with his grandparents for "a while," and "a while" had turned into almost three weeks.

Now his mother would have to sleep for "a while," and Paul wondered just how long that would really last. How much longer would "a while" be before his mother was well and they were both back in Kingsland with his brother and step-father? Paul loved his grandparents and his great-grandmother, but he loved his mother and brother, too, and he wanted to go back to Kingsland and live with them again.

"If you don't wanna watch *Hee Haw* with us, I guess you could go swing or somethin', Doll," Daddy C said. "I'd go out there an' swing you, but I'm kinda wore out from all that drivin'."

Paul got up from the couch. Big Mama swatted him gently on his bottom as he got up. "Now go out there an' have some fun," she said.

"You be careful, now," Mama Ray said. She was watching Lulu Roman blow into a whiskey jug on television. "An' don't let them dogs out," she added.

As Paul opened the sliding glass door, Dawn, Tinker, and Buster came running into the house. "Hello, Sweeties!" Mama Ray cried, as Dawn and Tinker jumped into her lap. "Y'all missed your Mama, huh?" Dawn and Tinker gave Mama Ray sweet sugar as Paul went out the door.

When Paul got to the swing set, he could tell that Cindy was coming out of her favorite spot. The bushes behind the old bus shell started to rustle immediately as he sat down in the swing. The rustling came toward him, until Cindy emerged with cigarette in hand. She walked up to the chain-link fence before Paul even started swinging. "Hi, there!" she said. "Why ain't you in there with your mother?" she asked. "I saw her come in earlier. She looked like she was about to tip over when she got out of that pickup to go into the garage."

"She's sick," Paul said.

"Oh, really? What's wrong with her?" Cindy asked.

Paul shook his head. "I don't know."

"She looked like she was gonna drop that stupid little dog. I was kind of hopin' she would." Cindy laughed, but she noticed that Paul didn't laugh with her. "It sure is awful when your mother's sick," she said. "But I bet she'll be okay. My Mama was real sick, too, a while back. She was in the hospital an' everything. The doctors thought she was gonna die, but she didn't. I was real scared." Paul stopped trying to swing higher. Cindy had caught his attention. "I bet your Mama will be okay, too," she added.

"You wanna come swing with me?" Paul asked.

Cindy took a drag off her cigarette and shook her head. "Hell, no, I ain't gonna go in there. You know your old granny would chase me off again."

"No, she won't," Paul said. "She told me this mornin' that you can come over any time you want to."

Cindy looked incredulously at Paul. "She didn't tell you no such thing," she said.

"She did, too," Paul said. "She was there in the kitchen with Big Mama when she said it. She knows I been goin' over to you an' LaVelle's, too."

"I don't believe it," Cindy said. "She told me not to ever come back, an' I don't intend to, anyway." Cindy took a last drag off her cigarette and threw it toward the gate. As it landed, the latch of the gate slid down and the gate swung open. Cindy and Paul both noticed it.

"Come on in," Paul said. "Mama Ray ain't gonna do nothin' to you. I promise."

Cindy hesitated, but finally she walked to the gate and inside the fence. She picked up the cigarette butt and extinguished it in the dirt. She threw it over the fence toward the abandoned bus shell and went over to the swing next to Paul. "If she comes out here with that broom, I'm gonna do to you whatever she tries to do to me," Cindy warned. Cautiously, she mounted the swing.

Paul smiled. "Ain't nothin' gonna happen," he said.

The two swung together for a few minutes before Cindy decided it was enough. When she became confident that Mama Ray was not going to come outside swinging a broom at her, she got bored. She was too old for swinging, after all, and a sudden attack from Mama Ray might have added a little excitement to such a monotonous activity as swinging back and forth without ever going anywhere. Just as Cindy started to leave, a handsome boy was walking up to the gate.

Cindy saw him first, and his sudden presence startled her enough to cause her to drop the cigarette that she had lit just a few moments before. After the initial shock of seeing him, Cindy was able to ascertain that the boy was very good-looking. He was tall and thin, with curly brown hair and eyes. He was carrying a duffel bag. "Who's that?" she asked Paul in a whisper.

Paul looked up to where Cindy was pointing. In mid-air, he jumped out of his swing. "Frank!" he yelled, as he ran to the gate.

"Hey!" yelled Frank. He flung open the gate and walked into the yard.

Paul reached up to hug his brother, but Frank patted him on the back instead. "I'm too big for hugs," he said. He looked over at Cindy, who had picked her cigarette up and was smoking it on the swing. "Who's your girlfriend?" he asked.

"What girlfriend?" Paul asked.

"Over there," Frank said, pointing to Cindy.

"She ain't my girlfriend," Paul said. "She's the neighbor's daughter."

"Paul, you told me we was goin' steady," Cindy yelled from the swing. "You been lyin' to me all this time?" She chuckled.

"Well, she's not bad lookin'," Frank whispered to Paul. "A little old for you, though."

"She ain't my girlfriend, anyway. She's just teasin'," Paul said.

Frank looked crossly at Paul. "When did you start sayin' 'ain't'?" he asked. "Mama's gonna skin your hide if she hears you talk like that," he added. Almost everyone in Texas spoke dialect, but in Texas there was correct Texas dialect, and hick Texas dialect. Both dialectical systems were distinct from those of the other states, but within Texas it was always fairly clear who was a hick and who was not, simply judging from the dialect a person spoke. When Connie had left her parents' house, she had vowed to learn to speak like an upper-crust Texan, as befitted her new location in the Kingsland suburbs. She had always taught her children to speak correctly, albeit with a very thick Texas drawl. She had always gotten cross with them when they had picked up hick words at school from their less fortunate classmates and decided to try those words out at home. It gave her the feeling that their roots were showing.

"Is Mama here?" Frank asked.

"I can say 'ain't' if I want to," Paul said. "Mama don't care what I say, anyway. She don't care nothin' about me." His mother had not shown him any sign that he even existed since his sister's death. Why should she care that he talked like a hick now?

"That's not true," Frank answered. "She's just been real sick. She misses you. She's cried every night since you've been gone. She won't let anyone go in your room or touch your stuff, keeps sayin' that we have to keep it the way it was till you come back. Is she here?" he asked again.

"Yeah, she's here," Paul said. "But she's sleepin'. She passed out on the floor, an' they had to carry her to bed."

"Is she all right?" Frank asked.

"I don't know," Paul replied. "They say she just needs to sleep a while." It seemed to Paul that his mother spent most of her life sleeping. When he had lived with them in Kingsland, Connie was normally still sleeping when they left for school, and she would still be in bed when they came home. In the afternoons, she would finally get up to start her day and feed them dinner around nine pm. That dinner usually consisted of sandwiches and potato chips, but sometimes Connie would get creative and serve them oatmeal with toast.

Frank walked over to the swings. He gave his hand to Cindy. "Hello, I'm Frank," he said.

Cindy was a little nervous. Frank seemed more polite than most of the boys she was used to. At first she didn't know how to react, but then she put out her hand and they shook hands.

"I'm Cindy," she said. She noticed how much Frank looked like his brother, Paul. It seemed to her that Paul would probably look just like his brother if he were only a couple of years older. "You gonna stay here for a while?" she asked.

"No, just till tomorrow," Frank answered. "I gotta be back for summer school on Monday."

Paul felt his heart drop. He had hoped his brother would stay longer. Now he was left with that terrible feeling that people have when hope is suddenly crushed.

Frank looked at Paul and noticed his disappointment. "Don't worry," he said. "I'll be back in a few weeks when summer school is over."

Paul suddenly felt happy again.

Cindy got out of the swing and put her cigarette out on the ground. She didn't leave the butt there, but put it in her pocket. "I gotta go get ready for a date," she said. She looked at Frank. "He's just a friend," she added.

"Well, you have fun," Frank said.

"We're just goin' to the movies," Cindy said. "Gotta do somethin' in this town to keep you from goin' crazy."

"It was nice meeting you, Cindy," Frank said.

"You, too," Cindy answered. "If y'all get bored, come down to see me an' my Mama, if you have time. Paul will bring you, won't you, Paul?"

Paul nodded. "Sure," he said.

"Okay. Bye," Cindy said. She went out the gate and closed it behind her. She took the cigarette butt from her pocket and threw it into the bushes around the old bus shell.

Paul and Frank went into the house through the sliding glass door.

Mama Ray was snoring in her recliner as the glass door slid shut. Dawn and Tinker, who had been sleeping in her lap, jumped up and started barking. When they saw Frank, they began to wag their tails. Lost in their own excitement, they inadvertently pranced on Mama Ray's face. Mama Ray raised up with a jolt and looked to see what had caused such a commotion. "Oh, my Word, Frank, is that you?" she asked, her eyes still groggy.

"Yep," Frank said. "It's me." He reached down and patted Dawn and Tinker. They gave his hand sweet sugar and continued to prance on top of Mama Ray as Frank brusquely ruffled their coats.

Mama Ray pushed the little dogs off the recliner. They danced around Frank's legs and jumped up on him. They never could get enough sugar from Frank.

"How did you get here?" Mama Ray asked, still surprised. No one had told her that Frank would be coming.

"I took a bus up from Dallas," Frank said. "I was there on a Boy Scout trip an' I called our step-daddy, an' he told me that Mama was here an' that she was sick, so I decided to take a bus up by myself." Frank didn't dare to tell Mama Ray that he had hitchhiked from the bus station in Sulphur Springs to their house. He had decided he would tell her that he had walked from the local station, if she should ask.

"Well, did you have a good trip?" Mama Ray asked. She yawned.

"I sure did," Frank answered. "Where's everybody else?" he asked.

"Well," Mama Ray said, "Big Mama done went home for a while, an' your Daddy C's in there takin' a nap in his room. Your Mama's still in her room sleepin', as far as I know. How long are you gonna stay with us?"

"Just till tomorrow," Frank answered. "I gotta catch a bus out in the mornin'."

"Well, we sure do wish you could stay longer," Mama Ray said.

"He's coming back in a few weeks," Paul said, "when summer school is over."

"Well, that'll be real nice," Mama Ray said. "We'll take y'all both out to Mrs. Celecia's to eat enchiladas for lunch, if your Mama's up to it. Daddy C mentioned it earlier, but I don't know if your Mama'll feel like goin' out to eat so soon. 'Course, Marie would love to see her. You wanna go put your stuff in your room?"

"Yeah," Frank said. He and Paul started to leave the den, but Mama Ray called them back.

"Ain't you even gonna come an' love your granny's neck?" she asked. She put her arms out and puckered her lips.

Frank turned around. "I'm too big for hugs and kisses," he said.

Mama Ray kept her lips puckered expectantly. "Come here an' give your old granny a wet one," she said. "Don't worry, I done put my teeth in this mornin'."

Frank and Paul both laughed. Mama Ray looked really funny with her lips puckered up and her eyes closed. She waved for Frank to come closer.

"Okay, I'll make an exception for you," Frank said. He went up to her recliner and kissed Mama Ray on the cheek. When he did, he felt Mama Ray's arms close around him. She squeezed tightly and rocked him back and forth. She kissed him several times on his cheek. His face felt wet from all her smooches.

Frank laughed. "Okay, okay," he said. "Enough." He tried to pull away from his grandmother, but she started to tickle him. Frank laughed even harder. "Stop!" he said.

Mama Ray let go, smiling. "That's what you get for saying you're too big to hug your poor old granny," she said. She slapped him playfully on the butt and said, "Now go on an' put that bag in your room, if you ain't too big to remember the way."

"She sure did show you," Paul said, still laughing, as they walked out of the den.

Tinker and Dawn started to follow them down the hall, until Mama Ray snapped her fingers and yelled, "Get back in here!" The two dogs ran back to their mother and jumped onto her lap.

As Frank and Paul passed Mama Ray and Daddy C's bedroom, they snickered at the sight of Daddy C asleep on top of the covers, in his T-shirt and underwear. They went into their bedroom, and Frank put his duffel bag in the chair at the foot of his bed.

"Let's go look in on Mama," Frank said.

Paul shook his head. "I think we should leave her alone," he said. She would always get cross with them if they tried to wake her up when they would get home from school.

"Don't be scared. We ain't gonna wake her up," Frank said. "We'll just have a look at her."

Frank left the bedroom, careful not to let Mama Ray spot him from the den. He tiptoed down the hallway to Connie's bedroom, and Paul tiptoed after him. At the end of the hallway, Frank gently turned the handle of Connie's door. He opened it slowly. It squeaked again halfway. Connie turned on her side, and her arm fell onto the mattress.

Frank went into their mother's bedroom and motioned for Paul to join him. Paul did so, but he was still afraid of waking his mother up and getting into trouble. Frank stood next to the bed, looking down at his mother's pale face. Paul tiptoed up and stood next to him. Their mother was so pale that, if she had not moved as they had opened the door, they could have mistaken her for a corpse.

Connie opened her eyes. "What are y'all being so quiet about?" she asked drowsily. Her voice was still weak.

"Hi, Mama," Frank said.

Connie turned her head to look around the room. "Where am I?" she asked.

"You're at Mama Ray and Daddy C's," Frank answered. He put his hand on his mother's shoulder.

"Oh, my God," Connie said under her breath. "How the hell did I get here?" The brown wooden panels and the paintings on the wall suddenly were familiar to her. She was in her own childhood bedroom.

"Daddy C brought you here," Frank answered. Paul was still afraid to speak, in case his mother became angry. "You're sick," Frank added.

Connie remembered. She had heard those idiots at the hospital talking. They were convinced that she had tried to kill herself. She had simply had too much to drink, and then she had taken a couple of those sleeping pills that the doctor had given her to calm her nerves. She had never thought that it could be deadly. She would never have tried to kill herself, especially when her children needed her to be strong for them. She had just wanted to sleep the pain away, and it had seemed like the best solution at the time.

"Oh, yeah," Connie said. She looked at her two children. There was one missing. "Where is Jennifer?" she asked.

Paul wanted to cry. He felt a lump welling up in his throat and a knot of pain in his stomach. It was too much for him. He remembered what Big Mama had told him, that he shouldn't mention Jennifer to his mother. Fighting back tears, he answered, "She's not here."

Frank and Connie both looked at Paul. They were confused. "She's at home with Bill," Frank said. Bill was their step-father. Frank winked at Paul without Connie noticing.

"I had an awful dream," Connie said. "Come sit down with me." Frank and Paul sat down on the bed with their mother. Paul was still on the verge of crying. Connie put her hand on each of them. "I dreamed I was in Big Mama's kitchen," she said. "We were sittin' around and talkin', waitin' for supper to cook. We were laughin' and carryin' on, and when we opened the oven to get the supper out, I saw that she had cooked my telephone. She had battered it just like she would a fried chicken." Connie laughed. "Can you imagine that? I pulled it out, and asked her, 'Now, Big Mama, why in the world would you want to cook my telephone?' She just shrugged her shoulders and told me it looked like a chicken to her, and, when she said that, the telephone rang.

"I picked up the telephone, and it was the police. They told me that y'all were all dead, and that it was my fault. I believed it, and I was so scared and mad, I threw the phone across the room, and it turned into an ugly snake that bit Big Mama on the leg. She started cryin' and told me that she was gonna die, too, and leave me alone with Mama Ray and Daddy C forever. I tried to leave the house, but when I did, I walked into another kitchen, but it was Mama Ray's kitchen, and I could hear her and Daddy C in their bedroom snorin', and those damned dogs were in there growlin' at me, and barkin'."

Paul put his hand on his mother's hip. "We're not dead, Mama," he said. He wiped the tears from his eyes.

Connie shook her head. "I know," she said. "But it was such an awful dream. I remember, I tried to leave the house, but when I did, a bunch of chickens came up and tried to attack me. It was awful." She looked at Paul and Frank. "Do they still have those crazy chickens?" she asked.

Frank looked at Paul, puzzled. "I don't know," he said.

"They haven't had 'em for a long time," Paul assured her.

Connie put her hand on her head. "Oh, man," she said. "I don't know what kind of dope they gave me at the hospital, but it sure did make me have a crazy dream. Babies, can y'all go in there and get your Mama some aspirins? I sure do have an awful headache."

Frank got off the bed. "I'll go get 'em," he said. "How many do you want?"

Connie turned her neck. It felt stiff. "Bring me six, Honey. It sure is a doozy." She patted Paul's leg. "You go with him, Baby. Your Mama needs to sleep some more." She looked at

Frank. "Don't forget a glass of water to wash 'em down with. Thank you."

Paul got up and went with Frank to the kitchen.

"What are y'all lookin' for?" Mama Ray asked.

"Mama needs some aspirins," Frank answered. "She's got a headache."

Mama Ray was a little worried. It seemed that her daughter had always been fast to numb herself to the smallest hint of pain. "They're over the sink, on the left," she said.

Paul carried the glass of water, and Frank carried the six aspirins to their mother. When they got to her room, she was already sleeping again. They put the water and the pills on the nightstand beside her bed, and then they left the bedroom.

Back in the den, Paul and Frank sat down on the couch. They didn't know what to do with themselves. Daddy C was still napping, and Mama Ray had turned on the television. The news was on, and it certainly didn't interest either of the two boys. They decided to make a Coke float, with ice cream and Coca-Cola. If there was nothing else to do, they might as well have ice cream and Coke.

"Don't y'all fill up too much on them thangs," Mama Ray said. "If we're gonna go an' eat at Mrs. Celecia's, you'll wanna fill up on her enchiladas." Paul and Frank were not worried. They knew that they had room enough for both ice cream and enchiladas. Mama Ray got up and put Dawn and Tinker in the back yard. She went into the kitchen to join her grandsons. "Make me one, too," she said." She hadn't had a Coke float in a long time.

"But you can't eat ice cream anymore," Frank said.

Mama Ray grinned. "My blood sugar's low today," she lied. "Ice cream'll help me to get it up again."

The three sat at the table drinking their Coke floats. After a few minutes, Big Mama came in through the sliding glass door of the den. "Y'all stay out there, now," she said to Dawn and Tinker as they tried to go inside.

Big Mama went into the kitchen. "Howdy, Frank," she said. Without warning, she walked up and planted a big kiss on his cheek. She squeezed him so tightly that he thought he would spit up his refreshment.

"Y'all stuffin' your guts without me?" she asked. She went to the freezer to pull out the ice cream. One rule that she adamantly lived by was that nobody was allowed to eat in her presence without her joining them. She got the Coca-Cola from the refrigerator and made herself a Coke float, too. "If I'd have known y'all was here stuffin' your guts, I'd have got here sooner," Big Mama said, putting her glass on the table next to Paul so that she could face her other great-grandson. "Of course, an old lady like me can't be in a hurry, you know. Your ganny told me you was still in Scouts, Frank. How you likin' it?" she asked.

"I like it a lot," Frank answered. "I'm training to be an Eagle Scout. When I make Eagle Scout, I'll get a letter from the President."

Big Mama chuckled. "He he! Your Daddy C will like that," she said. "You gettin' a letter of congratulations from a Republican."

Mama Ray grimaced. "Ain't that the truth," she said. "I don't even wanna think about it."

"We sure are proud of you," Big Mama said. "An' your mama an' step-daddy's probably real proud, too."

Frank nodded as he sucked his Coke float through the straw. Paul was not so sure. He didn't believe his mother and step-father were proud of anything that either of them had done. They certainly had never shown it.

"Do y'all still go campin'?" Mama Ray asked.

"Yeah," Frank replied. "We were up there at Lake Tawakonee up till this mornin', and then I took a bus on out here to check on Mama."

Big Mama shook her head. "It's a shame you can't stay but till tomorrow. We sure would love to have you longer."

"Yeah, me, too. But I've got summer school to finish up. I didn't do too well in math last year, and they made me take it over."

"I always hated math," Big Mama said.

Mama Ray laughed. "That's 'cause you never learned math," she said.

"I did, too," Big Mama said. "My mama taught us every day out there on the farm. She made us learn a lot more than most kids nowadays. I could speak both German an' English. An' I could sew an' plow, too. How many kids can do that these days?"

"Kids don't have to do that nowadays," Mama Ray said.

"Well, it seems to me they'd be better off if they could learn stuff they want to learn, instead of havin' to learn a bunch of stuff they don't even like. An' then the teachers call 'em dumb if they don't get it right the first time. Then they have to go back an' learn it again. Kids know what they need to learn. Maybe they could teach adults a few things if they'd shut up long enough to listen."

"True enough," Mama Ray said. "Maybe you'd be a lot smarter, too, if you'd just shut up an' listen." She laughed.

Big Mama smiled. She sucked up her frosted Coke through the straw, filling up her mouth until her cheeks puffed out. She turned to her daughter and aimed the straw at her face. Mama Ray's grin faded as she realized what her mother was going to do. Big Mama blew out with all her strength, covering her daughter in Coke and ice cream.

Mama Ray looked horrified. Paul and Frank were shocked. They didn't know what to do. Suddenly, Big Mama burst out laughing.

"What the hell was that for?" Mama Ray said.

"Honey, that's what happens when I shut my mouth too long," Big Mama answered. "I just have the need to let it all come out."

"You old battle axe," Mama Ray said. "If these boys wasn't here I'd show you what can happen when I open *my* mouth." She looked at her mother, who still had her glass in her hand. "You be careful not to spill that," Mama Ray said.

Big Mama looked at her glass. Suddenly, the glass somehow tipped itself in her hand, spilling the cold, sticky liquid onto her dress. At first, she was surprised by the icy, wet sensation, but then she felt pleased by her daughter's display of skill. "You really *do* remember everything," Big Mama said.

"I told you," Mama Ray replied. She was grinning with confidence. "Now you be careful with that glass, an' stop teachin' these boys how to act like an idiot." She calmly composed herself and blotted the liquid from her face and dress.

Paul and Frank looked at the two women. They were both stained with Coca-Cola and ice cream, and yet they were smiling at each other. Paul and Frank decided that they were in a madhouse. They wondered which of the four of them were the children, and which were the adults. Eventually, they, too, had to smile. It would have been insane to do otherwise.

When they had finished their drinks, Paul and Frank went into the den to watch television. Mama Ray went to change her shirt, but Big Mama decided just to wash her dress in the kitchen sink. Paul and Frank watched her from the sofa as she took her dress off and stood at the sink in her bra and panties. The two boys laughed as their great-grandmother began to jiggle while scrubbing out the ice cream and cola.

"Ain't y'all got no more manners than to laugh at a beautiful woman?" Big Mama asked. "If that's all y'all can think of, then y'all ain't gonna have much luck in romantic situations," she said as she continued to scrub her dress.

Daddy C walked into the den with Buster following behind. Tinker and Dawn began to scratch excitedly at the glass door from outside. Daddy C was dragging his bare feet and stretching his arms over his head. He, too, was in his underwear. Paul looked at his brother, and they began to snicker again. It seemed that everyone around them was half-naked.

"Howdy do!" Daddy C said, his eyes still sleepy. He looked at Frank. "Frank, is that you?" he asked.

"Yeah, it's me," Frank said, smiling widely. He was still amused by his grandfather's informality.

"Calvin, can you get me one of Wanda Ray's housecoats?" Big Mama yelled from the kitchen.

Daddy C looked toward the kitchen. "What are you doin' in there, Big Mama?" he asked. He could only see the top of her, because the counter was blocking his view. "They got you washin' dishes?"

"No," Big Mama answered. "Your wife made me spill my drink, an' I'm a washin' it out. Can you go in there an' get me one of Wanda Ray's housecoats, or ask her to get it?"

Daddy C scratched his head. "Sure, I'll get you one," he said. He turned back around and dragged his feet back down the hall. Buster wagged his tail and looked at Frank. The little dog didn't know whether he should stay or follow Daddy C. Finally, he turned around and trotted into the hall.

The boys could hear Daddy C knock on the bathroom door. "Wanda Ray," he yelled, "your mama wants a housecoat."

"What does she want a housecoat for?" Mama Ray asked from the bathroom.

"I don't know," Daddy C said. "She just wants one."

"Well, I'll be out in a minute, an' I'll take her one," Mama Ray replied.

Daddy C scooted back into the den and let the dogs inside. He sat down in his recliner and they jumped in with him.

Mama Ray came through the den toward the kitchen. She had changed her clothes and was carrying her purple housecoat. When she saw her mother in the kitchen, standing in her bra and panties, she said, "What in the world are you doin', Mama?"

"What do you think I'm a doin'?" Big Mama answered. "I'm washin' out the drink you made me spill."

"Well, my Word," Mama Ray said. "You'd think we lived in a nudist camp." She handed the housecoat to her mother. Big Mama dried her hands on a towel and put it on.

Mama Ray went into the den and looked at her husband. "Calvin, go put some clothes on, an' get ready to go to Mrs. Celecia's," she said.

Daddy C smiled at his grandsons and shrugged his shoulders. "If you wanna keep a good woman's love, sometimes you gotta do what she tells you to," he said. As he got up, he winked at them and went back down the hall to take a shower and put some clothes on. Mama Ray sat down. The dogs jumped out of Daddy C's Lay-Z-Boy and jumped into her lap. Big Mama put her dress in the dryer and sat down on the couch next to Paul and Frank.

"I'm gonna go see if Connie's still sleepin'," Mama Ray said. "If she ain't up yet, we'll just have sandwiches here."

"Don't do that," Big Mama said. "Y'all go on down to Marie's an' tell her I said howdy. I'll just stay here with Connie if she ain't up yet. My dress still ain't dry anyway."

"Well, okay," Mama Ray said. "But she might be up by now." Mama Ray got up to check on her daughter.

She opened the door of Connie's room, and saw that she was still sleeping. The glass of water on the nightstand stood empty and the aspirin tablets were gone. Mama Ray took the empty glass and went back through the den.

"She still ain't awake," Mama Ray said, taking the glass to the sink in the kitchen.

"Well, y'all just go on, then, when Calvin's ready, an' I'll eat me a ham sandwich with Connie when she wakes up," Big Mama said.

Mama Ray started to wash the dishes. She wondered how long her daughter would stay in bed. It seemed to her that Connie had spent most of her life sleeping. She wasn't sure why she had started to sleep so much. Connie had come down with mononucleosis when she was a teenager. She had had to miss a semester of school, and she had spent many weeks in which she hardly left the bed. Even after she had recovered from the illness, she never seemed to have the same zest that she had had before. For many years, Mama Ray had contributed Connie's withdrawal from the world to that illness.

Even after high school was over and Connie went to work, it seemed very hard for her to hold down a job. She just liked to sleep too much. It seemed to be her favorite way to cope with hard times, and, judging from the amount she slept, times were always pretty hard. Soon it became apparent that mononucleosis was not the cause of her problems. That illness did not lead Connie to drinking like she did.

Mama Ray knew that Connie loved her children more than anything else in her life. That made it even more difficult to understand why she couldn't seem to overcome her own problems in order to raise them better. She knew that her daughter, in her own way, was doing the best she could to solve her problems and be a better mother. It just didn't seem to be working for her. Mama Ray had hoped before that Bill would straighten her out. It even seemed to work for a while, even though Mama Ray now knew that one person couldn't solve the problems of another. After a while, Connie seemed to have gone past the bliss and hope of a new marriage, and found herself with the same problems as before.

Mama Ray hoped that she could somehow help her daughter to help herself this time. It was a little absurd, she knew, since she had also contributed largely to Connie's state because of the way that she had raised her. For a long time, Mama Ray had blamed herself, but she finally was able to accept that she had raised her daughter in the best way she knew how at the time, just like Connie had done for her children.

She knew that Connie would only be with them for a short while, but maybe it would be enough to get her started. She hoped that she could convince Connie to forgive her for her mistakes so that Connie could learn to forgive herself, and, thereby, make a better life for herself and the two remaining children that God had blessed her with.

Daddy C came back into the den dressed and ready to go. He, Mama Ray, Paul, and Frank loaded up in the car to go uptown. "Them dogs ain't gonna ride in my clean car," Mama Ray said. "Stay here, Sweeties."

Daddy C put Dawn, Tinker, and Buster back into the house with Big Mama, who put them out in the back yard as soon as Mama Ray's car left the garage.

"We'll stop off at the fruit stand to pick up some money," Daddy C said. He hadn't been by the fruit stand since the day before, just before he had left Sulphur Springs to pick up Connie. He didn't expect to have a lot, but there would be enough to buy them all some enchiladas.

"Okay," Mama Ray answered. She hadn't been by the fruit stand in a very long time. It was more a part of Daddy C's world than her own. Runny Joe and Cowboy would come by the house sometimes to help Daddy C unload some junk in their garage, and they would stay for supper. That was all Mama Ray really saw of them since she had stopped going to town. She wondered if the place had changed any, but she couldn't imagine that either Runny Joe or Cowboy had put much effort into decorating the place since she had last seen it. "They'll sure be excited to see you, Frank," Mama Ray said.

"Yeah, Cowboy thought I was you when he seen me," Paul said. He and Frank were in the back seat together.

"'When he *saw* me,'" Frank corrected. "Mama's gonna whoop your hide when she hears you talkin' like that." Frank loved his grandparents, but he knew his mother hated to let her children around them for too long. She was afraid that they would start to talk like Mama Ray and Daddy C. It seemed that her assumption was correct, in Paul's case.

"Ain't nothin' wrong with the way he talks, Doll," Daddy C said. "That's just the way we talk around here. Paul fits right in. People wouldn't know what to do if he went around talkin' like a city boy."

"Just don't let Mama hear it," Frank said. "She'll have a hissy fit."

Paul decided that Frank was right. He should try not to talk like Mama Ray and Daddy C. He didn't want to upset his mother any more than he had and, besides, he would only be with his grandparents for a little while, until his mother got well again. It wouldn't be a good idea to get used to talking like they did, as he would have to speak correctly again when he returned with his mother. It was better just to try to talk like his mother had taught him. It had only been a couple of weeks since he had arrived with his grandparents, but Paul was already forgetting how he was supposed to speak. He would try hard to remember, though.

Daddy C turned the car into the driveway of the fruit stand. Cowboy was sitting in the front playing with a little yellow dog. Everybody got out of the car and walked toward the entrance. "Howdy, Cowboy," Daddy C said.

"Howdy, Calvin," Cowboy answered. He looked at Mama Ray. "Mrs. Sewell," he said.

"Well, hello there, Cowboy," Mama Ray smiled.

Cowboy looked at Paul and Frank. "Now, if I ain't goin' crazy, then one of you is Frank. And I'll bet it's the tallest of the two."

Frank smiled. "Cowboy, you know it's me," he said. He walked up and shook Cowboy's hand. "How are you doin'?"

"Just fine, just fine," Cowboy answered. "Sure is good to see you. I bet your brother's tickled pink." Cowboy looked at Paul. Paul nodded with a smile.

"Where's Runny Joe?" Daddy C asked. "Did he run off with a girlfriend?"

Cowboy shook his head. "You know no woman in her right mind would have him," he said.

"Well, they say love is blind," Mama Ray said. "I guess it's crazy, too." She looked at Daddy C and put her arm through his. Daddy C didn't think too much of the comment.

Cowboy laughed. "Ha! Well, I guess that's right," he said. "Runny Joe went down to the store to get some baloney an' some tater chips for lunch. He done eat up all the potted meat this mornin'."

"Well, we're goin' to Mrs. Celecia's for lunch," Daddy C said. "I just came to empty the money box, if there's anything in it."

"Well, sure there's money in it," Cowboy said. "You know we done sold all them watermelons an' potatoes you brought.

We still got a few tomatoes you can take down to Marie, if you want."

Daddy C nodded. "That's a good idea," he said. "Wanda Ray, why don't you go an' get up some tomatoes an' jalapeños for Marie while I empty out that money box?"

"Okay," Mama Ray said. "Paul, you wanna come with me?"

Paul nodded. It was not as if they were really going somewhere to get the items. They were right there in sight, just a few feet away. He followed her to where they were. Frank went with Daddy C to collect the money in the back of the fruit stand. It was kept in an old shoebox next to the refrigerator. Cowboy stayed out front in his chair, watching the cars go by.

Paul looked around the place as Mama Ray filled a small sack with tomatoes and jalapeño peppers. It didn't seem as if much had been sold since Paul had last visited the fruit stand. Of course, only a day had past since he had been there with Daddy C, although it somehow seemed like longer.

"Let's go," Daddy C said, walking back to the front and stuffing the money in his pocket. "Cowboy, y'all done took some out for you, didn't you?" he asked.

Cowboy nodded. "Y'all tell Marie howdy for me an' Runny Joe. Tell her to come by the place sometime, if she can ever get away from that restaurant."

"Will do," Daddy C said.

"Frank, it sure was good to see you. Runny Joe'll be sad that he missed you," Cowboy said.

"Well, tell him hi for me," Frank said. "I'll be back again soon."

"Well, good," Cowboy said. "We look forward to it."

Mama Ray, Daddy C, Paul, and Frank got into the car again and headed toward Mrs. Celecia's.

They opened the door to the restaurant, and the place was empty. They looked around for Marie, but didn't see her. "You think she's closed?" Frank asked.

"No," Daddy C answered. "She's probably just back in the kitchen." He walked up to a table that was big enough for all of them. The others followed, and they sat down.

Frank looked around. It had been several years since he had been in Mrs. Celecia's restaurant, but the decorations were the same. The old posters of señoritas and bullfighters were still posted on the walls. He seemed to remember the place being busier than it was now. He wondered why they were the only people there at lunchtime. It seemed that there should be more customers in the place.

"Howdy," Mrs. Celecia said, coming out of the kitchen. She was drying her hands on her pink apron. "¡Ay, Dios mío!" she said. She ran up to Frank, put her arms around him, and planted a kiss on his forhead before he had a chance to protest. He cringed.

Mama Ray laughed. "He thinks he's too big for that now," she said.

Mrs. Celecia, still squeezing Frank, looked up. "Crazy," she said. She squeezed harder, and gave him another kiss. "Let me have a look at you now that I squeezed your good lovin' out." She looked Frank over. "You're real good-lookin'," she said. "I bet the girls go wild after you."

"Some of 'em," Frank said. He smiled and brushed back the hair on his head that Mrs. Celecia had ruffled.

"It runs in the family," Daddy C said.

"But he got it from *my* side of the family," Mama Ray said.

"What do y'all want to drink?" Mrs. Celecia asked.

"Iced tea for me," Mama Ray said.

"Me, too," Frank said.

Daddy C nodded. "Make it three."

Mrs. Celecia looked at Paul, who had been quiet the whole time. "Are you gonna have somethin' to drink, too, Cariño?" she asked.

Paul hadn't been paying attention. He had noticed a shadow at the kitchen entrance, and he had been looking at it. Someone seemed to be standing behind the doorway watching them. Paul turned to Mrs. Celecia. "What?" Paul asked.

Mrs. Celecia smiled. "You must be in the clouds today, Sugar," she said. "Whadda you want to drink?"

It took a moment for the question to register in Paul's mind. Mrs. Celecia was right. His head had been in the clouds. He had been transfixed by the shadow that seemed to be lurking at the kitchen entrance. Paul thought a moment. "Dr. Pepper," he said. He wanted to drink something other than iced tea for a change. He looked back over to the doorway. The shadow had disappeared.

Mrs. Celecia came back to the table with the enchiladas as Mama Ray, Daddy C, Paul, and Frank were eating their chips and salsa and drinking their drinks. Mrs. Celecia put the plates on the table.

"Take a load off, Marie," Daddy C said. "Sit down an' stay a while."

"Don't mind if I do," Marie said. She sat down in the chair next to Frank. "You ain't too big to sit next to me, are you?" She laughed.

Frank blushed as he shook his head. He dug into his enchiladas. They were delicious. It had been a long time since he had gotten his hands on some of Marie Celecia's enchiladas.

"Marie, Paul's havin' a birthday next week, an' we wanted to have him a little party," Mama Ray said.

Mrs. Celecia smiled. "I love parties," she said. "How old are you gonna be, Cariño?"

"Eight," Paul said.

Mrs. Celecia nodded. "A big boy," she said. "Still too young for me, though. He he! But not for my little granddaughter."

"I think Paul's got a way to go before he starts lookin' for a girlfriend," Daddy C said.

"He wouldn't know what to do with one," Frank teased as he took another bite of his beef enchilada.

"You wouldn't either," Paul said, laughing. He stuck his tongue out as his brother.

"We thought maybe we could just come out here an' celebrate Paul's birthday, if it's all right with you," Mama Ray said.

Mrs. Celecia became vibrant. "Good idea," she said. "It's a long time since there's been a party here." She looked at Paul. "We can get my little granddaughter to come, too."

As Mrs. Celecia mentioned her granddaughter, Paul noticed the shadow appear again in the entrance to the kitchen. It was moving slightly, as if flickering in the light from the kitchen. Paul had the sense that they were being watched, and he began to feel uncomfortable.

Mrs. Celecia noticed that Paul was looking toward the kitchen. She turned around in her seat and looked in the direction of his stare. "What is it, Cariño?" she asked.

Paul didn't answer. He watched as the shadow suddenly disappeared behind the doorway.

Mrs. Celecia yelled toward the kitchen. "Daniela, Honey, is that you?" There was no answer. Mrs. Celecia turned to the others at the table and said, "Don't y'all pay her no attention. She's just shy." Turning back to the kitchen, she said. "Daniela, come on out here, Cariño. Vente, Cielo, que no tengas miedo. Ándale."

Suddenly, Paul saw the shadow again from behind the doorway. It moved forward and a little girl with long dark hair appeared. She was wearing pajamas and rubbing her eyes.

Mrs. Celecia smiled. "Look what the cat dragged in. Daniela Rubio, you're supposed to be taking a nap, aren't you."

The little girl stood in the doorway, looking at the others who were seated at the table. She nodded her head shyly.

"Well, come on, Honey. I won't tell your Mama," Mrs. Celecia said.

The little girl walked forward cautiously, still looking at the four strangers at the table. She walked up to Mrs. Celecia and sat down in her lap. Mrs. Celecia put her arms around her.

"This is my little granddaughter, Daniela," she said. "I already told y'all about her."

"Hi there, Daniela," Daddy C said.

Daniela looked at the old man who was smiling at her. "Hello," she said.

"I'm Calvin," Daddy C said. "These here's my grandsons."

Frank smiled at the little girl. "I'm Frank," he said. Daniela nodded. Paul didn't say anything, but simply stared at the girl in Mrs. Celecia's lap. She was pretty, with dark brown eyes and a soft, round face. She seemed familiar to him. He tried to remember where he had seen her before, but he wasn't sure. Frank nudged Paul with his elbow. "Introduce yourself," he said.

Paul was jarred back into the present situation. "I'm Paul," he said.

Daniela smiled timidly and snuggled closer to her grandmother.

"I'm Wanda Ray, Paul an' Franks granny," Mama Ray said.

Mrs. Celecia looked down at Daniela. "Her mama and daddy live next door, and she was *supposed* to be takin' a nap." She smiled. "You know how children listen to their parents."

"I guess she knows when she needs to take a nap," Daddy C said.

"But a girl's got to have her beauty rest," Mrs. Celecia said. "It ain't always easy to look this good, is it, Wanda Ray?"

"Not with all the men a wantin' somethin' all the time. Bacon grease an' toilet cleaner ain't the best things for a lady's skin."

"That's why us men are so purty," Daddy C said, swallowing a mouthful of frijoles. "We don't bother with none of that stuff. We done learned all the beauty secrets. Stay away from cookin' an' cleanin'. An' naps is recommendable, too." He laughed.

"Yeah, Honey," Mama Ray said to Daniela. "Just look at ol' Calvin here. This is what takin' naps and avoidin' cookin' an' cleanin' has done for him. Highly recommendable." She and Mrs. Celecia both chuckled. Daddy C wasn't sure whether to laugh with them or not.

"Yeah, Sweetie. Just do like the men do, and you won't never need a nap," Mrs. Celecia said.

"We need naps all the time," Daddy C said.

"Yeah, but only when you're supposed to be workin'," Mama Ray said.

"What's the point of workin'?" Frank chimed in. The others looked at him, surprised.

"Good point," Daddy C said, smiling at his grandson. "I guess there ain't no point in workin', unless you're doin' somethin' you really like to do."

"I'm gonna be a Boy Scout leader," Frank said.

"I'm gonna be a magician," Paul said. Daniela smiled at the notion. Paul remembered the magic he had made the evening before, and he wondered whether he would be able to do it again.

"What are you gonna be, Honey?" Mama Ray asked Daniela. The little girl put her head in Mrs. Celecia's chest.

Mrs. Celecia looked at the others and smiled. "She's just real shy." She stroked her granddaughter's arm and said, "Answer her, cariño. She ain't gonna bite you."

"Well, I might bite, but I ain't poisonous," Mama Ray said with a grin. "I wouldn't bite a sweet little thing like you, anyway."

"Don't worry if she *does* bite you, Doll," Daddy C said. "Her teeth would come loose before she could get a good grip on you."

Paul and Frank cracked up with laughter. Daniela, despite her shyness, started to laugh, too.

"Shut up, you old fart," Mama Ray said.

"That's right, Calvin," Mrs. Celecia said. "You tryin' to make these kids think that *you* don't have false teeth?"

"Oh, Wanda Ray knows I'm just teasin'," Daddy C said. He looked at Mama Ray. "You know you're my Number One, Honey."

"I guess at your age I'm your *only* one," Mama Ray said.

"And always have been," Daddy C said. He winked at his wife as he chugged down the last of his iced tea.

"In a bank," Daniela said. The others looked at her, surprised to hear her speak.

"What, Honey?" Mama Ray asked.

Daniela pushed herself up toward the table and said, "I wanna work in a bank."

Mama Ray nodded her head. "Well, that's good, Honey. You like to work with money?"

Daniela shook her head. "They give little kids candy at the bank," she said. "They give me a sucker when I go with my mommie to the drive-through."

Mama Ray smiled warmly at the little girl. "Well, that's real good. All the little kids will be happy to see you, then," she said.

"Just make sure you got time to take a nap now an' then," Daddy C said. "Don't let 'em work you too hard. 'God maketh me to lie in green pastures.' Ain't that how it goes, Wanda Ray?"

Mama Ray nodded.

"Shows how far we've got from what the good Lord put us on the Earth for, don't it?" Mrs. Celecia said. "It's hard to believe nowadays that God made us to lie in green pastures."

"It sure is," Mama Ray said. She didn't mind too much that she was sitting in Mrs. Celecia's restaurant instead of lying in a green pasture somewhere. She had always enjoyed her soap operas, and she didn't think that she would get good TV reception from a green pasture, anyway. She understood the point, though. She had worked her whole life, and it wasn't until she had become sick and been forced to quit working that she had really felt like she was in control of her own life.

It was a strange paradox that, through her illness, Mama Ray had finally been able to feel well. Before that, she had never imagined it possible to leave her job and still survive. She had thought many times that her job, or better said, her reaction to it, had made her ill in the first place. She had worked on the same sewing machine for fifteen years in that factory and, the minute she couldn't turn out another shirt for them, her paychecks magically stopped coming just as quickly as they had started. They had sent her a blouse and a get well card, and then they were through with her. Mama Ray wiped her mouth again and put the napkin down onto her empty plate.

"Let me up, Cielo," Mrs. Celecia said to Daniela. Daniela got up and helped her grandmother clear the table.

Big Mama was sitting in Mama Ray and Daddy C's living room with LaVelle, who had come over to keep her company while the others were out at Mrs. Celecia's restaurant. LaVelle was concerned because she hadn't seen Cindy since the day before. "She was just standin' there in the kitchen," LaVelle said. "Then she just disappeared into thin air, just like a ghost." LaVelle knew that Cindy would show up again, and that she could not hold onto her daughter like she had when she had been alive. But it was still hard for her to accept that she could only see her daughter when Cindy was sleeping.

Big Mama understood. She had had the same problem when she had passed on. It was typical. At first, she hadn't even known that she was dead. She had found herself trying to do everything as she had before: walking through doors by turning the handle; talking to her relatives in the same way that she had before she had passed on. She hadn't known any other way to live before. She had become so frustrated and angry when the physical world had stopped responding to her. She could see everything perfectly well and clearly, but the people she loved suddenly passed by her as if she did not exist.

Big Mama had been lucky to establish contact with her mother, Gertrud, before she herself had passed on. Her mother had been there upon Big Mama's physical death, and guided her through the transition. Although Big Mama had recognized and trusted her mother's guidance, she at first had noticed no change in her own physical form. She had seen her own body lying there in the hospital bed, but she could also see herself standing there next to Mama Ray, Connie, Lorene, and Daddy C, watching the doctors work on her. It had been as if there were two of her — the body that was standing watch, and the body that was lying on the hospital bed. Her consciousness had left the body on the hospital bed, and was standing in the body, *her* body next to herself.

It had been confusing to her. She had thought that she was in a dream. Her mother came to her in the hospital room, and told her that she, too, had passed on. Big Mama did not believe it, because she saw herself not as a spirit, but still as flesh and blood. Her own body still looked and felt as it had before. Her mother had tried to explain to her that her mind was still alive in her soul, and that her mind continued to create the *impression* of having a body, which seemed to be of flesh and blood as it had been when she still lived in the physical world.

Big Mama did not believe her mother in the beginning. She had thought that she somehow was still in a dream state. That was how the whole transition had seemed, really. She would slip in and out of consciousness, feeling sometimes as if she were dreaming and other times as if she were wide awake. She would find herself moving from one place to the next, without knowing how she had gotten there, just like in a dream. She had left the hospital room, and somehow had found herself in Mama Ray's den as her daughter was watching television with Tinker.

She tried to speak to her daughter, but Mama Ray was deaf to her. Big Mama talked louder and louder, pleading with her daughter for help, but Mama Ray would not listen. She simply sat there watching television and stroking Tinker's back. Scared, and angry that her own daughter wouldn't listen to her, Big Mama began to cry. In desperation, she tried to open the sliding glass door and run away from there, but she couldn't even grasp it. It was as if she was reaching out through a hologram, an object that did not exist. She suddenly found herself in the back yard, but not the back yard of Mama Ray's house. She found herself at the farmhouse of her childhood. Her mother Gertrud, young and strong, took Big Mama into her arms and wiped her tears away.

Soon Big Mama learned how to deal with her new reality. She became astute at manipulating her new world, and even mastered communication with her loved ones who were still in the other. She was able to accept that this communication was different from the way she had known it before, and even learned that it could be more effective than the means of communication that she had previously known.

Big Mama had been there to help her own daughter, Wanda Ray, to accept her own death. She stood by her every second as Mama Ray lay dying in the Hereford Beulis Memorial Hospital in Dallas. Big Mama had expected that it would be difficult for her daughter to accept the new reality. Mama Ray had always been very stubborn and, therefore, in her own way a master manipulator of her own reality. Mama Ray had already known that she was dying. She had chosen to die, in a sense. About a year after Daddy C had passed on, Mama Ray decided it was time to go off the dialysis machine. Even though Mama Ray had known that she was going to die, it had still been a very difficult challenge for Big Mama to help her daughter adapt to the new reality. In time, however, — if one can speak of the new reality in terms of time — Mama Ray seemed to have accepted the new situation, and even seemed to enjoy it.

Although Mama Ray had seemed to adjust to the fact of her own passing, her grandchild's funeral had seemed to trigger in her a regression to the ways of the old existence. This became apparent to Big Mama when Mama Ray invited her over to kill a chicken in celebration of Paul's arrival. Big Mama wondered what had made Mama Ray bring those chickens back to that house, especially since she had always hated them, but soon it became clear that her daughter had forgotten that she was dead.

"Don't worry about Cindy, Honey," Big Mama told LaVelle. "You know how kids are. She'll be comin' round again before too long."

LaVelle could not help but worry. It had not been a long time since she had died in the car crash. She had been killed instantly, but Cindy, who was with her in the car, had survived. LaVelle knew from the beginning that she was dead. She had hovered over her own body and seen that her daughter was unconscious in the passenger seat. She tried to pull Cindy out, but her hands couldn't grasp her daughter's body. LaVelle watched horrified and helpless as the paramedics put Cindy onto a stretcher and carried her off in their ambulance. She was so concerned about Cindy that she felt no sadness as they covered her own body and carried it away. She somehow knew that her body was useless to her at that point. She stayed with Cindy in the hospital, and had been able to establish a strong connection to her daughter from early on. There were times when Cindy left her own body and sat beside her bed with LaVelle, who was holding vigile over her.

Since Cindy's recovery, they had seen each other regularly; but Cindy did not seem to remember that her mother had died.

"I know she'll come back," LaVelle said. "But I just can't find her nowhere. I call an' call her, but she don't answer."

Big Mama smiled. "You know how it is, Honey. They get caught up in their world and tune us out sometimes. It ain't nothin' personal. She has a life of her own, just like you do."

LaVelle nodded. Indeed, she felt lucky to be able to follow her daughter's progress in life. She hadn't thought it possible before her life had ended. "I grew up a Christian, you know," LaVelle said. "An' I believed in Heaven an' all that, but I just never thought it would be like this."

"But that's the beauty of it," Big Mama said. "You can have it however you want it to be. Just like the other life. Just think what it could've been like before if we'd have known that that life could be Heaven, too." Big Mama lifted up on the sofa and pulled a cushion out from under her. "You're lucky. Most folks ignore their relatives after they've died. They don't wanna hear nothin' from 'em. Lots of people become dead to the world just by gettin' old. Don't nobody even care that they're still livin'. At least you've got a daughter that still comes an' visits you."

It was true. LaVelle knew of plenty of others who had passed on without having had contact with their families for many years before their actual deaths. They reacted in different ways. Some of them were like her. They still took an interest in their loved ones' affairs and visited them in dreams. The visits were real and beautiful, even though the "living" didn't typically remember the visits in their waking lives. Those who did remember the visits experienced the memory only as a dream. Others who had passed on had transcended so high and were so busy doing other wonderful things in their new reality that they had little awareness of what was happening in the other realms.

LaVelle still did not want to lose contact with her daughter, and she was grateful that she didn't have to.

The door to the living room opened. LaVelle and Big Mama turned to see who was there. Connie walked in. She seemed fresh and showered, and her blond hair was still damp. She had even put makeup on her face.

"Well, howdy do," Big Mama said. "Did you sleep well?"

"I could've slept a lot longer, " Connie replied. She looked curiously at LaVelle. "I'm Connie," she said.

LaVelle nodded. "You're Paul's mother, ain't you?" she said. "He's such a sweet little boy. Me an' my daughter Cindy just love him to death. I'm LaVelle Willbrook. I live next door."

Connie walked toward the couch. "Nice to meet you," she said as she sat down next to Big Mama.

"I was hopin' to meet you," LaVelle said. "I wanted to see who had brought such a sweet little boy into the world."

Connie smiled. "Don't look at me," she said. "He didn't get it here. And, Lord knows, he didn't get it from his father."

"Is his father the one there in Kingsland?" LaVelle asked.

Connie chuckled. "Well, he's one of 'em," she said.

LaVelle nodded. "Say no more," she said. "I've done had my share of serial marriages."

"Me, too," Big Mama said. "I think I invented the word divorce, he he! I was about the only one to ever get divorced back in my day. I think I started the trend." Big Mama had made her way through her fair share of husbands. In the beginning, it had so scandalized the town that all the married women were on their guard, afraid that their husbands would be her next target. As time went on, divorce became more common, and she was not the only divorced man or woman around. "You gotta keep doin' it till you get it right, is what I say. 'Course, it's a good idea to learn a thing or two before you go into the next one."

"I'll say," LaVelle replied. "First you gotta know what the hell you want out of it, 'fore you can know what the hell to expect from it."

Big Mama looked at Connie. Although she was freshly showered, she still looked tired. "Honey, do you want somethin' to eat?" she asked.

Connie shook her head. "I'm all right," she said. She had been trying to follow the conversation, but she was thinking of the strange dreams she had had while she was sleeping. In the last dream she remembered, she could have sworn that those doctors from the hospital had been right there in the bedroom with her. She had looked up from her bed and seen three doctors standing over her, talking with each other in low voices. She actually had felt relieved when she woke up in her old bedroom, even though it meant that she was back in her parents' house. At least it was a familiar place, not the cold and sterile confines of the hospital room that they had put her in before they had released her to leave with Daddy C.

"You feelin' any better?" Big Mama asked.

Connie thought about the question. She could barely remember how she had felt before. It seemed to her that she had seen Big Mama in the kitchen when she arrived, but she wasn't sure. "I guess so," she answered. "I don't even remember getting to my bedroom."

Big Mama laughed. "I didn't figure you would. Seems like they had you pretty doped up at the hospital."

"Oh, yeah," Connie said. She seemed to remember the nurse giving her a pill. She ran her fingers through her damp hair to help it dry. "Was that what it was?" she asked.

"You said it was. Said they gave you some kind of tranquilizer or somethin' at the hospital."

Connie shook her head. "Beats all I ever saw, givin' tranquilizers to somebody who was in there for takin' too many of 'em in the first place."

"Well, I guess they thought you needed it," Big Mama said. She knew that Connie had not been given a tranquilizer at the hospital. She had still been under the effects of the pills that she had taken before they had admitted her to the hospital, and she simply didn't know the difference. "You had a little spill on the kitchen floor," Big Mama said.

Connie put her hand on her face. "Oh, my Word," she said. "I think I said somethin' that wasn't too nice to Mama, didn't I?" She looked at Big Mama. "Or did I just dream that?"

Big Mama laughed. "Don't worry none about that, Honey. Wanda Ray knew you was doped up. She didn't take it personally."

LaVelle perked up. She may have been dead, but she still liked to hear gossip from time to time. "What'd you tell her?" she asked sneakily.

Connie smiled at LaVelle. "I'm not real sure," she said. "I don't think it was too nice, though."

LaVelle wasn't satisfied with Connie's answer. She turned to Big Mama and asked, "What'd she say, Martha?"

"Oh, she just called her an old bitch," Big Mama said. "It wasn't the first time she'd heard that, he he!"

"Oh, your mother's changed an awful lot," LaVelle told Connie. "She's a real sweetheart now."

"I can't imagine that she's changed too much," Connie said. "But that doesn't mean I should have said that, especially not in front of my kids." Connie didn't remember that Frank had not yet arrived when she had made her grand entrance in the kitchen.

"Well, you can always tell her you're sorry," Big Mama said.

Connie hadn't thought of apologizing to her mother. The concept was uncomfortable to her. It seemed that they had had many ugly exchanges in their time, and it had never occurred to either of them to say that they were sorry.

Instead of commenting, Connie simply looked down at her hands. She noticed that the red polish on her nails was chipping off. She would have to paint them again. "Where is everybody, anyway?" Connie asked.

"They went down to Mrs. Celecia's to eat lunch," Big Mama said.

Connie seemed puzzled. "Is she still alive?" she asked. It had been several years since Connie had been in Sulphur Springs, but it seemed to her that she had heard that Mrs. Celecia had passed away.

LaVelle and Big Mama looked at each other. It was strange that Connie appeared to remember Mrs. Celecia's death but did not remember that Big Mama and the others had also passed away. "Well, she was in the hospital a while back, but she's okay now," Big Mama said. Big Mama did not actually lie to Connie. Mrs. Celecia *had* been in the hospital briefly, and she *was* doing fine now. Big Mama just neglected to mention that Mrs. Celecia had died during her brief stay at the hospital. She didn't think it was the right time to explain the situation, especially since both Frank and Paul were also involved.

"Oh," Connie said. "I thought I'd heard she didn't make it. But I guess there's lots of gossip in a small town."

"Ain't that the truth," LaVelle said. "I wouldn't have it any other way. You got any good gossip, Honey? I don't get around much anymore."

Connie laughed. "You don't get much gossip from a hospital bed," she said.

"I guess that's true," LaVelle replied.

"LaVelle's got herself a real cute daughter," Big Mama said. "I reckon she's about Frank's age, maybe a little older."

Connie nodded as she scratched away at the polish on her fingernails. "What's her name?" she asked.

"Cindy," LaVelle answered. "I guess I'll be seein' her tonight, maybe."

"You mean she doesn't live with you?" Connie asked.

"No, she lives with her daddy now," LaVelle said.

"I'm sorry," Connie said. "I don't know what I'd do if I didn't get to see my kids every day."

"Oh, I get to see her just about every day," LaVelle said. "But she's at that age now where she thinks she's too big for her breeches."

"I've got a little girl, too," Connie said. "Her name's Jennifer."

Big Mama smiled.

"How old is she?" LaVelle asked.

"She's four," Connie said. "She'll be five in January."

LaVelle felt sadness in her heart. She remembered Cindy at four. They were living together in that same house where LaVelle still lived, on the corner of Texas Street and Bellview. She wished that she could see her daughter off every time she had a date, and be there waiting in front of the television when she came back home. "Well, you just wait about ten more years," she said. "She'll be chasin' the boys like crazy. Cindy's probably out right now tryin' to see what kind of excitement she can rustle up."

"Why don't you put a stop to it?" Connie asked.

LaVelle smiled. She had had the same maternal fear before she had died suddenly. "Why should I?" she said. "It's her life. She has to live it. Of course, it's normal for a mother to worry. But, if I tried to stop her from doin' somethin', she'd just resent me for it an' do it behind my back. I have to just be patient an' let her do what she's gotta do, an' open my arms wide up when she needs a shoulder to cry on."

"What if she comes home pregnant?" Connie asked. She herself had given birth to Frank at a very young age, before she had finished school. She had never forgotten the shame of going to high school in the late sixties in East Texas with a swollen belly and no wedding ring. Everyone knew what she had been up to. Even the teachers treated her like she was a disgrace. Even those who were nice to her had trouble looking her in the eyes. Perhaps they were afraid that the same would happen to their children.

Mama Ray stopped going to church until several months after Frank was born. It took several years for her to forgive Connie for the embarrassment she had caused.

"I was old as dirt when I had Wanda Ray," Big Mama said. "I didn't think I could have children. Lord knows I enjoyed tryin', though. Every minute of it, he he!" She smiled gleefully. "I thought I had bone cancer or somethin' awful like that, when I went to the doctor an' he said I was expectin'. I was happy as a lark."

"I know lots of people who wait to have a baby till it's too late," LaVelle said. "They're too busy savin' up money that never comes, or whatever. One of my friends was waitin' till her husband got a better job, an' then she had to have a hysterectomy when she was twenty-five, if you can imagine that." LaVelle shook her head as she remembered her young girlfriend, working hard to save every penny that came her way, hoping that the best would come. Then all her money, along with her uterus, were taken away with one quick incision at the hospital. The woman and her husband were probably still paying off those doctor bills. "You might think this is crazy," LaVelle continued, "but I'd be thrilled if Cindy came home an' told me I was gonna be a granny."

LaVelle knew that this was a radical idea, but she had already learned about the uncertainty of life. She had spent her whole life thinking about the future, until her car suddenly met head-on with another. Being dead makes a person look at things in a different way.

Connie was surprised. She had never heard a mother say that she would be pleased to have her little girl come home pregnant. "But she's so young," Connie said. "She's too young to be a Mama."

LaVelle laughed. "Honey, she's fifteen, almost sixteen. She's been havin' her period for about three years now. What do you think her body's been doin' all this time? Warmin' up for when she's forty?"

Connie shook her head. She had left high school almost two years before graduation to have Frank. She left early, partly because of the embarrassment of being pregnant, but also to work in the blouse factory where Mama Ray had gotten her a job. Suddenly, at sixteen, she found herself stuck with a child and many medical bills. She had always expected to have a man there to help her, but she had to do it on her own in a society in which she had become an outcast. The stress of it became too much. Finally, she ended up in bed, trying to cope with everything, but she found that she became less and less able to find the strength to even lift herself up from the mattress. "But she can't bring a kid in this world and expect to clothe it and feed it at fifteen. Life doesn't work that way. I know from experience."

"I know it, Honey," LaVelle said. "It's hard as hell to do a lot of things nowadays. I ain't sayin' she should go out an' get knocked up, but it wouldn't have to be the worse thing in the world if she did. If a woman can have a baby at twelve or thirteen, but can't afford to feed it in this world till she's forty, then it's the world that's screwed up, an' not the woman, if you ask me. A woman's body knows when it's ready to have a baby. What do people think them eggs are for that's comin' out once a month, anyway?"

Connie laughed. "I hope I have at least another eight or nine years before I have to start worryin' about Jennifer's eggs," she said. "But, it looks like you better start worryin' about Cindy's."

Big Mama also laughed. "Ha ha! Well, I guess Connie's right, 'cause it looks like her eggs are pretty hot on the market right now."

"Well, I done told her all about how to take care of herself," LaVelle said. "Now, whether she does it or not is another thing."

"That's the truth," Big Mama said. She shifted her weight on the sofa. "You can tell a person whatever you want, but that don't mean they're gonna do it just because you told 'em to. They might be our children, but they got minds of their own. I guess we always think we know better 'cause we're the parents. But, what makes us think that what we've done has made us any happier than our children are?"

Connie had heard enough. She knew that she wasn't the model of happiness, but there was no point in mulling that over while she was still recovering. Lots of things were true in life, but that didn't mean that people had to talk about them. "I'd kill for a cigarette," Connie said. She had quit smoking before Paul was born, but she started up again after he left Kingsland.

"Well, Honey, I got plenty of cigarettes, if you want one," LaVelle said, "but I think this house is a non-smokin' establishment."

"Yeah," Big Mama said. "I don't think Wanda Ray would like it too much if you was to light up in her livin' room."

"Just come on over to my house next door whenever you get a cravin'," LaVelle said. "Or if you just wanna get away for a while."

"You got an extra bed there?" Connie joked. "I might be there more often than you think. I don't know if I can handle it here for too long." Since she had moved away to Kingsland to marry her third husband, she had only brought the children back to visit their grandparents on holidays. She never looked forward to it, and she made the visits as brief as possible. Thus, it was very surprising that her husband had called Daddy C to come get her. He hadn't even consulted her before he made the call.

"Well, you know your mama's glad to have you here," Big Mama said.

"Yeah, right," Connie said. "Just like she'd be glad to have another hole in her ass."

"Now, that's an interestin' thought," Big Mama giggled. Her face then turned serious. "Connie, Honey, your Mama misses you."

Connie couldn't believe that her mother was capable of missing her. Mama Ray had seemed glad to be rid of her when she had finally found a man who would take her. It seemed to have made it easier for her mother to act as if the scandal of Frank's illigitimate birth had never happened, so that she could eventually hold her head up high in the community again. It didn't seem to matter to Mama Ray that Connie had married a poor excuse for a husband the first time out. He was always stoned out of his mind and had even tried to run over Connie with his pickup. "Just stay with him, Honey," Mama Ray had said. "He's all you've got."

The paradox of it all was that Mama Ray and Daddy C had taken care of baby Frank throughout Connie's first marriage. Her husband hadn't wanted the burden of raising a son that was not his own. Mama Ray loved to have a baby boy around the house, and the fact that Connie was finally married somehow made it acceptible that Frank existed. The fact that Connie was married seemed to erase the fact that Frank had been born out of wedlock. It didn't matter that Connie's new husband didn't want baby Frank around the house. At least she was married, and the shame of Frank's illegitimacy, according to the standards of the time, could finally be swept under the rug.

When Connie left her first husband, she came back to take Frank away for good. By this time, Mama Ray and Daddy C had grown to think of themselves as Frank's parents. Of course, Connie was still his mother, and had never thought of letting him stay with his grandparents forever. Mama Ray was so upset by the prospect of losing baby Frank, that she started legal proceedings to get custody of him. To do this, she had to accuse Connie of being unfit to take care of him, and to cite the time that he had stayed with them as evidence of her inability. Connie simply took Frank from the daycare while Mama Ray and Daddy C were at work, and she moved off to Dallas to live with a friend of hers from school.

Daddy C had never wanted the problems in the first place. He loved Frank dearly, and he understood the hurt that both his wife and daughter were going through. He finally was able to convince Mama Ray to drop the suit for custody, telling her that, if she didn't end the suit, she might never see Frank or Connie again. It was years before they were able to regain contact with Connie and Frank, however. By that time, she was already married again, and had given birth to baby Paul.

"Did my husband call while I was asleep?" Connie asked.

Big Mama shook her head. "No. He's probably waitin' to give you some time to settle in. I bet he knew you'd need some time to sleep it all off."

It was true that Connie was famous for sleeping. She spent about half of her day in bed. There just seemed no point in being awake in the daytime. What was there to do? She found solace in the quiet times of night. It was then that she could sit alone and do what she wanted without being disturbed. Connie had done her best to take care of the children before they were old enough to go to pre-school. She had even breast-fed Jennifer. Of course, she loved her children more than anything. She just never found the energy to spend more time with them. Luckily, her third husband had enough money to send them all off to pre-school when each of them reached three years old. This allowed her to sleep most of the day, and to somehow conjure up the energy necessary to face the children when they came home from school.

"A nap sounds good right now," Connie said. "I think I'll go rest for a little while. I don't think that dope has worn off yet." She was not really tired, but going back to bed seemed like the best thing to do, especially if she couldn't smoke a cigarette. She was tired of talking about pregnant teenagers, anyway.

"Well, do you want me to go get you up if your husband calls?" Big Mama asked, not calling Bill by his name. She always had trouble remembering the names of Connie's husbands. It had been hard enough to keep track of her own husbands' names while she was still living. As luck would have it, two of them had had the same name, Albert. Therefore, it was no problem for Big Mama to recall the name Albert. One of the Alberts had been bald, and the other had worn a bushy gray moustache. While she could remember the name easily, she sometimes had trouble remembering which Albert had been the bald one, and which had worn the moustache.

"Just tell him I'll call him back," Connie said. She got up from the couch and looked at LaVelle. She had a feeling that her husband, Bill, would not call, anyway. They hadn't been on the best of terms lately. "I'll take you up on that offer to come to your house," she said. "I don't think I'll make it for too long without a cigarette."

"Just come by anytime," LaVelle said. "An' enjoy your nap."

"I will," Connie said. "Tell the boys to come and get me up when they get back," she told Big Mama.

"Will do," Big Mama said. "They oughta be back any time now."

"It doesn't matter," Connie said. "I'm just gonna go lay down and rest my head. I'm not gonna sleep." Connie walked out the door and went back to her bedroom.

"I wish she'd eat somethin'" Big Mama whispered, when Connie had left the living room. "I sure do hate to see her waste away like that."

"I guess her body'll tell her when it's time to eat," LaVelle said. "What's wrong with her, anyway?" LaVelle asked.

"She's got a big ol' chip on her shoulder, for one thing," Big Mama said. "She don't think nobody loves her. How could she *not* think it, when she don't even love herself?"

"I've seen a lot of cases like that. Of course, it ain't easy to sit back an' watch when it's your own granddaughter."

"You got that right," Big Mama said. Just because she was dead didn't mean she had stopped caring about the people she loved. On the contrary, she cared about them even more. Now she could see how much there was to be happy about, and that their suffering was senseless. "An' I guess that deep down she knows what happened to Paul, even though she don't let on to it. All the tranquilizers in the world couldn't have flushed that out of her."

"When are you gonna tell her?" LaVelle asked.

"I don't know," Big Mama said. "I guess we'll wait till Frank goes back. But I guess that's up to Wanda Ray an' Calvin, too."

"Are you sure that Wanda Ray's got back to her senses?" LaVelle asked. She had been surprised when Big Mama had told her of Mama Ray's regression. It was normal for those who had recently died to not know what had hit them, but Mama Ray had already gone through the change. LaVelle had never expected that Mama Ray would return in her mind to her old world, insisting that things were as they had always been.

"Oh, she's back, all right," Big Mama assured LaVelle. "This mornin' she turned my drink over on me just by lookin' at me, right there in front of the boys. I'd forgotten how strong she was. 'Course, what can you expect from someone who's so hard-headed?"

LaVelle laughed. "Did the boys suspect somethin'?" she asked.

Big Mama shook her head. "No, they was too busy laughin' at two old ladies havin' a food fight."

"Well, that don't surprise me," LaVelle said with a laugh. "I'd be laughin', too, just as long as you didn't throw nothin' on me."

LaVelle and Big Mama heard the garage door open and Mama Ray's car drive up. "Well, they're back," Big Mama said.

"You think I should slip out the front door?" LaVelle asked. She still was not sure whether Mama Ray had really come back to her senses. When Mama Ray realized the first time that she was dead, she was easy to get along with. Before that, she had always disliked LaVelle, because LaVelle had had a pretty rough reputation around the town. In her earthly lifetime, Mama Ray hadn't thought it very Godly to consort with the likes of LaVelle Willbrook. However, when Mama Ray had accepted her death, she began to understand that everything with a kind heart was Godly, and she and LaVelle became good friends. Then, suddenly, when Mama Ray had her relapse, LaVelle went onto her blacklist again.

"Don't worry none about Wanda Ray," Big Mama said. "I done told you that she's back full force. *Too* full if you ask me."

LaVelle laughed. "That's what I'm afraid of. I guess I'll stay to say hello. I ain't seen her since she had her little breakdown."

The two women went into the den. As they entered, the door to the garage was opening. "Oh, shit," Big Mama said. "I forgot about them dogs." She snapped her fingers and Tinker, Buster, and Dawn appeared on the couch. They shook their coats. Tinker wobbled a little as if she were dizzy, and then she quickly jumped off the couch and ran to greet Daddy C at the door.

"Hi there, Tinker," Daddy C said. Tinker jumped up at his waist. "You smell enchiladas on me?" he asked. He looked up and saw that LaVelle was there. "Howdy, LaVelle," he said.

"Hi, Calvin."

The others all filed in from the garage. "Well, did y'all get your guts full?" Big Mama asked.

"Sure did," Mama Ray said. "Marie said to tell you hi."

"Did you tell her howdy for me?" Big Mama asked.

"Yep," Mama Ray answered. She noticed that LaVelle was there, and she smiled warmly at her. "Well, hi there, LaVelle," she said. "How are you doin'?"

LaVelle smiled back. "I'm just fine," she said. "It's good to see you back to your old self."

"It's good to *be* back to my old self," Mama Ray said. "Where's Cindy?"

"Oh, I don't know. She was here this mornin', but, you know how it is. It might be a couple of days before I see her again."

"It's hard to get used to, ain't it?" Mama Ray said. "Like anything else, you gotta just enjoy 'em while you can, 'cause they might be gone tomorrow."

"Ain't that the truth," LaVelle said.

Paul was confused. He had just seen Cindy only a few hours before. She had told him and Frank that she was going back to LaVelle's house. "I seen her outside right before lunch," he said. "She was swingin' with me when Frank come up."

"Don't talk like a hick," Frank said.

"Honey, she's just gone off to visit her daddy for a little bit," LaVelle lied. She looked at Frank. "You must be Frank, the famous older brother."

Frank nodded.

"You boys sure are the spittin' image of each other," LaVelle said. She had never seen two brothers who looked more alike, except for twins.

"It runs in the family," Frank said.

"That's true," LaVelle said. "If your mother was to chop all her hair off she'd probably look just like the two of you."

It was a strange thought for Paul and Frank. They had never imagined what their mother would look like if she cut all her hair off.

"Well, Frank, it sure was nice to meet you," LaVelle said. "You're welcome to come by an' visit any time, but I reckon you'll want to spend as much time here with your family as you can."

"But I'll be back again in a few weeks," Frank said. "Maybe I'll come by then."

LaVelle nodded and started for the glass door.

"LaVelle, you're welcome to come back over for supper," Mama Ray said.

"That's a good idea," Daddy C said.

"It'll just be a light one, seein' as we done stuffed our guts on Marie's enchiladas," Mama Ray added.

LaVelle shook her head. "I sure do appreciate the invitation," she said, "but I never know when Cindy will be comin' back. I don't want her to think I've gone an' run off with the circus."

Mama Ray nodded. "Well, come back again another time."

"I will," LaVelle said. "You'll need all the help you can get."

"Tell her about Paul's birthday party," Daddy C said.

"That's right," Mama Ray said. "I'd forgotten. We're gonna have a party for little Paul's birthday down at Marie's place, an', of course, you an' Cindy are invited."

LaVelle smiled. "I wouldn't miss it for the world," she said. "An' I know that Cindy would love to come."

"It's next week," Big Mama said.

"Okay." LaVelle turned again to leave. "Oh, Martha, don't forget to get Connie up."

"I won't, Honey," Big Mama replied.

"I'll see y'all, an' Frank, you have a nice stay."

"Thank you," Frank said. "I will."

LaVelle turned and went out the glass door.

"Connie, get up, Honey," Big Mama said as she opened the door to Connie's bedroom. When she looked inside, she noticed that Connie was not in her bed. "Connie?" she said. She heard the commode flush from the bathroom, which was attached to Connie's bedroom. It was actually the master bedroom of the house, but Mama Ray and Daddy C had chosen the bedroom in the back of the house, as it was farther away from the street. Big Mama noticed that the bedroom smelled of cigarette smoke. Connie emerged from the tiny bathroom, drying her hands on a towel.

"Are they back already?" she asked.

"Yeah, they just got here," Big Mama answered. "You oughta leave that bathroom window open and shut the door to let that smoke out."

"I done took care of it," Connie said.

Big Mama smiled. "Just like when you was little," she said. "You had your mama chasin' you all over town."

Connie laughed. "She never could catch up with me, though. I was always too quick for her. And for every trap she could think of, I knew an escape route. I've been in and out of that bathroom window more times than I can remember."

"I remember," Big mama said. "You thought she didn't know what you was up to, didn't you?"

"She was too busy prayin' to know what I was doin'," Connie said.

"If she was prayin', she was probably prayin' for you, an' beatin' herself over the head for never knowin' how to do to suit you."

"I didn't ever need her prayers," Connie said.

Big Mama sat down at the foot of Connie's bed. "Honey, I ain't gonna take nobody's side," she said. "Lord knows I ain't one to criticize nobody. All I know is that she done her best with what she had an' what she knew at the time. That's the problem about havin' children, isn't it?"

"What's the problem with havin' children?" Connie asked. She was feeling a bit peevish after having lain down for a few minutes, and her headache had returned. She didn't really want to get into a discussion about Mama Ray and child rearing.

Big Mama smoothed out the bedspread with her hand. "The problem is that any idiot has the ability to have children from the minute their body starts pumpin' out hormones. It's okay to be an idiot. Lord knows I've been an idiot plenty of times in my life. The truth is, most of us are more ignorant than we let on. But, my Lord, the minute we have a child, we're supposed to suddenly know everything there is to know about everything." Big Mama looked Connie directly in the eye. "The problem is, it don't work that way. Your mama was just a kid herself by today's standards when you was born. There ain't nobody in this world that's perfect. I know that your mama loves you."

Connie lit up another cigarette and stood in the doorway of the bathroom, holding the cigarette out the bathroom window. "She had a great way of showin' it," she said.

"Honey, there's lots of people who don't know how to show people that they love 'em," Big Mama said. "Sometimes you just gotta look deeper."

Connie and Big Mama heard a knock at the door. "Mama," Frank said from the other side. "Are you up?"

"We'll be out in a minute, Honey," Connie replied. Then she looked at Big Mama. "You know what she did to me when I was Frank's age?"

Big Mama shook her head. There was no telling what her daughter had done. She supposed that any child could come up with a long list of attrocities committed by their parents.

"We were in the kitchen and I was about to go out to the movies, and she said I had on too much makeup," Connie said.

"That sounds like her," Big Mama said. "I didn't ever let her wear makeup till she was married. Of course, she was done married at sixteen."

"I told her I was goin' out anyway and that she could just shut up and eat her dinner." Connie flicked an ash out the window. "Well, she didn't shut up and eat her dinner," she said. "She got up and grabbed me by the hair and dragged me to the sink. She turned the water on and stuck my head under the faucet. Then she scrubbed my face with soap and a scouring pad." Connie pulled her hair out of her face and rubbed a small scar over her eyebrow. "I still have this scar from where she busted my head open on that faucet," she said. She laughed bitterly. "I didn't go to the movies that night."

Big Mama frowned. What could she say? She had hit Mama Ray plenty of times when she was a child. Mostly, she had just spanked her, but there had also been times when she had slapped her daughter. She hadn't known any other way to discipline a child. That was simply how it was done.

"Why do you think she did that to you?" Big Mama asked.

Connie shook her head. "Do you think I know?" she asked.

"Can you think of a situation when you might have done somethin' that wasn't too nice to somebody, but it was the only thing you could think to do at the time?" Big Mama replied.

Connie felt angry. She knew what Big Mama was trying to do. It didn't matter that her grandmother had a point. Connie hadn't come home to forgive her mother for bashing her head open on the kitchen faucet, nor for treating her like an embarrassment when she was pregnant with Frank.

"We're not talkin' about me," Connie said.

Big Mama saw that Connie was angry. She didn't want to pursue the matter, but she hoped that she had at least made her granddaughter think about the question. If Connie could arrive at a point in which she could forgive her mother at least a little bit, then perhaps she could also start to forgive herself.

Big Mama got up from Connie's bed. "Well, you come an' join us in the den when you're finished with your cigarette," she said as she started toward the door.

"Big Mama?" Connie said.

"What, Honey?" Big Mama asked.

"Do you think I'm a good mother?"

Big Mama looked at her granddaughter and smiled. "I think we're all good mothers," she answered. "We just have our good days an' our bad days like everybody else. Maybe we ought to try for more good days."

"I'll be out in a minute, when I finish smokin'," Connie said.

"All right, Honey," Big Mama said. She left Connie's bedroom and shut the door.

When Connie came into the den, Big Mama, Mama Ray and Daddy C were relaxing. Daddy C had opened his belt and unzipped his pants to let his stomach breathe, as he usually did after a big meal. Buster was lying next to him with his head resting on Daddy C's leg. Connie cringed to think that Paul might have picked up that habit from her father. She would be horrified if her son suddenly decided that it was okay to open his pants up and pass gas after a meal the way her father did. Daddy C had done that ever since she could remember. "Hope that don't stink," he would say, after passing gas while watching his favorite television programs in his armchair. It was no wonder that Mama Ray had spent so much time in church.

Connie had decided she would take Paul back with her the next morning. She didn't know why she had agreed to let him spend the summer with his grandparents in the first place. Neither of her parents was in the best of health, and she didn't want her son to end up eating all their greasy food and talking like a hick as they did. She was no longer feeling doped, and she could sleep at home just as easily as she could sleep there at her parents' house. There was no point in staying in Sulphur Springs any longer.

"Well, looky there," Daddy C said, as Connie walked into the den. He scratched his stomach. "You feelin' any better?" he asked.

"Yeah, I guess," Connie answered. She hadn't really felt very bad in the first place. She had just felt a little doped up, and then that feeling had subsided into a headache. But even the headache was gone now. She was left with just a feeling of regret that she would have to tell her parents of her decision to leave.

"I'm feeling much better now," Connie said. "In fact, I'm gonna call Bill and tell him to pick us up in the morning."

Daddy C looked at Mama Ray and Big Mama.

"Are you sure that's a good idea?" Mama Ray asked. Tinker and Dawn, who were on either side of her, perked their ears up as she spoke.

"I'm real sure," Connie said. "It was nice of y'all to let me come here, but it's not necessary, really. I've got to get home. I've got another kid there who needs her mama."

"Well, Bill's there takin' care of her, an' he's got a good babysitter to look after her," Mama Ray said.

Connie shook her head. "I'm not gonna leave Jennifer with Pauline," she said. Pauline was the teenage girl who lived down the street and looked after the children when Connie and her husband Bill went out. "She's a good kid, but she can't take care of Jennifer for such a long time."

"Well, we was just gettin' excited about havin' you back," Daddy C said.

"I know it, Daddy, but I've got to get back home," Connie replied.

"What about little Paul?" Mama Ray said. "He's so glad to have his mama back with him."

"I'm gonna take him back with me," Connie said. "He's been visitin' here long enough. I thank y'all for takin' care of him, but he's going back with me tomorrow."

"Honey, you can't take him back with you," Mama Ray said.

"The hell I can't," Connie said. "I'm his mother, and I guess I can take him wherever I want to."

"She don't remember nothin' about it, Wanda Ray," Big Mama said.

Mama Ray nodded. "That's what we were afraid of," she said.

"Sit down, Honey," Big Mama said to Connie.

"No, I'm gonna go and get Paul and Frank," Connie answered. "Where are they?"

"Honey, come sit down by me," Big Mama repeated.

"Where are they?" Connie insisted.

Mama Ray got up from her recliner. She started to cry. Dawn and Tinker, confused, did not get up. "Honey, why don't you just sit down an' let us talk for a while," Mama Ray said. She looked at Big Mama. "She really don't remember nothin'," she added.

"Remember what?" Connie asked. For some reason she was getting angry. All she wanted now was to tell her children to get their bags packed. She didn't want to wait till morning. She didn't need her husband to come and get them. She would take a bus back to Kingsland if she had to and, if she couldn't get a bus back that night, then she would get a hotel room for her and the boys. She didn't want to spend another moment in that house. How could they tell her that she couldn't take Paul back home with her? It scared her, because it reminded her of when they had tried to take Frank away from her after her first marriage.

"Honey, Paul has to stay here with us," Mama Ray said. She walked toward her daughter.

"The hell he does!" Connie shouted. "Where are they?" Connie went to the glass door and looked outside. She saw her two sons on the swing set. She opened the door and shouted, "Paul, Frank, y'all get in here right now!" As Connie shouted, Dawn and Tinker, sensing trouble, ran outside to safety. Buster jumped from Daddy C's lap and ran out after them, barking.

Both Frank and Paul looked up, surprised. They jumped from the swings and ran toward the house.

Connie turned around, leaving the glass door open. By now she was furious and ready to leave in an instant.

Big Mama got up from the couch. "Honey, I wish you would sit down," she said.

"I ain't gonna sit down!" Connie screamed. "Y'all can sit down all you want. I'm gonna get the hell out of this shithole!"

Frank and Paul came into the den, and Frank shut the glass door.

"Honey, you can go if you want, but little Paul has to stay here with us," Mama Ray said.

"The hell he does!" Connie said. "You already tried that once with Frank, and you see what it got you."

"What are y'all talking about?" Frank asked.

Mama Ray's face turned red as tears started to stream down. "Honey, why do you think Paul is here with us?" she asked Connie.

"To spend the summer," Connie answered. "But he's been here long enough. I'm not gonna have him learnin' to live like a back-woods hick." She turned to her two sons. "Y'all go get your bags packed," she said. "We're gettin' out of here this instant."

"But, I'm takin' the bus out tomorrow," Frank said.

"We're leavin' right now," Connie said. "We'll get a motel room if we have to. Now go and get your bags packed."

Paul and Frank were shocked. They had walked into a madhouse. Their grandmother was crying, and their mother was in a rage. They didn't know what to do.

"Go!" Connie shouted.

Mama Ray turned to the boys. She tried to wipe the tears from her eyes, but even the lenses of her glasses were soaked. "Y'all do what your mama tells you," she said weakly. She didn't know what else to say.

Paul and Frank went into their bedroom, without saying another word. They were too confused to speak.

When the boys had gone into their room, Daddy C stood up and began to zip up his pants. "Paul lives here with us now, Doll," he said to Connie. "We're takin' real good care of him."

Connie shook her head. "He doesn't live here with you. I'm takin' him back with me right now."

"You can't take him back home with you 'cause he's done passed away," Big Mama said. She had wanted to tell Connie in a more gentle way, but the situation called for the blunt truth.

"You're all crazy!" Connie screamed. She walked out of the kitchen and down the hall. "Hurry up!" she yelled to Paul and Frank, as she passed their bedroom. She went into her own room and slammed the door shut.

When she turned around, Big Mama and Mama Ray were both sitting on her bed. She was shocked. It was impossible for them to have passed her in the hallway and beat her to her bedroom. She tried to open her bedroom door again to escape, but the handle would not turn. "What the hell is goin' on here?" she screamed. "Help me!"

"Honey, please come an' sit down with us," Big Mama said.

"The hell I will!" Connie said. She continued to beat on the door. "Help me!" she repeated.

"They can't hear you, Honey," Mama Ray said. Her voice was trembling. "Please sit down an' let us talk to you for a while."

Connie turned around again. Tears were streaming down her face, but she was not sad. She was enraged. "What the hell do you want me to sit down for?" she asked. "You want me to sign some papers to give you custody of Paul?" She could no longer control herself. "You goddamned bitch!" she screamed. "Did you think all this time that you were a better mother than I am? Good mothers don't bash their kids heads open on the kitchen sink!"

Mama Ray's face turned red as tears streamed down them. She had always regretted having filed for custody of Frank. He had lived there for almost a year, and she and Daddy C had grown so close to him. She hadn't been able to bear the thought of losing him after having bottle fed him and changed his diapers every day. He had become the son that she had never had. When she realized that she was going to lose her own daughter if she proceeded with the custody suit, she dropped it. It hadn't helped to drop the suit, however. The deed had already been committed, and Connie had never been able to trust her again.

Mama Ray shook her head. She wiped her tears back with her hand and tried to steady her voice. "No, Honey, it ain't about that," she managed to say.

"They're *my* kids!" Connie screamed. "Frank an' Paul an' Jennifer are *mine*, an' you'll never get your filthy self-righteous hands on 'em again. Do you hear me?"

"Honey, don't nobody wanna take your kids away," Big Mama said. "We just wanna talk to you about little Paul. That's all."

"Liar!" Connie shouted. She tried to open the door again.

"Honey, just sit down an' let's talk a minute," Mama Ray said.

"You sit there an' talk all you want," Connie said. "but I'm gonna stand right here. I ain't goin' anywhere near you. And my kids aren't, either. An' we're gonna get the hell out of here."

Connie turned to the door again. The handle still did not budge. She screamed out again. "Help me!"

"Try to calm down, Honey," Big Mama said. "Ain't nothin' gonna happen to you."

Connie turned around to face Big Mama. She was frightened now, and desperate to leave. "Big Mama, help me get out of here," she pleaded. "*Please* help me out of here."

"I *will* help you. I promise," Big Mama replied. "But, sit down first, an' let us have a little talk with you."

Connie was afraid to sit down. She wanted out. Why would the door not open? She remembered the dream she had had about being stuck in her parents' house again. She looked at her grandmother, who returned her stare with a peaceful expression on her face. Mama Ray was still choking up with tears.

"Tell me what you have to say," Connie said finally. "But I'm stayin' right here by the door."

"Okay," Big Mama said. "What do you remember about when you came here?"

"I was drunk," Connie said. She was still holding onto the door handle. "And I took some tranquilizers because I couldn't sleep."

"Where'd you get them tranquilizers?" Big Mama asked.

"From the doctor," Connie answered.

"And, why'd he give 'em to you?" Big Mama asked.

Connie started to answer, but then she stopped. She couldn't remember why the doctor had prescribed the tranquilizers for her. "Because I had trouble sleeping," she lied.

"Why'd you have trouble sleepin'?" Big Mama asked.

"I don't remember," Connie said. She really *didn't* remember. Now that she thought about it, it *did* seem strange that she would have taken tranquilizers because of insomnia. She had never in her life had trouble sleeping. On the contrary, most of the time she found it difficult to stay awake. Connie's anger started to fade. Now she felt drained of energy and upset, as if she had been tortured for a long time and finally left to rest. It scared her that she could not remember why she had been taking the tranquilizers.

"Are you sure you don't want to sit down, Honey?" Big Mama asked. She put her arm out and patted the bed next to her.

Connie looked at the bed. She suddenly had the feeling that she would faint if she didn't sit down. She walked over to the bed and sat down about a foot away from Big Mama and Mama Ray. She was afraid to get too close to them.

Mama Ray turned to Connie. "Honey, do you remember what happened that day at your house, down at the water?"

Connie shook her head. "What do you mean?" she asked.

"Paul and Jennifer were down there playin', weren't they?" Big Mama said.

"When?" Connie asked. The children often played together at the lake with her and Bill.

"About three weeks ago, I guess," Big Mama answered. It was always difficult to keep track of time where she and Mama Ray lived.

"We didn't go out to the lake about three weeks ago," Connie said.

"I know you didn't, Honey. But *they* did," Big Mama said.

Connie shook her head again. "They wouldn't go out there without me or Bill," she said.

"Honey, they *did* go down to the lake while you was in bed," Mama Ray said.

"Well, Pauline must have been with 'em, then," Connie said. Her children knew that it was strictly forbidden to go down to the lake without supervision.

"She wasn't with 'em, Honey," Big Mama said. "And Frank was away with the Boy Scouts."

"Why in the hell are you tellin' me this?" Connie shouted. What business was it of Big Mama's and Mama Ray's that the children had walked down to the lake? She supposed that they were looking for another opportunity to accuse her of being an unfit mother.

"Because that's how it happened," Big Mama said.

"How *what* happened?" Connie asked.

Big Mama reached out her arm to her granddaughter, but Connie jerked away from her.

"How *what* happened?" Connie repeated.

"Do you remember the funeral?" Big Mama asked.

"What goddamned funeral?" Connie asked. She was becoming irritated again by all the questioning that seemed to be leading nowhere. "I didn't go to any goddamned funeral!" she said.

"They buried little Paul right out there in the cemetery, there in Kingsland, Honey," Big Mama said.

Mama Ray started to sob again at the thought of the funeral. It had been too much for her to see her little grandson put into the ground. She had wanted so much to go over to her daughter on that day and comfort her, but she had known that Connie would not see her. When they went to get Paul after the funeral, something seemed to snap in her. It was the first time she had directly dealt with death since she herself had died. Somehow it just seemed logical to her that Paul was alive. He looked the same as he always had, and she fould it easier to believe his version of what had happened. It felt comfortable to feel "alive" again.

Connie got up from the bed. She bolted toward the door and tried to open it again, but it would still not budge. "Let me out of here!" she screamed. "Let me the hell out of here!" She beat on the door. She pulled on the handle again, but she simply could not open the door. She felt her heart race and her skin turned hot. Tears began to roll down her face.

"They can't hear you," Big Mama said. She wanted to cry, herself. It broke her heart to have to tell Connie. She couldn't let her out, because Paul still didn't realize himself that he was dead. He had thought the whole time that he had been sent away because his little sister had died, and he had even thought that he had caused her death.

"Honey, *please* come back over here an' sit down," Big Mama said. Her voice trembled as she tried to fight back her own tears. She had been dead for a long time, but she still could not stand to see the living suffer. "Come sit down, an' let's talk about it."

"Come on, Honey," Mama Ray said. She was so upset that the words came out garbled.

Connie stopped banging on the door. She felt helpless. All she wanted to do was run out of that house and take both Paul and Frank far away from there. She knew that her mother and grandmother were right, that she couldn't take Paul with her. How could she have forgotten? When she had walked into the kitchen and seen Paul looking so healthy and alive, she had simply thought that she had dreamt it all while she had been in the hospital. She immediately forgot all about that terrible dream in which she had found him floating face-down on the water. Connie put her head against the door and sobbed. The brown wood of the door became stained with her tears. "Oh, God," she said. "He's just a little boy."

Connie turned again toward Mama Ray and Big Mama. "Please just let me take him back with me," she pleaded.

Both Big Mama and Mama Ray were heart-broken. "You can't take him back, Honey. It's too late," Big Mama said.

"*Please*," Connie insisted. "I'll watch him all the time. I promise." She looked at her mother and grandmother intensely. "I'll get help," she said. "I know that I wasn't the best mother before, but, please, just give me one more chance."

"Oh, Honey," Big Mama said. Her own tears were now streaming down her cheeks. "We can't. We would like for him to go back with you, too, but he can't."

"He has to stay with us now," Mama Ray said. Her chest was heaving, and her voice trembled uncontrollably.

"Please," Connie repeated. "*Please*, let's just forget it happened, and let me take him back with me. Just give me one more chance." She started to walk toward her mother and grandmother. She wanted to grab them, to plead with them, but as she approached them she lost control of her body and fell unconscious onto the floor.

Then the crying started again.

Mama Ray and Big Mama noticed that Connie's body began to fade away. They thought they were going to lose her that instant. Suddenly her body stopped fading, and her presence began to return. Relieved that she was still with them, Mama Ray and Big Mama got up from the bed and pulled Connie up from the floor. They started to walk her to the bed. "I'm okay," Connie said. "Let me go."

They continued to try to help Connie to the bed. "I'm okay, really," Connie repeated. Big Mama and Mama Ray let go of her arms as Connie tried to regain her composure.

Connie used her hand to brace herself against the foot of her bed. "I couldn't take it anymore," she said.

"I know it, Honey," Mama Ray said. She put her arm on her daughter's back.

"A couple of weeks after the funeral, I got real drunk, an' I looked at that bottle of pills. I just couldn't sleep that night." Connie raised herself up and turned around. "I reached into that bottle, an' I took some," she said. "The next thing I knew, I was in the hospital. Then Daddy showed up an' brought me here."

"You're still in the hospital," Big Mama told her. "You just ain't conscious in that world."

Connie turned toward the door. "What's that noise?" she asked. She could hear a noise coming from down the hall. It sounded like a little girl crying.

"That's Jennifer," Big Mama said.

"Where is she?" Connie asked.

"She's with you, I guess," Big Mama answered.

"What are you talking about?" Connie demanded. Suddenly, they heard shouting from Paul and Frank's bedroom. Connie grabbed the door handle and turned it. This time the door opened. She, Big Mama, and Mama Ray went down the hall to the boys' room.

Daddy C and Paul were in the room, sitting on Paul's bed. Paul was crying, and Daddy C was holding him.

"What's goin' on?" Connie asked.

"Frank's gone," Paul said, sobbing.

Connie looked at Mama Ray. "Where'd he go?"

"He just disappeared," Paul said. His face was red and tear-stained. He was shaking as he spoke.

"What do you mean, Honey?" Connie asked. "Where'd he go?"

Paul shook his head. "I don't know," he said. "We heard Jennifer cryin'. We started lookin' for her, but we couldn't find her nowhere. Then Frank yelled, 'I'm comin!' An' then he just disappeared."

"Oh, my God," Connie said. She didn't know what was happening anymore. She thought she must be in a crazy dream caused by the tranquilizers she had taken. She didn't know what was real and what was not. She walked over to Paul and touched his shoulder. He felt warm and real to her. She sat down next to her son and put her arm around him. He moved away from Daddy C and buried his head in his mother's bosom. She could feel the wetness of his tears begin to seep through her blouse. She could smell his hair as it brushed against her face. She was sure that she was not dreaming.

Connie looked up at Mama Ray. "Where is Frank?" she asked.

Paul raised up. "He disappeared, I told you! Why don't you believe me?"

Paul had never yelled at his mother like that before. He yelled so loudly that it made her ears ring.

"Baby, I believe you," Connie said. "I just want to know where he is."

"Mama Ray don't know," Paul said. "She wasn't here when it happened. It ain't her fault. Stop blamin' her for everything."

Connie pulled Paul to her. "I'm not blamin' anybody, Baby," she said. "I just want to find him. That's all."

"He's probably back at the hospital," Daddy C said.

Connie and Paul looked up at Daddy C.

"Why would he be at the hospital?" Connie asked.

"I seen him there asleep in the waitin' room when I went an' got you," Daddy C said. "He was there with Bill an' Jennifer. Bill was pacin' back an' forth holdin' Jennifer in his arms, an' Frank had dozed off. I guess he was wore out."

"I thought he was in Dallas on a Scout trip," Connie said.

Mama Ray shook her head. "He wasn't on no Scout trip," she said.

"He was just dreamin', Honey," Big Mama said. "In his dream, it was the only logical way he could explain how he got here."

Connie was stunned. She remembered everything now. She remembered pulling Paul from the lake, and going to his funeral a few days later. Frank had just gotten back from his

Boy Scout trip, and they had had to tell him the terrible news about his brother. Frank had been heart-broken over his brother, just like the rest of them.

Connie looked at Big Mama. She was petrified. She didn't want to ask the question that was in her mind, but she had to know the answer. "Am I dead?" she asked.

Paul looked up at his mother. Why would she ask such a question?

Big Mama shook her head. "No, Honey," she said. "You're just in a very deep sleep. You ain't gonna be with us much longer."

"Oh, my God," Connie said. She squeezed Paul tightly. She couldn't bear the thought that she would have to leave him. She thought in that moment that, if she held him tightly enough and didn't let go, then perhaps she would be able to take him back with her.

"That hurts," Paul said. He tried to push himself out of his mother's grasp. "Mama, let go."

Connie let go of her son. "How long do I have with him?" Connie asked.

"Not much longer," Big Mama said. "When you fainted there in your bedroom, I thought we was gonna lose you just like Frank. I think you're gettin' stronger."

"What are y'all talkin' about?" Paul asked. "Where did Frank go?" Big Mama had taught him a lot about magic, but he had never seen a person disappear into thin air before.

"Honey, Frank went back home," Connie said.

"He did not," Paul said. "I saw him right there. He didn't go nowhere. He diasppeared."

Mama Ray looked at Connie. She was trying not to cry. "He don't know nothin' about what happened," she said. "He don't remember."

"Oh, dear Lord," Connie said. She turned to her mother, who was still standing in front of the dresser. "What are we gonna do?"

"I think you should talk to him alone, at first," Mama Ray answered. "You're still his mother." She looked at Connie intently. "You always will be."

"What are y'all talkin' about?" Paul demanded. He was tired of everybody walking around the truth. He wanted a direct answer.

Daddy C got up from the bed. Big Mama and Mama Ray began to follow him out.

"Big Mama?" Connie said, as her grandmother started to leave the room.

Big Mama turned around. "Yeah, Honey?"

"Could you stay here?" Connie asked. She didn't want have to address the problem alone. She didn't understand what was happening to them. She wanted to be a mother to Paul, at least this one last time, but she had no idea how to comfort him. Perhaps Big Mama would be able to help them understand.

Big Mama walked back into the room and sat down on the bed opposite Paul and his mother. Mama Ray and Daddy C shut the door to give them their privacy.

"Are we still goin' home?" Paul asked when the door had closed.

Connie tried not to cry again, but she could already feel her eyes getting wet. She shook her head. "I have to go back soon," she said, "but it looks like you'll have to stay here."

"It's because of Jennifer, isn't it?" Paul asked.

"What do you mean?" Connie asked.

"It's because I killed her," Paul said. He started to cry, too. "Mommy, I didn't mean to let her die. I told her not to go down to the water."

"Oh, baby, you didn't kill your sister," Connie said. "She's fine."

"But I saw her," Paul said. "An' you told me it was my fault."

"Baby, what are you talkin' about?" Connie asked.

"You came runnin' down an' pulled her out of the water, an' you told me it was my fault." Paul could remember it just as if it had happened yesterday. He had watched helplessly as his mother ran frantically down from the house and jumped into the water. She swam out to where his sister's body was floating and pulled her to the shore of the lake.

Connie shook her head. "That's not what happened, sweetheart," she said.

"Yes, it is," Paul said.

"Honey, your sister wasn't in the water. I pulled *you* out of the water." Connie began to sob again. It was too much for her. She had never imagined that she would have to explain to her own son that he was dead. She could still remember his cold skin as she held him on the shore. He was so wet, it had seemed to her as if the water had saturated all the pores of his skin. She remembered looking up at the sky and crying out, "How could you let this happen?" At that moment, even as she called out to God, she knew in her heart that it had not been God, but she herself, who had let it happen.

"That's a lie," Paul said. He had watched from the shore as his mother had pulled Jennifer in from the water. Now she was trying to tell him that it had all been in his mind. "I *saw* you pull her out," he said. "You made the neighbors come an' get me, 'cause you didn't want to see me no more. You said it was my fault."

Connie shook her head. She wiped the tears from her face, but they continued to flow. "Baby, I didn't send you off to the neighbors." She paused. How could she explain it to him? "I couldn't have sent you off to the neighbors, because you were dead."

"They wasn't your neighbors, Honey. They was your sweet little angels," Big Mama said. "They came to take care of you before your Mama Ray an' Daddy C could get there."

"That ain't true!" Paul said. "I ain't dead! Jennnifer's dead!"

"Paul, Honey, Jennifer's fine," Connie said. "She came to get me an' tell me that you were in the water."

Connie remembered it so clearly now. She was taking a nap when, suddenly, she felt Jennifer's little hand pulling at her. "Mommie, Paul's in the lake," was the only thing that she was able to say. It was enough. Connie bolted out of bed and ran out of the house without even putting her shoes on. She could see Paul's body floating on top of the lake as soon as she reached the back porch. The back yard was covered with grass burs, but Connie ignored their sting as she ran through them toward her son. She was too late. Paul had probably died before Jennifer had even gotten up to the house to tell her mother that he was in the lake.

"I saw you holdin' her," Paul said. "She wasn't movin'."

Connie shook her head again. "I was holdin' *you*, Baby," she said. "I got out there and found you in the water. You were just out there floating with Jennifer's ball beside you." Connie wiped her eyes again. "You must have jumped in to get her ball, and then you just—." Connie had to stop and take a breath. "You just didn't come back out again."

His memory of that day was hazy, but Paul remembered seeing Jennifer's ball floating on the water. He had found Jennifer standing on the shore. He knew that he would get into trouble if his mother found out, because he was supposed to be watching her. He ran toward her from the house. She was standing by the lake, and he was afraid that she would try to jump in after the ball. He screamed at her to stop. When he got down to the lake, he pulled her away from the shore. Then, he jumped into the water to fetch the ball, hoping that his mother would never know that he had let his sister out of his sight. The next thing he remembered was standing on the shore, watching his mother jump into the lake and pull his sister back to land. Connie sat on the shore and held his sister's wet body as she screamed into the air.

"I saw you holdin' her," Paul said. "I was standin' right there beside the lake when you jumped in an' pulled her out."

"Baby, your sister came to the house to get me. I made her stay there when I came down and found you. Jennifer wasn't even near the water when I —" Connie's voice quivered, but she had to finish. "When I pulled you out," she said.

Big Mama shook her head. "What exactly did you see, Honey?" she asked Paul.

Paul turned to Big Mama. "I was standin' by the lake when Mama came runnin' out an' jumped in the water. I saw her pull Jennifer out, an' then she started screamin'." Paul's face was bright red by now, and the salty tears stung his cheeks. "She looked right at me, an' she said, 'How could you let this happen?'"

"Oh, my Word," Big Mama exclaimed. She understood now why Paul had been so confused. He had thought all along that his mother had pulled Jennifer's body from the lake, when she had actually pulled *his* body from the water. It had been similar for her. She had not believed that she was dead in the beginning, because her new body had seemed just as physical and real to her as the old one. Of course. It had been the only logical explanation that Paul could think of. How could his mother have dragged him out of the water, when he was standing by the shore watching her the whole time? He didn't realize that he had drowned, because his soul was very much alive.

"What's wrong?" Connie asked Big Mama, who seemed to be deep in thought.

Big Mama looked over at both Paul and Connie. "Paul, Honey, do you remember what your sister was wearin' that day when she drowned?"

"Jennifer didn't drown," Connie insisted.

"Wait a minute, Honey," Big Mama told her.

Paul thought for a moment. He remembered that he had helped her to get dressed that morning, because their mother was still in bed. Jennifer had insisted, as usual, on wearing her favorite pink summer dress. Paul remembered that the dress had dirt stains on it, and so they had chosen another one. Jennifer loved to wear dresses. What dress had they chosen for her that day? He could see it now. They went to the dryer and pulled out her new baby blue dress that had a little elephant on the front. He put the dress on her himself. He had even put the matching bonnet on her, but she had insisted on taking it off. "No hat," she had said. She pulled at it until it fell to the floor. He picked the bonnet up from the floor and tossed it back into the dryer, because he didn't want to have to fold it and put it away with her other clothes.

"She was wearin' her blue dress with the elephant on it," Paul said.

"An' what was she wearin' when your mama pulled her out of the lake?" Big Mama asked.

"What do you mean?" Paul asked.

"Was she wearin' the blue sun dress when your mama pulled her out?" Big mama repeated.

"I guess she was," Paul said.

"Think about it, Paul," Big Mama said. "Think back an' tell me exactly what she looked like when your mama pulled her out."

"No!" Paul shouted. He didn't want to remember the way Jennifer had looked there on the shore, limp and doubled over in Connie's arms. It was too much to think about.

"Please try, Honey," Big Mama said.

Paul didn't want to try, but just the fact that Big Mama had asked the question somehow sent his memory flying back to that day. He could see his mother, drenched and crying, sitting on the shore with the body in her arms. He could see the body now, too. It wasn't clothed in a blue sun dress, but in a white T-shirt and blue jeans. He couldn't see the face, but the hair on the head was not blond like Jennifer's, but brown like his. He realized that his mother was right. It wasn't Jennifer's body which lay in his mother's arms on the shore, but his own.

Paul looked up. He couldn't believe what his memory had just shown him. Tears rolled down his cheeks. He opened his mouth to speak, but he couldn't catch his breath. He wanted to ask a question. There were so many things that he wanted to be answered. Suddenly he began to tremble, as if his whole body were rejecting what he had just seen in his mind. His chest started to heave violently, and he began to scream. "I'm not dead!" he shouted. "It wasn't me!"

Connie pulled Paul into her arms and put her hand over his face. "It's okay, Baby," she said. "Don't be scared." She wanted to promise him that she would stay with him, but she knew in her heart that she wouldn't be able to fulfill that promise.

Paul began to tremble more and more. His body buckled back against Connie's chest as he screamed. "I'm not dead!" he repeated.

Connie tried hard to hold him in her arms, but Paul started to shake more violently. He slipped out of her grasp and lay on the bed, his torso convulsing against the mattress as he went on shouting.

Connie got up from the bed and reached down to try to hold her son against the mattress. "What's happening?" she asked Big Mama.

"I don't know," Big Mama answered. She was frightened. She got up from the other bed and went over to Paul. "Calm down, Honey," she said. Paul continued to shake and scream violently. "I'm not dead! Y'all are lying!"

"What's wrong with him?" Connie asked again.

Big Mama shook her head. She put her hand on Paul's forehead to try to calm him, but he continued to shout. "I'm not dead!"

Big Mama saw that saliva was dripping from his mouth. "Come back, Honey," she said to Paul. "Come back to us."

Suddenly the lights above them shattered. Connie screamed as shards of glass fell onto her head. The boxes in the closet started to fly across the room. One of them flew toward Big Mama, but she blocked it with her arm. "Stop that, Honey," Big Mama said to Paul.

"What is that?" Connie asked. The lamp on the nightstand flew across the room and crashed against the dresser, breaking the mirror into pieces.

"It's Paul," Big Mama said. "But he don't realize that he's doin' it." She looked at Paul again, and grabbed him quickly to her chest. "Stop it, Honey. *Please!*"

Paul pulled away from his great-grandmother. "Leave me alone!" he screamed. "I want to go home!" He turned to his mother. "Mama, take me home," he said.

Connie shook her head. "I can't, Honey," she said.

Paul screamed out again. The walls started to shake this time, and the bed collapsed beneath him. The door to the bedroom opened, and Mama Ray and Daddy C walked into the room. As they entered, the bedroom window shattered. The bottoms of the curtains blew out violently, waving from the curtain rod like navy blue flags in that sudden gust of wind. Finally, there was silence. Big Mama let out a sigh of relief.

"Oh, my Word," Mama Ray said, as she looked at the aftermath.

Big Mama sat down on Frank's bed again with Paul in her arms.

"Are y'all all right?" Daddy C asked.

Connie looked at Paul, who was listless. "Paul, Honey, are you okay?" she asked.

Paul didn't respond, but at least the commotion had stopped.

Big Mama nodded. "He's fine," she said. She let out another sigh. "It just takes a while to get used to somethin' like this, as I'm sure you can imagine." She looked around at the mess that Paul had made. "I guess we'll have to give him a few more lessons about the difference between black an' white magic."

"He sure is strong," Mama Ray said. "I didn't think we'd be able to stop him."

"We could feel it all over the house," Daddy C said.

"Well, you can imagine what it felt like in here," Big Mama said, "with all them heavy things flyin' all over the place."

"Did Paul really do that?" Connie said. She still didn't understand how her son could have made all of those things move around the room and break without even touching them.

Big Mama nodded as she rocked her great-grandson in her arms. "Yeah, it was him," she said. "But he didn't mean to do it. He didn't even know that he could."

Big Mama stood up from the bed with Paul in her arms. "Wanda Ray, will you an' Calvin take care of this mess?" she asked. "I'm gonna go an' lay little Paul down in his mother's bed."

Mama Ray nodded.

"Come on with me, Connie, unless you wanna see how your parents work miracles." Big Mama laughed.

Connie got up and followed Big Mama out the door. She had seen enough miracles for one day. They went down the hall and lay Paul down in Connie's bed. "I'll stay with him," Connie said. She pulled down the covers again and slid into bed next to Paul. Big Mama left the room and shut the door. Soon both Connie and her son were fast asleep.

That evening everyone sat in the den. There was a terrible silence all around. Connie felt as if she were in two worlds. She was seated on the couch holding Paul. Big Mama was on the couch, too, on the other side of him.

Paul was so quiet that Connie was scared for him. She didn't know how he was processing everything. She still couldn't absorb it all herself. She knew that she would wake up soon. She couldn't stand to leave Paul, but she was also worried about Frank and Jennifer. She knew that they must be awfully upset there in the hospital, waiting for their mother to wake up. They had already lost their brother, and now they were probably wondering whether their mother was going to die, too. She felt unbearable guilt, first for having left her children alone that day when Paul had drowned, and then for having taken those pills that had sent her into the hospital. She had not really wanted to kill herself. She had just wanted to escape.

Her escape began with the bourbon. Then, as she sat there alone in the living room in the middle of the night — her sadness numbed by about eight glasses — she decided that she wanted to just fall asleep. She opened the bottle of tranquilizers and took three of them. Only in that moment of taking the pills had the thought occurred to her that if she took another one, she might never wake up. Impulsively, she swallowed three more, just in case one more was not enough to do the trick. In any other moment but that one single instant, she was sure that she would not have even opened the bottle of pills. But she *had* opened it, and now her husband and two children were probably still sitting there in the hospital waiting room, holding onto the hope that their wife and mother would come back to them.

Connie couldn't stand to sit any longer in the silence of the den, but she didn't want to break that silence, either. She had to get out of there. She wanted to go somewhere with Paul, but she was afraid that, if she left the house, she would end up in a strange place, like in her other dreams. She wasn't sure how anything worked there. If she walked outside, would she still see the neighborhood that she had known as a little girl? Or would she find a barren place, filled with blackness and the howling madness of nightmares?

"What's outside?" she asked.

They had been sitting in silence for so long that Connie's voice startled Mama Ray. It was a logical question. She herself had taken a long time to get used to how it worked there where they were. Sometimes she would find herself in strange and frightening places, not knowing how to find her way back home, until she finally learned that it was her own imagination that produced these landscapes.

"Honey, you can see what you want to see around here," Mama Ray said. Dawn and Tinker were sitting in her lap again.

"What do you mean?" Connie asked.

"Well," Mama Ray said, "it's all what you make of it. If you wanna see the town you grew up in, then all you gotta do is think of it." She paused. "You can see Kingsland, too, an' you can even go back to the hospital to see Frank an' Jennifer, but I don't recommend it. You won't be able to talk to 'em, because they won't be able to see or hear you."

"Is this supposed to be Heaven, or what?" Connie asked.

"You could call it that, if you want," Big Mama said.

"Where's God, then?" Paul asked.

"Oh, God's everywhere, Honey," Big Mama answered. "Under every rock, an' in every breath you take."

"'On Earth as it is in Heaven,'" Daddy C said. "Ain't that how it goes, Wanda Ray?"

Mama Ray nodded. "That's how it goes," she said. "'Thy Kingdom come, Thy Will be done, on Earth as it is in Heaven.'" Mama Ray looked at her daughter. "It would be a lot better if people would realize that Earth can be Heaven, too."

Big Mama laughed. "Most people have to die a few times before they figure that out," she said.

"Well, I'm not lookin' for a tour of Heaven right now," Connie said. "I just want to go outside is all, an' maybe see the old neighborhood. I thought I'd go on a walk with Paul, but I'm afraid of —"

"You're afraid of gettin' lost, ain't you?" Daddy C said. Connie nodded.

Daddy C smiled. It had been a long time since he had died, and he had wandered around himself for a long time. For a while, he had no idea where he was, or where he was going. Thanks to Big Mama he learned to create his surroundings with his own will and imagination. When Mama Ray died about a year later, he had already recreated their old house, right there next to Big Mama's. It had made it much easier for Mama Ray to integrate.

"Just let Paul show you, Honey," Big Mama said. "He already knows his way around here. Y'all can go out an' get a Slushy if you want."

Connie looked at her son. He looked so tired. She thought the events of the day must have completely drained him. "Baby, do you wanna go and have a walk with me?" she asked.

Paul looked up. He was still puzzling over everything that had happened. He tried to put all the pieces together. It had occurred to him that his mother and granparents had made up a lie in order to keep him there in Sulphur Springs forever to prevent him from returning to Kingsland where he belonged.

He had accepted by now that he had fallen into the lake. He knew that the body that he had seen in his mother's arms was his own, and not Jennifer's. He still couldn't understand how he could have seen his own body right there in front of him, nor did he understand how the body that he was in seemed just as real as his other one, if he was really dead. He certainly didn't feel dead. He felt the exact *opposite* of dead. He was there with his mother on the couch, and his heart ached with love for her, and with the fear that she would soon leave him again.

"Baby, are you all right?" Connie asked.

Paul nodded, although he really wasn't all right. His emotions had exploded that day to the point where he couldn't even feel sad anymore. What was left was numbness. Paul got up from the couch without a word. He turned to his mother and looked at her intensely, as if he wanted to absorb her somehow into his soul and keep her there. It just wasn't fair that she was going back to the others and leaving him there.

Connie got up from the couch, too. She could see that her son was not all right. She got down on her knees and hugged him. "I don't want to go, either, Baby," she said. She began to cry.

"Honey, you don't have to leave," Big Mama said. "Not forever, anyway."

Connie wiped her eyes. She was tired of crying, but the tears continued to fall. "What do you mean?" she asked.

"Well, you can come back an' visit all the time," Big Mama answered, "just like Cindy does. It's real easy. We can call you here in your dreams."

"How will I know that you're callin' me?" Connie asked.

"You'll know it, Honey," Big Mama said. "Everybody knows when they're bein' called. Some people just ignore it, 'cause they don't want to be around dead folks."

Mama Ray nodded. "I was callin' you for a long time before little Paul passed on," she said. Her own eyes started to water. "But you didn't wanna have nothin' to do me."

"Mama, I didn't know you were callin' me," Connie said. She let go of Paul and stood up again.

"People most always forget about it when they wake up," Big Mama said. "But, now that you know, you can start to call on Paul even when you're awake. Just like I used to visit with my mama after she had passed on."

"How can I do that?" Connie asked. She had never heard of calling on dead people.

"Just say howdy to him in your mind, an' he'll come." Big Mama took Paul's hand. "Won't you, Honey?"

Paul nodded. He still didn't know exactly how that type of communication worked, but he was sure that Big Mama would show him.

"Do you remember that dream you had when you was in my kitchen an' you pulled that telephone out of the oven?" Big Mama asked.

"Yeah," Connie said. "How did you know about that?"

Big Mama chuckled. "I know about it 'cause I was in it, Honey," she said.

Connie shook her head. She was at a loss for words.

"You remember the telephone that was in the oven?" Big Mama asked.

"Of course, I remember it," Connie said. "I'd never seen such a thing. I couldn't figure out why you'd breaded and baked a telephone."

"Well, it wasn't a telephone," Big Mama said. "Not really. It was just somethin' that your mind invented as a way to bring you that information."

"I don't get it," Connie said.

Big Mama nodded. "Yeah, it's real hard to understand, at first," she said. "It took us all a long time, didn't it?"

"It sure did," Daddy C said.

Mama Ray nodded.

"Well, talkin' on the telephone is just as real as talkin' to somebody in your mind," Big Mama said. "When you're talkin' on the telephone, you ain't really talkin' to a person. Your mind just thinks you are."

"Wait a minute," Connie said. "That's too much for me already."

Big Mama grinned. "Okay, Honey," she said. "We'll talk more about it on your next visit. You should enjoy the time you have with little Paul. My point was just that the real basis of what we call communication is somethin' called telepathy. The telephone is just an invention in our minds to make a bridge over physical distance. The truth is that we don't need a telephone to communicate. All you got to do is talk to Paul, an' he'll hear you. An' you can hear him, too, if you listen."

Connie had never heard Big Mama talk that way before. In fact, she had never heard *anyone* talk that way. Before she had found herself in that house with her dead family and son, she would have simply believed that anybody who said such a thing was crazy. Now, she wasn't so sure. She actually believed what Big Mama had just said. She just wasn't sure whether she actually understood the concept. She would have to give herself time. Like Big Mama had said, she should focus now on spending time with her son in this strange dream, before she had to go back to the hospital.

"Will you take me for a walk?" Connie asked Paul.

Paul smiled and took his mother's hand.

"Y'all be careful," Mama Ray said. "Just call us if you need us."

"We will," Connie said. She and Paul went through the living room and out the front door.

So far, everything was exactly as Connie had remembered it: the driveway to the house; the street in front. It was a marvelous recreation of the neighborhood she had grown up in. She had difficulty believing that she wasn't really there. Since she had realized that she was dreaming, she hadn't been able to discern what was real and what was her imagination. It occurred to her that there was no difference, that perhaps one thing was just as real as another, or that perhaps nothing at all was real. Maybe she wasn't really dreaming, after all. Or, perhaps, every part of her life had been a dream.

"It's as dry as I remembered," Connie said to Paul, as they turned the corner onto Texas Street. They could no longer see Mama Ray and Daddy C's house.

"It's hot, too," Paul said.

"Yeah, they don't live right on a lake like we do," Connie said. "The lake sure cools things off a lot." At that moment, as soon as the words left her mouth, she regretted having mentioned both the lake and their house in Kingsland.

"I miss the lake," Paul said.

Connie looked down at her son. "I know you do, Baby," she said. "Maybe you can come an' visit us there. I don't know exactly how it works, but maybe there's a way."

"If I do come an' visit, are you gonna ignore me like Mama Ray said?" Paul asked.

Connie stopped on the sidewalk and turned to Paul. "No, Baby. I would never do that. You just come an' you holler at me as loud as you can. I'll hear you," she promised. She was afraid that the trembling in her throat would betray her fear that she wouldn't be able to hear her son when he called to her. "You talk to LaVelle an' ask her how she gets Cindy to come an' visit her," Connie said. "Maybe there's a special way to do it. I promise you I'm gonna listen as hard as I can, an' the minute I hear you call me, I'll be there." She took her son's hand again, and they continued down the sidewalk.

"Big Mama said she could feel her mama around her body," Paul said. "I felt her, too. Maybe when I come an' visit, you can feel me like that."

Connie was just a little girl at the time, but she could remember that Big Mama had told her that she communicated with her mother, who had already died. She had told Connie to keep it a secret from Mama Ray. Connie hadn't paid much attention to Big Mama. She had just thought her grandmother was kooky, but she had always enjoyed keeping secrets from her mother, and so she had delighted in hearing the stories that were kept from Mama Ray. Now she realized that Big Mama must have been telling the truth all that time, that she really had been able to communicate with her dead mother. Connie knew that there were books on the subject of communicating with those who had passed on, and she told herself that she would read as much as possible on the subject in order to not lose contact with Paul.

"Honey, I'll do everything I can," she said. "I promise."

"Me, too," Paul said. "Big Mama will show me how."

"I know she will," Connie said. She smiled as they continued walking hand in hand.

When Connie and Paul got back from their walk, Paul had a cherry Slushy in his hands, and Connie was carrying a paper grocery bag.

"Well, I guess y'all made it to the Super Handy," Mama Ray said. She was still seated in her Lay-Z-Boy, but Big Mama and Daddy C were not to be found.

"We sure did," Connie said. "I think I like this world. We went into the store and started to pay. I could have sworn I didn't have a penny on me, but I reached into my pocket and had exactly enough to pay for all this stuff."

"That's how it works around here," Mama Ray said. "I'm surprised Helen even charged you. She probably did that just 'cause you're an out-of-towner."

"Where's Daddy and Big Mama?" Connie asked.

"I'll give you three guesses," Mama Ray said. "An' the first two don't count."

Connie laughed. "Well, I guess Daddy's in bed," she said.

"Yep," Mama Ray said as she nodded.

"And there's no tellin' where Big Mama is," Connie said.

Mama Ray nodded again. "Right again," she said. "There just ain't no tellin'." She got up from her recliner and went to the glass door to let Dawn and Tinker in. "Big Mama's kind of all over the place," Mama Ray added. "She passed on so long ago that she can be in several places at once now. Even when she's here, she's probably in about four or five other places, visitin' with kin folks an' friends, or just fartin' around somewhere."

That wasn't exactly the answer that Connie had expected. "I don't think I even want to know about that," she said. "Not now, anyway."

"It don't matter," Mama Ray said. "You've got plenty of time. I still don't quite understand it all, myself."

"No wonder," Connie said, shaking her head.

"I know how she does it," Paul said.

Both Connie and Mama Ray looked at Paul, surprised.

"How?" Connie asked.

"She just believes that she can," he said. "An' that's how she does it."

Mama Ray smiled.

"Well, if it's that simple," Connie said, "then I guess I'll be able to do it soon enough." She laughed. "I believe that anything's possible after this trip."

"It is," Paul said. "Big Mama done showed me how to make magic."

"Well, that's good," Connie said. "Maybe you could make some dinner appear in the kitchen, 'cause I'm hungry."

"What do you want to eat, then?" Paul asked, smiling.

"Don't do that!" Mama Ray said. "I done fixed us some supper." She looked at Connie. "You ain't gonna leave my house without eatin' my good down-home cookin' at least once."

Connie smiled. "I wouldn't dream of missin' your down-home cookin'," she said. "Not for one minute." She reached into the paper bag and pulled out a can of snuff. She handed it to her mother. "I wanted to get you a little gift at the store," she said. "They didn't have much there, but I know how much you used to like snuff."

Mama Ray held the can up to the light. "How in the world did you know that I dipped snuff?" she asked. She had dipped snuff almost all her life, but she had always hidden the fact from everyone. She and her cousin Hermann had started sneaking snuff from Uncle Norbert's cans when she was just a little girl. As far as she had been aware, she and Hermann were the only ones who knew about that. Not even her first husband or Daddy C had been privy to it, as far as she knew. She had always been very discreet, only dipping when no one was around, and drinking Listerine when she had finished.

Connie laughed heartily. "Lorene and I have both known it all our lives," she said. "We used to laugh when we'd come in and your teeth were stained with it. You didn't think we noticed, 'cause we were just little kids."

"I didn't think nobody knew about that," Mama Ray said, shaking her head.

"We even found a can of it in the bathroom behind the towels," Connie said. "We'd laugh as we'd check it from time to time and saw that it got emptier and emptier."

"Well, my Word," Mama Ray said, shaking her head again. She had to laugh. "It's been a long time since I thought about havin' me a dip of snuff." She opened the can and sniffed. "Good Lord," she said, pulling it away from her nose. "I don't know what the attraction was. It smells like a bunch of horse shit to me now."

"I guess everybody likes to have a secret," Connie said.

"Well, I guess it wasn't a big secret, if you an' Lorene knew about it all this time." Mama Ray laughed.

"Mama?" Connie said.

"What, Honey?" Mama Ray asked.

"I'm real sorry about how I treated you earlier," Connie said.

"It's okay, Honey," Mama Ray replied. "I know I gave you plenty of reasons to be upset with me in my lifetime."

Connie laughed. "I guess I wouldn't have been so hard on you if I'd have remembered that you were dead." It was true. The moment she remembered that her mother had died, her anger seemed to have vanished. She had been left with a feeling of remorse for not having been more forgiving before.

Mama Ray laughed, too. "That's the way it usually is," she said. "We don't appreciate nothin' we have until we ain't got it no more." Mama Ray walked past Connie and stopped near the counter. "I was the same way before Big Mama died," she said. "Thank God I had the chance to see her again an' make it right."

"I decided I'm gonna get some therapy when I get out of the hospital," Connie said.

"Well, that'll be good for you," Mama Ray said. "You're lucky to have a husband who can afford it, an' who's willin' to pay for it, too."

Connie nodded. "I know it," she said.

"Don't forget to tell your therapist what a snuff-dippin' ol' bitch I was," Mama Ray said, laughing.

Connie smiled. "Well, I guess you weren't all that bad," she said. "Not all the time, anyway."

"But I reckon I wasn't no Harriet Nelson, neither," Mama Ray replied.

"Probably Harriet Nelson wasn't even Harriet Nelson," Connie said.

"Ain't that the truth," Mama Ray said as she walked into the kitchen. Tinker and Dawn followed her. Mama Ray put the can of snuff down beside the sink. "You don't mind if I wait till after dinner to dig into this stuff, do you?" she asked, nodding in the direction of the can.

Connie shook her head. "You don't have to use it if you don't want to," she said. "You can just keep it as a souvenir, if you want."

Mama Ray laughed. "You never know when I might get a hankerin' for a dip of that stuff. It *has* been a long time."

Paul came into the kitchen and sat down in a chair against the wall. Mama Ray looked at him and smiled. "You don't mind eatin' your granny's cookin' tonight, do you, Honey?"

Paul shook his head and smiled at Mama Ray.

"I'll let you do the cookin' tomorrow," Mama Ray said. "We'll see what kind of magic you can rustle up for us."

"Okay," Paul said. He was excited to see if his magic would work again. He heard something growling under the table. He looked down and saw Tinker. He kicked his foot out and pegged her softly on the nose. She turned around and ran up under Mama Ray's feet.

Mama Ray turned to her daughter, paying no attention to Tinker. "Now, look at all these pots here, Honey," she said. "I got all your favorite things in 'em. Everything you used to love when you was little."

Connie noticed that all the pots were covered, and she wondered what kind of down-home treats her mother had concocted.

Mama Ray picked up the first pot and held it out to her daughter. "Now, what do you think is in this one?" she asked.

Connie shook her head. "I don't know, Mama," she said.

"Let me put it this way," Mama Ray said. "What's your favorite dish in the world?"

"Linguini and clams," Connie said, laughing.

Mama Ray frowned. "You know you ain't gonna get no linguini an' clams around here," she said. "What was your favorite dishes when you was a little girl?"

Connie smiled. "Let me see. I think my favorite thing you made must have been chicken fried steak."

Mama Ray lifted the lid and revealed a heap of steaming-hot chicken fried steaks. She was so pleased with herself that she had to smile.

"Oh, my Word," Connie said. "How did you know?"

"What did you like to eat with chicken fried steak?" Mama Ray asked.

"Mashed potatoes and cream gravy, of course," Connie answered. "And maybe some green beans on the side."

Mama Ray smiled again. She lifted the lids of all the other pots to reveal cream gravy, mashed potatoes, and green beans. "Good choice," she said, still smiling.

"How on earth did you know?" Connie asked.

"I didn't know," Mama Ray said. "You're the one who put 'em there. I just lifted the lids off."

"What?" Connie asked.

"It's your dream, Honey," Mama Ray answered. "You make whatever you want of it." Mama Ray turned to Paul.

"You remember that when we have your birthday party, Sugar Pud," she said. "That way you'll make sure you get whatever you want when you open your presents."

Paul smiled, delighted by the thought of getting whatever he wanted at his birthday party. His mind immediately began to think of wonderful toys that he could have. "Can I do that all the time?" Paul asked.

"Sure you can, Honey," Mama Ray answered. "All you gotta do is use your imagination. We'll let you choose the dessert." She looked at him earnestly. "But you be careful what you create with your imagination," she said, "because, whatever you think about will happen. Just like when I brought those durn chickens back when I was about half out of my mind."

"What chickens?" Connie asked.

"I enjoyed them chickens," Daddy C said, walking into the kitchen. He was in his T-shirt and underwear. "They was my friends." He sat down and started to scratch his leg. Buster lay down underneath his chair.

"Calvin, don't walk around half naked in front of your daughter an' grandson," Mama Ray said. "Put some clothes on."

Both Connie and Paul laughed.

Daddy C stopped scratching his leg and got up. He turned around and started to drag his feet back out of the kitchen.

"You don't have to go away to do it no more," Mama Ray said. "They both know what's goin' on."

Daddy C sat down again. When he did, he was fully clothed, wearing a blue shirt and a pair of khaki trousers pulled up with suspenders. Paul laughed with delight.

Connie smiled and shook her head. "I'm not even gonna ask how you did that," she said.

"There's nothin' to it," Daddy C said. "It's all in the mind."

Suddenly, the sliding glass door of the den opened. Big Mama's loud voiced rattled through the house. "Y'all better not be in there stuffin' your guts again without me," she said. She walked into the kitchen and sat down next to Daddy C. "I thought I smelled food in here. Connie, Honey, would you hand me a plate?"

The four of them ate dinner together. When they finished, Paul chose blackberry cobbler and ice cream for dessert. "This sure is good," Daddy C said, as he filled his mouth with another spoonful of cobbler.

"Tomorrow I'll make sloppy Joe's an' tater tots," Paul said.

"Oh, my Word," Mama Ray said. "I don't know if I'll ever get used to eatin' junk food. Why don't you fry up some chicken livers instead?"

Big Mama and Connie laughed as they continued to eat their cobbler.

That night Paul slept with Connie in her king-sized bed. When they went to bed, Connie held her son close to her. As she closed her eyes in the darkness of the room, she feared that she would wake up in another place far away from Paul. Her fear of leaving him kept her up most of the night. As they lay there in the stillness, Connie moved her hands along Paul's shoulders to make sure that he was still there with her. Eventually, however, she drifted off to sleep.

When the bright morning light shone through the curtains, Connie awoke again. Although she was awake, she still felt very tired. At first, she was afraid to open her eyes. She simply moved her hands over toward Paul. All she felt was the mattress. Hesitantly, she opened her eyes. She turned to her side and saw that Paul was gone. She looked around and recognized that she was still in her old bedroom, there in her parents' house in Sulphur Springs. Her eyes wandered around the bedroom, but she couldn't find Paul.

Terrified, Connie screamed out. "Paul!" she shouted. "Paul, where are you?"

She heard the toilet flush, and Paul came out of the bathroom that was attached to her room. She sighed with relief.

"I was just peein'," Paul said.

"I'm sorry, Honey," Connie said. "I was just scared that you were gone."

"I was scared that you'd be gone, too," Paul admitted. He smiled. "But I knew you wasn't gone," he said, "'cause I could hear you snorin' up a storm most of the night."

"Come here, you little booger," Connie said, laughing. Paul climbed back into the bed and snuggled with his mother. Connie put her arm over Paul, and she drifted quickly back to sleep. Paul was no longer sleepy, but he lay there with Connie, anyway. It was comforting to be in his mother's arms. He simply lay there and felt his mother's warm skin around him, and listened as her breathing became softer.

Although Paul's eyes were closed, he heard his mother's breathing stop and felt her arm suddenly fade away from his chest. He knew that she had slipped away from him, just as Frank had disappeared the day before. Paul didn't open his eyes, but lay still in the bed and tried to imagine his mother's face and her beautiful smile. "I love you," he said, his eyes still closed. When Connie did not answer, he began to cry.

That morning Mama Ray and Daddy C came into Connie's
bedroom and found Paul lying alone on top of the sheets.
"Come into the den with us, Honey," Mama Ray said. Slowly,
Paul got up from the bed and followed his grandparents down
the hall and into the den.

"Don't' worry about your mama, Doll," Daddy C said, as
he sat down in his recliner. "She's fine."

"She's back there with Frank an' Jennifer, an' your step-
daddy," Mama Ray said. "But I guess you know that."

Paul didn't respond. He just sat on the couch and looked
out the glass door to the back yard. Through the glass he could
see Buster, Tinker, and Dawn lying in the sun. He missed his
mother and his family. He had already cried himself out that
morning, and all that was left was an emptiness as dry and
barren as that grassless yard.

"You'll see her again," Mama Ray said.

Paul turned to his grandmother. "When?" he asked.

Mama Ray smiled. "At your birthday party, just a few days
off," she said.

Paul shook his head and folded his arms. "She ain't gonna
come," he said.

"Oh, yes, she is," Mama Ray insisted.

"How, then?" Paul asked.

Mama Ray stretched her arm out and snapped her fingers.
"With a little bit of white magic," she said. "We're gonna suck
'em out of their dreams just like we did with your brother
Frank an' Uncle Norbert, an' just like Mrs. Celecia did with
her granddaughter, Daniela." Mama Ray shrugged her
shoulders guiltily. "It's sort of against the rules," she said, "but
we do it all the time."

"How do you do that?" Paul asked.

"Easy," Daddy C said. "We'll just go to 'em while they're
sleepin' an' invite 'em to one heck of a birthday party at Mrs.
Celecia's." Daddy C grinned. "They won't be able to resist a
party like the one we're gonna throw. An, Lord knows, they
won't pass up the chance to see you."

Paul smiled widely. His birthday was only a few days away, and he was excited to see his family again.

"Just make you a list of all the people you want to come, an' me an' Daddy C an' Big Mama will go an' round 'em up for you," Mama Ray said.

"Okay," Paul answered. He got up from the couch to look for a pen and some paper.

"We gotta break you from that habit, Doll," Daddy C said.

Paul turned around. "What habit?'" he asked.

"From tryin' to look for things that's right in front of your nose," Daddy C said.

"I'm lookin' for pen an' paper to make a list," Paul said.

"It's in your pocket," he said.

"Bull corn," Paul said. He was still in his pajamas. "I ain't even got no pockets."

"You do now," Daddy C said. He laughed.

Paul looked down at his pajama bottoms. He grinned as he reached into the pocket and pulled out a pen and a pad of paper. He sat down and smiled as he looked out the window. "Look, Mama Ray," he said.

"What, Honey?" Mama Ray asked.

"There's a bunch of chickens in the back yard," Paul said.

"Oh, my Word!" Mama Ray exclaimed. She got up from her Lay-Z-Boy and ran to the glass door to look out. She looked around but didn't see anything except for her dogs, which were happily soaking up the late morning sun. "I don't see no chickens," she said finally.

Paul grinned. "Just jokin'," he said.

"That ain't funny, Honey," Mama Ray said. She waved her finger at him. "Now that you're learnin' magic, don't ever let it occur to you to bring them durn chickens back to this house. If there's one thing I can't stand, it's to have a bunch of durn chickens flappin' around an' squawkin' an' leavin' chicken shit all over the yard."

Paul and Daddy C bellowed with laughter at the sight of Mama Ray so passionate over chickens.

"It ain't funny," Mama Ray repeated as she sat back down in her Lay-Z-Boy.

Paul picked up his pad and pen and started to make a list of people to invite to his birthday party. Still laughing at his grandmother, he tried hard to steady his pen as he wrote out his mother's name.

"Don't you hear the bells now ringing?
Don't you hear the angels singing?
'Tis a glory hallelujah to believe
in that far-off sweet forever,
just beyond the shining river,
when they ring the golden bells for you and me.
When our days shall know their number,
when in death we sweetly slumber,
when the King commands the spirit to be free;
never more with anguish laden,
we shall reach that lovely Eden,
when they ring the golden bells for you and
me."

"When They Ring the Golden Bells"
by Dion de Marbelle, 1887